Peter Abelard, O. W. (Orlando Williams) Wight

Lives and Letters of Abelard and Heloise

Peter Abelard, O. W. (Orlando Williams) Wight

Lives and Letters of Abelard and Heloise

ISBN/EAN: 9783337016333

Printed in Europe, USA, Canada, Australia, Japan

Cover: Foto ©Raphael Reischuk / pixelio.de

More available books at **www.hansebooks.com**

LIVES AND LETTERS

OF

ABELARD AND HELOISE.

BY

O. W. WIGHT.

"Mès ge ne croi mie, par m'ame,
C'onques puis fust une tel fame."
Roman de la Rose, t. ii., p. 213.

NEW YORK:
M. DOOLADY, 49 WALKER STREET.
M DCCC LXI.

RIVERSIDE, CAMBRIDGE: PRINTED BY H. O. HOUGHTON.

PREFACE.

THIS book, written ten years ago, is faulty in style, but contains, it is believed, an accurate history of Abelard and Heloise, and a new translation of their famous letters. It was first published under the title of "The Romance of Abelard and Heloise," and has long been out of print. The title was unfortunate, inasmuch as it gave rise to the impression that we had been rhapsodizing about the renowned lovers, instead of writing their lives. We respond to the demand for a new edition, and send it forth with a new title, with revision, and with much additional matter.

In translating the letters, we left in the original Latin a very few passages that we did not care to render literally. A paraphrase would have been no translation. The concluding pages of the correspondence were omitted simply because Abelard and Heloise left themselves, left the subject of their misfortunes and their love, and entered upon a dry-as-dust discussion of monastic institutions. Abelard's letter about nunneries is as dreary a piece of composition as any mortal ever had the misfortune to read, and none but a professional antiquary could regret its omission here.

The story—the *whole* story—of Abelard and Heloise will be found in these pages, told in the ambitious style of youth; and if any one is inclined to censure, let him blame the Muse of History rather than us. The Ages have preserved the record of their passionate love, their tears have been embalmed for us in the burning language of the heart; let those who are able extract wisdom from a faithful picture of human experience.

"CEDAR-GROVE," Rye, 1860.

CONTENTS.

———•◆•———

LIVES AND LETTERS

OF

ABELARD AND HELOISE.

————•♦•————

I.

GENESIS.

REAL romance is in real history. Life, as it is lived,
is more wonderful and touching than life as it is
shaped by the fancy. History gives us the substance
of existence; fiction gives us nothing but its shadow.
The highest conception of genius is meagre, when
compared with the drama that humanity is enacting
in time and space.

Most of us have lived a romance more beautiful
and pathetic than ever yet has been described by the
pen of man. Experience is the light whereby one is
able to read all romantic history. We know when
the historian writes fiction instead of truth, for within
us is a test. Truth to life, we always demand. The
romancer must faithfully give us the experience of

1*

his own heart, or faithfully report the experience of
others.   Nothing less than the history of real life will
satisfy us.   Truth is stranger than fiction, and truth
we must have.

Life is not new ; there is nothing new under the sun.
No doubt, life was more complete and satisfying in
the garden of Eden, millenniums ago, than it is to-day,
here in the United States of America.   Was there
not a woman's heart in the beautiful bosom of Aspasia?
Was there not a man's brain in the Roman head of
Cato ?   Human nature is the same every where.
Humanity, through a thousand variations, is ever
humming the same old tune of life.

The remoteness and obscurity of the Middle Age
then, cannot be objected to us in our present undertaking.   Abelard and Heloise were human, and have
for us a human interest.   In the Middle Age, heaven-
facing speakers and actors walked the earth, that
looked quite similar to those who are moving to and
fro to-day.   Man then felt, as he now feels, that it is not
good to be alone.   Then the precious heart of woman
deeply yearned, as it always yearns, for sympathy,
with which she is blessed, without which she is
wretched.   Down upon thy brother and thy sister,
looked, calmly and sweetly, the same stars, that each
night keep watch over thee.   The wind that kissed
the cold cheek of the Alps then, kisses it still.   The
same hymn of nature that now goes up from the hills

of New-England, and the deep-bosomed forests of the West, to greet the morning; then went up from wold, plain, and mountain, touching the heart of the early worshipper, and melodiously uttering for him the praise that his soul would give to Deity. Then, too, each son of Adam, and each daughter of Eve, needed food and raiment, for which they toiled, slaved, enslaved, trafficked, cheated, stole, talked, wrote, preached, fought, or robbed. The breath of passion swept the chords of life, and the answering tones of joy or woe were heard. Reformers disturbed conservatives in church and state, and statesmen preserved kingdoms, as politicians now save the Union. Then, too, men wept and prayed, laughed and sung. There were then marriage and giving in marriage, wars and rumors of war, loves and hates, the cries of childhood and the complainings of age. The enchanting spirit of beauty flooded heaven and earth; and the solemn mystery of things filled the soul with awe. The old sphinx was still sitting by the wayside, and the children of earth strove to solve the tough and ever recurring problem of destiny. Stars were silent above them, graves silent beneath; and the soul was compelled to answer as she could, to the imperative questionings of sense. The Middle Age was an age of humanity, and has an interest for us, for human things touch the heart.

Our freedom has its roots in the twelfth century.

Then through the influence of the *communes** began
the enfranchisement of the people; with Heloise,
the most devoted and one of the greatest of her sex,
began the enfranchisement of woman; with Abelard,
one of the most eloquent of men, began the enfranchisement of human thought.   Woman, recognized in
the Middle Age by the state under the degrading title
of the weaker vessel (*vas infirmior*),—woman cursed
in the eleventh century by the church, the heroic Heloise in the twelfth century proved, by her example and
her writings, to be equal with man,—equal as a whole,
compensating for lack of energy and strength by superior devotedness, patient endurance and love.   With

---

* Thus have been called the towns that sprung up at the
foot of the castles of the great lords, the inhabitants of which
purchased from their masters a few privileges. "Needy and
wretched as they were," says Michelet, "poor artisans, smiths,
and weavers, suffered to cluster together for shelter at the
foot of a castle, or fugitive serfs crowding round a church,
they could manage to find money; and men of this stamp
were the founders of our liberties." Kings sometimes, in
their contests with the feudal lords, called in the aid of the
commons, and, in requital for service, gave new privileges.
Noble is the language put by the author of the Romance of
the Rose in the mouths of these commons, in regard to their
lords: "We are men as they are, we have such limbs as they
have, and quite as great hearts, and can endure as much."
Michelet's History of France, b. 3, c. iv.
Rob. Wace, Roman de Rou, v. 6025.
Thierry: Lettres sur l'Histoire de France.
Guizot: Fifth vol. of his Cours.

Abelard commenced a movement that triumphed with
Luther, after the martyrdom of Hüss, and how many
more !

With the philosophy of Abelard we shall not
trouble ourselves here. Abelard and Heloise—the
greatest man and the greatest woman of the twelfth
century—were brought by fortune into romantic relations with each other, and, as lovers, they possess for
each soul of us an extraordinary interest. The
heart is not human that does not love. There is no
use in denying the fact, that happiness or misery is,
somehow, strangely connected with conditions of the
heart. Woman asks no more in this world than to be
sincerely loved. When she is queen of one devoted
heart, then she has a kingdom that sufficeth for her
ambition. When all is well with her affections, she
thanks God for his abundant blessing, and is happy.
Man is as restless as the wind until his soul is anchor-
ed in woman's love. Without it there is for him no
rest, no peace. When equally mated with one that is
faithful, he is ready for any trials that " outrageous
fortune " may prepare for him, and the common adversities of life are tossed aside as " a lion shakes the
dew-drops from his mane." The Powers Invisible
have such blessings in store for only a limited number ; hence the misfortunes of Abelard and Heloise
have a fresh interest for each new generation. They
enacted upon the earth a real romance, a faithful history

of which we have undertaken to write. The curious, the students of human nature and history, and those who like to amuse themselves with a romantic narrative, may come here and get from a brother man such help and pleasure as he can give and they receive.

II.

BIRTH-PLACE.

INASMUCH as we have determined to follow the chronological order, which is perhaps the only true order in all veritable history, it is necessary to commence with Abelard's birth-place. We must describe the place where the first scene of the first act of the drama of his life is laid.

After leaving Nantes in Brittany, and before arriving at Clisson, we come to a little village which is called Pallet. There is but one street. That street, however, is long enough, if it were sufficiently divided, to make a village of the usual form. We are about to leave the place behind us without observing any thing remarkable. Let us stop, however, and survey that church on our left, that overlooks the street below. It is a simple church, but men are accustomed to worship there the Maker of heaven and earth. It stands, as it were, at the gateway of the village, and we will respect the temple of the Infinite. Some of its parts seem to be remarkable for their antiquity; we will go, and, if may be, find some monument of an earlier age

What mean those remains of thick walls, and those vestiges of ditches, upon the hill back of the church? They are overgrown with ivy, and seem to be very old.   Never mind the church, let us ascend the hill.   The dilapidated walls, and half-filled fosses, indicate an ancient and strong construction.   They inclose a cemetery, now abandoned, and overgrown with weeds and shrubs.   Tread softly: beneath us sleep the dead, those who once thought, felt, and acted, as we now think, feel, and act.   The earth is a vast burial-ground; every step we take, we press beneath our feet dust that once has been ensouled with the breath of Jehovah.   We will go and stand by that old stone cross, erected in the midst of a few modest tombs.

Here* dwelt, and here still dwell, the lords of Pallet.   Times have changed, but they heed it not. Their sleep is deep.   They were brave knights and true, but they have for ever laid aside the armor and the lance.   The war-trump may sound, Europe may again and again be the theatre of conflict, but not a finger will they lift, either for the new cause or the old.   Some other than a *war*-trump must be sounded to make them answer the call.   Sleep on, thou lord of Pallet, thy *villain* shall not disturb thee more, unless some injury thou hast done him, shall yet be paid for

* Abelard, par Charles de Remusat, t. I., p 1.

out of thy soul's joy. Thinkest thou that he will be
thy villain hereafter ? Tears and toil were appointed
unto thee also, upon the earth; the Eternal has not
commanded me to curse thee; peace be to thy
ashes.

Upon this place, too, war laid its heavy mailed
hand. It was destroyed, history tells us, in 1420.
Margaret of Clisson made an attack upon John V.,
duke of Brittany, and wars followed. Here in the
eleventh century, stood a small fortified chateau,
which commanded the town. The chateau was on
the highest part of this hill, overlooking the narrow
river Sangueze. This name was given to the river, because it was often died with the blood of the combatants who fought upon its banks. Many a time the
blushing stream carried along to the inhabitants below evidence of a hard-fought battle between the Bretons and the English.

In this chateau, in the year 1079, Peter Abelard
was born. Philip I. was king of France, and Hoël
IV. was duke of Brittany. Many more kings and
dukes were then upon the earth, but the sun will probably shine to-morrow, if their names are not mentioned. Beranger, the father of Peter Abelard, was lord
of the chateau, and the name of his wife was Lucie.*

* See second paragraph of the *Historia Calamitatum*, or the
first letter of Abelard. Guizot gives a different interpretation ; see *Essai Historique sur Abailard et Heloise*, p. xi.

Peter was the first-born child. There in that chateau on the hill, above the river, often reddened with the brave blood of warriors,—in the chateau that commanded the little town of Pallet, once more was manifested the continually recurring miracle of life. A new flower of humanity bloomed upon the banks of the stream whose dyed waters often told the tale of death. Has that young life no interest for thee? Then thou art still a sleeper; the mystery of things has never laid an awakening shadowy hand upon thy soul. A young mother's heart was there bursting with joy, while the propitious fates kept closely veiled the unhappy future. Who but a father knows what was the meaning of Beranger's silence, and self-satisfied look. Two more sons and a daughter were given to them, but the experience of clasping to their bosoms a first-born could never be repeated.

There nature made an effort, once more, to produce a man. Millions of efforts she makes, but in every instance she fails as well as succeeds. A perfect man she never produces, and therefore always fails. She never fails in making a good attempt, and therefore always succeeds. The perfect, or ideal man, the standard of which nature in every instance comes short, is the type of the unity of the soul, while nature's failure in different degrees, produces variety in unity Her method is simple, her operations are manifold. She proceeds in every thing else, as she does with man. She is infinitely economic, and at the same time infinitely prodigal. The child Abelard had one meaning for his parents, another for the world, and another for Deity. His history was, no doubt, already written in the quality of his infant blood, and the structure of his infant brain; but we must follow him, and see in what manner he will coin himself into real acts in the mint of life. His good and his evil deeds will interpret for us ours, and may make us wiser and better.

Here, among the lords of Pallet, sleeps Béranger; but far from here, in a more frequented place, we shall find the tomb* of Abelard, to which lovers, both fortunate and unfortunate, still pilgrim.

* See the *Notice Historique*, etc., par M. Alex. Lenoir, imprimée à Paris en 1815, p. 4, et seq.

III.

LOGICAL KNIGHT-ERRANTRY.

> " 'Tis not in man,
> To look unmoved upon that heaving waste,
> Which, from horizon to horizon spread,
> Meets the o'erarching heavens on every side,
> Blending their hues in distant faintness there.
>   " 'Tis wonderful !—and yet, my boy, just such
> Is life. Life is a sea as fathomless,
> As wide, as terrible, and yet sometimes
> As calm and beautiful. The light of heaven
> Smiles on it; and 'tis decked with every hue
> Of glory and of joy. Anon dark clouds
> Arise; contending winds of fate go forth ;—
> And hope sits weeping o'er a general wreck.
>   " And thou must sail upon this sea, a long
> Eventful voyage. The wise *may* suffer wreck,
> The foolish *must*."

THE father of Abelard before commencing the occupation of arms, had received some instruction, and never lost a taste for letters.* He was desirous that the military education of his sons should be preceded by some intellectual culture. Love for his first-born,

---

* Vie d'Abelard, par M. de Remusat, p. 3.

inspired him with particular care for the instruction
of that son.   The bright, fair boy more than answered
the hopes of his parent.   He early showed a subtlety
of mind that promised a glorious future, and a brilliant career.   As he increased in strength and years,
the bias for letters, that had been given by his father,
also increased.   He renounced a military life, and
abandoned to his brothers his inheritance, and his
right of primogeniture.   Philosophy first wins the
passionate love of the beautiful brilliant boy, and
never will she let go her strong hold upon his fiery
heart.   He abandons Mars for Minerva, and will
write his history with tears instead of blood.   Dear,
fair-haired, beautiful-browed boy, thou dost not yet
know the cost of wisdom ; other years shall teach thee
that it must be paid for in the fusion of the brain,
over the burning of the heart !   And what, if a vase
of ashes shall at length take the place of thy heart, and
thy brain congeal to stone !   With thee, also, fate
opens an account ; take what thou wilt, but payment
thou shalt not escape, even to the uttermost farthing.
Choose thy principles of action, but know that thou
must abide the results.

Abelard was a real Breton.*   Every man must
inherit his country and his times.   In arms and in

* Ouvr. ined. d'Abelard, par M. V. Cousin, *Dialectic.* p. 222
et 591.

philosophy, the Bretons have always manifested a character of unconquerable resistance; obstinate firmness, and fearless opposition. The true Breton is a compound of the Greek and the Celt. Pelagius*, the first churchman who was an avowed champion of liberty, who provoked the attacks of St. Augustine and St. Jerome, who denied original sin, and would not admit the doctrine of redemption, who unconsciously would have robbed Christianity of her piety and her heart, the purity of whose life was regarded by the fathers in the church, as increasing the danger of his heretical doctrines; this giant, as he is described by one of his opponents, with the strength of Milo of Crotona,—who spoke with labor yet with power, was a native of Brittany, a man of the sea-shore, as his name implies, of that shore where the sea wails for ever, and beats as it were upon the heart of the beholder, imparting to it her own untamable energy, and unsubduable spirit of freedom. Descartes, who philosophized with as much intrepidity as he fought under the walls of Prague,* was a Breton. By the strong-breasted and hard-headed Bretons, the Northmen and the English again and again were repulsed. Believers and unbelievers, orators and poets, Brittany has produced. The last exclamation heard at Water-

* St. Augustin, t. xii. diss. de Primis Auct. Haer. Pelagianae.

† M. Cousin's History of Modern Philosophy, t. i., p. 44.

loo, it is said, was uttered by a Breton,—"*The guard dies, but does not surrender.*"* Abelard has the blood of his Breton mother in his veins. Mars he has renounced, but for the goddess of wisdom he will fight, with such arms as she will permit. To the science of dialectics, the art of intellectual warfare, he devotes himself, preferring a logical combat to a conflict of arms; preferring to triumph over a re-futed rather than a slaughtered enemy. Have a care, brave boy, thy brain is not the whole of thee; thy soul is larger than thy warlike logic.

Still a mere lad, Abelard availed himself of every opportunity to engage in the contests of reasoning. Such was his natural ability, and such his acquired skill, that no champion could be found in the neigh-borhood to stand before him. Like a fearless knight, leaving the paternal mansion, he went from province to province,† searching for masters and adversaries, marching from controversy to controversy, eager to enter the lists for a dialectic tilt, putting lance in rest, with or without provocation, unhorsing, beardless as he was, every logical combatant. He was a peripatetic, whose walk extended from end to end of the kingdom. He was a real logical knight-errant, every where seeking philosophic adventures.

* Michelet: Histoire de France, l. iii.
† The Guizot edition of the Abelard and Heloise letters: the first letter of Abelard, p. 5.

In the eleventh century, dialectics were called an art.* The one who was skilled in dialectics was called a master of arts,—a title which is still in use. This art rivalled theology in importance, and we might add, with a little exaggeration, in power. Theology sometimes consented to be served by dialectics, but always showed signs of uneasiness when in the presence of her subtle foe. The former was based upon authority; the latter demanded an exercise of free thought. Mother Church has always hated and cursed every independent thinker, so it is necessary for thee, thou youthful knight-errant of logic, to beware. Authority† gives thee, on the one hand, the premises,— on the other, the conclusions; it will not be safe to question the former, nor to transcend the latter. Talk as it may please thee about genus, species, difference, property, and accident; about categories or predicaments; about the universal principles of language; about reasoning and demonstration; about the rules of division; about the science of discussion and refutation,—go from premises to conclusions by what route thou wilt, but do not rashly venture further; within this charmed circle it is permitted thee to obey reason and God; out of it close thy clear eye, and follow the voice of the siren that calls thee to

* Vie d'Abelard, p. 5.
† M. Cousin: His. Ph., t. II., lecture ix.

her bosom. It is hard I know, but upon no other condition shalt thou have any fellowship with thy generation. It may be, some German will hereafter journey far to listen to thy eloquent voice, whose descendant, in a more propitious age, shall conquer for men the privilege of obeying God. Go on, then, in thy logical knight-errantry; thus unconsciously shalt thou teach others to freely think and freely act. Aristotle, Porphyry, and Boethius, cannot afford thee the best of mental nutriment, and thou art not skilled to read nature and the soul; yet, if thou wilt persevere, all the men of thy times shall soon be left behind. I fear thou art sadly neglecting one book, but never mind now, Mother Church will not curse thee for that.

Abelard, in the course of his philosophic adventures, must have met with the celebrated John* Roscelin, who first pushed *nominalism* to its extreme consequences. In 1092, when Abelard was twelve years of age, the doctrine of Roscelin had been condemned by a council held at Soissons. Denying the *reality of universals*, it seems, endangered some of the dogmas of the Church. St. Anselm, Abbé of Bec, in Normandy, who was highly esteemed among the religious orders, and enjoyed a great reputation as a philosopher, who was expecting to succeed Lanfranc

---

* M. Cousin: Introduction to the Ouvr. ined. d'Ab., p. 40.

2

as Archbishop of Canterbury, had from the beginning supported *realism* against the *nominalism* of Roscelin. Anselm served the Church and gained the object of his ambition. Roscelin sought for the true in itself, and was banished. We do not know precisely when, or where, or how Roscelin, and Abelard met. They were brother Bretons, and perhaps thought it were not best for Greek to encounter Greek. Abelard heard the lectures of Roscelin, who was then canon of Compiegn, and probably carried away in his retentive memory the arguments that were used to substantiate a new system.

Thus are spent the youthful days of Abelard. Philosophy he is serving with the devotion of a true lover; but time shall teach him that Life cannot be fathomed by any plummet of Thought.

IV.

AN EPISODE: THE FIRST CRUSADE.

WHILE Abelard was pursuing his philosophic adventures, Peter the Hermit was preaching the first
crusade. The young logical knight-errant did not
seem to be affected by the movement that was convuls-
ing all France, nearly all Europe. Like a true philosopher, he was unmindful of every thing that did not
pertain to thought, to the everlasting principles of
mind.

The first crusade—all the other crusades were
only repetitions or imitations of that—was the greatest movement of the Middle Age. The preaching of
Peter the Hermit in the year 1095 was not its beginning. It had its origin in one of the constituent principles of the society of the times. Ideas are at the
basis of every human organization, whether in church
or in state. Modern society has taken the place of that
of the Middle Age, because the ideas of men have
changed. Belief in the benefit of pilgrimages and
crusades was one of the characteristics of those times.

Man's condition of being on this planet is that of a pilgrimage. Each age has its place, to which it joyfully, yet often painfully, wanders. Wearily, wearily journeys the Arab to Mecca. Cold is the heart of that Christian who has never desired to gaze upon the tomb of his Redeemer. In the middle age, pilgrims, with staff in hand, journeyed to Jerusalem, willing to endure any fatigue, braving dangers, bearing humiliations. " Happy he who returned! Happier still he who died near the tomb of Christ, and who could exclaim in the presumptuous language of a writer of the time, ' Lord, you died for me, I die for you.' "

The pilgrimages to Jerusalem commenced about the year 1000. At first the pilgrims were kindly received by the Arabs, and soon their numbers became immense. " About the same time so countless a multitude began to flock from every quarter of the globe, to the sepulchre of our Saviour at Jerusalem, such as no man could before hope for—the common people .... middling classes .... kings and counts .... bishops .... many nobles, together with poorer women .... It was the heartfelt wish of many to die before they returned home."* When the Caliph Hakem, the son of a Christian woman, pretended to be the incarnation of the Divinity, Christians and Jews were alike persecuted by

---

* Pierre D'Auvergne, ap. Raynouard, Choix de Poesies des Troubadours, iv. 115.—Rad. Glaber, L iv. c. 6, ap. Scr. R. Ser. x. 50. Quoted by Michelet.

him. The former persisted in believing that the
Messiah had come, and the latter persisted in believing that he was to come. Both, consequently, opposed the pretensions of the Caliph Hakem. By his
command, no one could approach the holy sepulchre
except on the condition of defiling it. The danger
increased, and the desire to visit Jerusalem also increased. Whole armies of pilgrims sometimes failed
to reach the sepulchre. There often remained only a
few worn-out survivors, to tell of the hardships and
heroic death of their companions, thereby exciting
others to undertake the same perilous, yet glorious
journey. At length, in the last quarter of the eleventh
century, the Turks obtained possession of Jerusalem
and massacred Christians and Alides,—all believers
in the incarnation.

Shall pilgrimages to the holy city cease then?
Will Christian Europe incur the penalty of leaving
the Redeemer's sepulchre in the hands of infidels?
No; the invasion of the East must be re-enacted in a
vaster form, and for the realization of a loftier idea.
The Greeks invaded Asia for the purpose of conquest,
for the purpose of extending their civilization. The
cause of the Past and the cause of the Future then
met, but the ideas that animated both sides were political ideas, merely those of Empire. In the
Middle Age the East and the West must again meet,

again must draw the sword, but a religious principle lies at the foundation of the contest.

When Peter the Hermit began to preach the crusade, western Europe was ripe for the movement. France was the seat of the greatest excitement. Urban II., who was then pope, was a Frenchman. In France the whole populace was ready to take up arms. Four hundred bishops or mitred abbots were present at the Council of Clermont. "The lower order of people," says a cotemporary,* "destitute of resources but very numerous, attached themselves to one Peter the Hermit, and obeyed him as their master, at least so far as matters passed in our country. I have discovered that this man, originally, if I mistake not, from the city of Amiens, had at first led a solitary life under the habit of a monk, in I know not what part of Upper Gaul. He set out thence, by what inspiration I am ignorant ; but we then saw him traversing the streets and burghs, and preaching every where. The people surrounded him in crowds, overwhelmed him with presents, and proclaimed his sanctity with such great praises, that I do not remember like honors having been rendered any one. He was very generous in distributing whatever was given him. He brought back to their husbands wives who had wronged them, not without adding gifts from himself, and re-

---

* Guibert: Nov. l. ii. c. 8. Quoted by Michelet.

stored peace and a good understanding between those who had been disunited, with marvellous authority. In whatever he did or said, there seemed to be something divine in him, so that they would even pluck the hairs out of his mule, to keep as relics.... He wore only a woollen tunic, and above it a cloak of coarse dark cloth, which hung to his heels. His arms and feet were naked; he ate little or no bread; and supported himself on wine and fish."

Every one mounted the red cross upon his shoulder, and some imprinted the mark of the cross on themselves with a red-hot iron. Every body was seized with the crusade mania. The ties of kindred and the love of country were forgotten. "Thus," says the one from whom we have quoted, "was fulfilled the saying of Solomon,—' the locusts have no king, yet go they forth all of them by bands.' These locusts had not soared on deeds of goodness so long as they remain stiffened and frozen in their iniquity; but no sooner were they warmed by the rays of the sun of justice, then they rose and took their flight. They had no king. Each believing soul chose God alone for his guide, his chief, his companion in arms. Although the French alone had heard the preaching of the crusade, what Christian people did not supply the soldiers as well?.... You might have seen the Scotch, covered with a shaggy cloak, hasten from the heart of their marshes.

"....I take God to witness, that there landed in our parts barbarians from nations I wist not of; no one understood their tongue, but placing their fingers in the form of a cross, they made a sign that they desired to proceed to the defence of the Christian faith.

"There were some who at first had no desire to set out, and who laughed at those who parted with their property, foretelling them a miserable voyage, and more miserable return. The next day, these very mockers, by some sudden impulse, gave all they had for money, and set out with those whom they had just laughed at. Who can name the children and aged women who prepared for war ; who count the virgins and old men trembling under the weight of years ?...
..... You would have smiled to see the poor shoeing their oxen like horses, dragging their slender stock of provision and their children in carts; and these little ones, at each town they came to, asked in their simplicity—' Is not that the Jerusalem that we are going to ?' "

Walter the Penniless, and the German Gotteschalk, also had their followers. While the princes, barons, and knights, were slowly putting their armies on the march, the multitude, countless in number, under the guidance of Peter the Hermit, began to descend the valley of the Danube. Every unfortunate Jew that happened to fall in their way, was mercilessly slaughtered, as having inherited the sin of crucifying the Redeemer.

The crusade has now left France, the scene of our story, and we cannot pursue it further.

Six hundred thousand men started, bearing the cross. Europe and her elder sister Asia, the West and the East, met. Jerusalem was taken. But what became of the more than half a million that composed the great army of the crusaders? Their route through Hungary, the Greek Empire, and Asia Minor, was marked by their bones; only ten thousand returned! And where were the little ones who asked at each town on their way —" Is not this the Jerusalem that we are going to ?"

Was then the crusade a disaster and a failure?

We cannot here speak of all its benefits. Islamism, that, especially on the side of Spain, more than once had invaded Europe, was condemned to remain at home, among her Saracens in the East. Christianity, endowed with eternal youth and beauty, met a daughter of earth, and pronounced the sentence of her decay. The men of Europe, who long had been engaged in warfare among themselves, learned the great lesson of their brotherhood under the tuition of danger and misery. The serf and the lord, learned to recognize each other as belonging to the same humanity, when fighting side by side in a common cause, under the walls of Jerusalem, or dying side by side on the pestilential plain. Thus European liberty grew up in

2*

a soil enriched by the blood of so many thousands of men. It is said that an oriental town was walled with the bones of the crusaders. Let us speak of them with respect and gratitude, for we are to-day drinking out of their skulls the wine of freedom.*

* Michelet: Histoire de France, l. iv., c. iii.

V.

TO PARIS.—PARIS AT THE BEGINNING OF THE TWELFTH CENTURY.

IN the year 1100, or not far from that, Abelard journeyed to Paris. Where were the crusaders? Most of them had arrived at a better Jerusalem than the *old*, we hope. Loyal to his mission, Abelard did not trouble himself about the work of others. His pilgrimage was after free thought. Reason was then buried, and the armed soldiers of Mother Church were keeping watch at her grave. He who would make a pilgrimage thither, was compelled to insult the divinity that he would worship. Reason, however, was only sleeping in the sepulchre, was waiting for a resurrection—was waiting to reappear, in the white robes of Christianity, restored to its original nobility through the power of the redemption. O lion-hearted Breton youth! I fear thou hast undertaken a dangerous pilgrimage, for thou wilt encounter worse than Saracen foes,—thy own passions and the darkness of thy times! Persevere nevertheless; a sight of the shrine which thou seekest shall bless thine eyes, but its capture shall be the work of a braver than Godfrey of Bouillon, of a heroic Teuton, who shall gather up in his own experience the whole antecedent history of the world, who shall fear neither Duke George, the Council at Worms, nor pope Leo X.,—neither men nor devils; who shall obey God alone and emancipate the soul!

Abelard was little more than twenty years* of age when he arrived in Paris. Although he was so young he was still a veteran in controversial experience and dialectic skill. Paris was then the centre of letters and arts, for northern and western Europe. The ardent young logical knight-errant was attracted by the city which contained the most celebrated schools, and was the home of the most distinguished professors of philosophy.

As every one who has visited Paris knows, and as any one who will open a map of it may see, there is an island in the Seine, at the centre, which is called Cité. When Abelard first visited Paris, it did not extend beyond this island.† It was joined to the right bank of the river by the *grand-pont* (great bridge) and to the left bank by the *petit-pont* (small-bridge). Upon this famous island was then concentrated all

---

* Vie d'Abelard, p. 8.
† Among the Documents ined. sur l'hist. de France, see Paris sous Philippe le Bel. Vie d'Ab., pp. 40—44.

that was greatest and best in the kingdom. It was
the seat of royalty, of the church, of the administration
of justice, and of instruction. On the left bank of the
river arose the hill whose summit was crowned with
the abbey of Sainte-Genevieve. On the right bank, between the ancient churches of Saint-Germain-l'Aux-
errois and Saint-Gervais, was the quarter where foreign
merchants dwelt. Here and there upon the neighboring plains, were springing up establishments of piety or
learning, destined to great renown. The abbey of
Saint-Germain-des-pres, on the west, perpetuated the
memory of that bishop of Paris whose fame rivalled
that of Saint-Germain-d'Auxerre. Down the left
bank of the Seine, in the neighborhood of this abbey,
where the school of Fine Arts and the University now
stand, not far above the present site of the Palais Bour-
bon, was the playground of the scholars and clerks;
thither they repaired, to engage in those exercises and
rude sports that were fitted for the robust nature of the
men of the times !*

Towards the lower end of the island, was the palace of the early French kings. On the end of the
island, between the palace and the river, was the garden of the palace. It was not much like the modern
gardens of Paris. It was a place planted with trees,
which was opened on certain days as a public prome-

* Hist. Univ. Paris, t. II., p. 750, et seq.

nade. In front of the palace was the ancient church of Notre-Dame,—an imposing structure, although very inferior to the immense church which has succeeded it. When one would speak a word about Notre-Dame he remembers Victor Hugo's romance, and remains silent. "There is one," says Michelet, "who has laid such a lion's paw on this monument as to deter all others from touching it; henceforward, it is his, his fief, the entailed estate of Quasimodo—by the side of the ancient cathedral he has reared another cathedral of poetry as firm as its foundations, as lofty as its towers."*

Where the Garden of the Tuileries, the Champs Elysées, and the Avenue de Neuilly leading out to the Arc de Triomphe, now are, there was an unbroken marsh 750 years ago, at the beginning of the twelfth century. Every thing changes ; the earth is metamorphosed under the busy hands of man. At the period of which we are speaking Paris is small, still she is the cherished capital of the nation. Abelard comes up from the forests and the villages of Brittany, and gazes upon her for the first time with wonder and delight. His blood flows faster, and his ambition is inflamed anew. How many sons of genius shall follow him—to fame and misery ! Dear, deceptive, gay, graceful

* See the third book of Victor Hugo's Notre-Dame de Paris.

city! thou shalt increase in wisdom and beauty, in strength and sin; thou shalt invite the lovers of pleasure from the ends of the earth, to enjoy thy charms; thou shalt drink the wine of poesy and wit, and eat the food of learning, and take the lead in the world's civilization; thy night revels shall be revolutions, and thy fair bosom more than once shall be drenched with the blood of heroes contending for thy smile; thou wilt banish thine own children and nourish those that come unto thee from afar; thou shalt be the loved and the envied among the capitals of the nations; but the rose of innocence thou wilt not wear upon thy ravishing breast; thy queenly face shall fade, thou shalt at length sleep with thy elder sisters, with Nineveh, Athens and Rome; the hand of retribution shall touch thee, and through long years of mourning thou shalt decay; the eyes of strangers shall gaze upon thy ruins, and foreign feet shall tread carelessly upon thy dust!

VI.

ABELARD STUDIES AT THE SCHOOL OF NOTRE-DAME, AND QUARRELS WITH HIS MASTER, WILLIAM OF CHAMPEAUX.

WHEN Abelard first entered the capital of France, he sought the celebrated episcopal school of Notre-Dame,* whose master was the famous William, of Champeaux. There was then no University of Paris. There were in the city many schools, however, which were under ecclesiastical supervision. The largest and the most renowned among these was the one that we have just named. Students flocked to Paris from every part of middle and western Europe. Thither young men went, not only from every part of France and Gaul, but also from England, Germany and Italy. The instruction at the episcopal school, as in a modern German University, consisted mostly of lectures. The auditors listened to the lectures of the master, then talked or disputed among themselves.

The students assembled in a cloister, not far from the habitation of the Bishop. This was called the

* Vie d'Abelard, p. 10.

cloister of Notre-Dame, and was formed by an inclosure that extended from the Metropolitan church to the garden of the Archbishopric.*

The chief of this school, William of Champeaux, was Archdeacon of Paris. He taught with much success and eclat, and the students were proud of their unrivalled master. He excelled in dialectics, and was first in the school of Notre-Dame to apply the forms of logic to the teaching of holy things. William of Champeaux was therefore the first to introduce scholastic theology in Paris.†

Abelard soon attracted the attention of his master. A teacher always loves a disciple, who understands him, and can reproduce him with skill; but woe to that pupil who sets up any notions of his own. The disciple, in order to please his master, must have a genius for being moulded to the pattern of another mind. Abelard soon distinguished himself among his fellow pupils. His intellect had already been somewhat disciplined by his dialectic encounters, and many things had been learned in the various provincial schools that he had visited. By nature he was endowed with a rare subtlety of understanding. His speech flowed with graceful ease, and his illustrations were singularly beautiful. Of course he was praised

* Paris ancien et moderne, par de Marlès, t. I., c. i., p. 51, et c. ii., p. 139.

† Abelard's Works: *Dialectic*, passim.

by his teacher, admired, loved, and envied by the
other scholars. Those who occupy a position of outward equality with us, will begin to hate us when they
are compelled to acknowledge our superiority. He,
whose life is a continual progress, has most to fear
from those that he is passing.

Abelard, as it seems, was only waiting to fathom
the mind and to comprehend the system of William of
Champeaux, before giving him battle. He separated
himself from his teacher and attacked some of his doctrines. The skilful young logical knight-errant more
than once unhorsed his proud master. The chief of
the great episcopal school of Paris, a school renowned
among distant nations, regarded the hardy young dialectician with indignation and fright. Some of his fellow-
students looked upon him with jealousy and treated him
with defiance; yet others, as is usually the case, probably looked upon him as a hero, and secretly wished
him success. Force of mind is never lost; place the
really strong man where you will, and his influence
must be felt.

The soul of William of Champeaux was tortured by
the presence of one who possessed a more subtle mind
than his own. In a church in the city of Rouen, "you
see, on one and the same monument, the hostile and
threatening figures of Alexandre de Berneval, and of
his pupil whom he stabbed; their dogs, couchant at
their feet threaten each other as well; and the ill-

starred youth, in all the sadness of an unfulfilled destiny, wears on his bosom the incomparable rose in
which he had the misfortune to surpass his master."
Young artist, beware of the veteran who has won the
confidence of men; thy soul may be tempered with
the fire of genius, yet a smile of triumph might make
thee an enemy whose envy would supply the fuel of
his hatred. Young divine, who art ambitious to
serve thy master, take care not to disturb the repose
of leaders that have the ear of the public, that have
outlived their energy, that are, above all, impatient of
rivals; any sin may be forgiven thee, except that of
excelling too much in eloquence and learning; hide
thy gifts for a season, and do not question the right
of men who hold stations for which they are not fitted.
Every man is in danger from those who govern in
church or state, just in proportion to his power to disturb them. Abelard dated his misfortunes from the
time when he incurred the opposition of his master
and his fellow-pupils.

At that period, Abelard was full of vigor and hope,[*]
and did not succumb to adversity. The whole field
of human knowledge was open before him, like the
world before a conqueror. He sought an acquaintance with the mathematics, astronomy and music, for
he seemed to be already master of all other sciences.

[*] See his own account in the *Historia Calamitatum.*

Mathematics, through want of natural aptitude, dislike, or too much preoccupation, he did not succeed in. He was ridiculed by his mathematical teacher, and gave up the study in thorough disgust.*

Whither now will he go? what course will he pursue? Will he be contented with knowing what there is ready at hand to be known, or will he show himself a man by exploring new fields, and exhibiting a spirit that can rely upon its own energies? Between him and the master of the great school of Paris, there shall be warfare and continual enmity; other foes await him, too, who shall dig the sepulchre of his hopes, and build the charnel-house of his joys!

* See the article, by Sir Wm. Hamilton, in the Edinburgh Review, for January, 1836, "On the Study of Mathematics, as an Exercise of Mind;" also republished in his "Discussions on Philosophy, etc.," p. 257.

VII.

MELUN AND CORBEIL.

ABELARD was not in the least disheartened by the envy and opposition of his master and fellow-pupils. He even conceived the idea of becoming a master himself, which, in his times, was considered as a hardy notion for a youth only twenty-two years of age. He had that which is always a characteristic of genius, self-reliance. It seemed to be a necessity with him, to seek to realize his ambition. He was not contented to indulge in dreams of glory, without putting forth any efforts to gain the object of his desire; still less did he passively complain about the wrongs received at the hands of others, and succumb to misfortune. He was born for action and had no disposition to play the whiner.

Paris, where teaching was under the supervision of the head of the school of Notre-Dame, was of course interdicted to Abelard. He could not there erect a chair of philosophy, and lecture to those who might be willing to receive his instruction. He turned his attention to Melun, which was then one of the

most important towns of France, and was during part
of the year, the residence of the royal family. The
chief of the episcopal school,—the master whom Abelard was abandoning, had the penetration to perceive
that his own reputation was in danger. He did not
wish to have the brilliant pupil, who more than once
had silenced his teacher, establish a rival school in a
neighboring town.* Although William was on the
point of renouncing his chair of philosophy, although
he was about to quit the world for a convent, still he
used every effort to prevent the accomplished youth
from commencing a course of instruction in a place so
near Paris. He hoped at least to drive the young
Breton farther off.

The archdeacon brought to bear every influence
possible to have Melun also interdicted to Abelard.
His secret manœuvres, however, were of no use. A
young man, if he is gifted and heroic, has the sympathy
of the public. Men like to see an old leader giving
place to a new. The genius of Abelard was exagger-
ated on account of his extreme youth. His antagonist had powerful enemies who were in the possession
of political influence. The very manner in which a
young philosopher was pursued by an envious master,
rendered him the more interesting to those who took

---

* Cousin's Introduction to the Ouvr. ined. d'Abelard,
p. 13.

his part. He was also a born nobleman, and for that reason was sympathized with the more by the court.

Abelard gained the object of his wish. He established his school at Melun, and succeeded in his teaching. His renown soon threw into the shade the nascent reputation of his fellow-disciples, and the established celebrity of his former teachers. His fame, to use his own language,* " effaced all that the masters of art had little by little acquired." His auditors were numerous, and no one seemed to them worthy or capable of being his rival in the art of dialectics.

Becoming more and more confident of final success, and triumph over his adversary, he removed his school from Melun to Corbeil. He was then near enough to harass the school of Paris with his arguments. The young knight-errant of logic, was not contented to satisfy his own disciples, it was necessary for him to be near enough to tease and worry his enemy. The philosophic citadel of Paris was invested by one whose heart knew no fear, whose youthful spirit could not be conquered.

Philosophy as well as war has its heroes. It is difficult to tell whose fame is the greater, that of Alexander or that of Plato. War is only the bloody encounter of ideas. The great hero is the representative of a great principle. It was not Cæsar that conquered

* Epistola Abælardi, in the Guizot edition of the letters. p. 6.

at Pharsalia ; in the person of Cæsar human liberty conquered Roman liberty. Ideas were at war in Abelard and William of Champeaux. The battle, which they were fighting at Paris, may have been fraught with greater consequences to the world than that of Arbela or that of Waterloo. The question is not to be decided, by giving a picture of events, but by examining the ideas that were contending for dominion. A philosopher surrounded by his scholars, does not make so great a show as a commander followed by a brave army, but the importance of any thing in this world is not to be judged by external appearance. The Apostle Paul when he was in bonds at Rome, no doubt seemed very insignificant in comparison with the Emperor, but we are now able to judge whose importance was in reality the greater. " Things are not what they seem," and wise is he who looks through the appearance at the reality. That philosophic quarrel at Paris in the first years of the twelfth century, was really one of the most important events of the Middle Age. It was the cradle of scholasticism, and the first decided declaration of the independence of human thought in modern as distinguished from ancient history. After centuries of darkness, there arose once more a champion of unextinguishable reason.

> " As all Nature's thousand changes
> But one changeless God proclaim,

So in Art's wide kingdom ranges
  One sole meaning, still the same :
This is truth, eternal Reason,
  Which from Beauty takes its dress,
And, serene through time and season
  Stands for aye in loveliness."

VIII.

PHILOSOPHY AND SICKNESS.

A RELIGION is the main source of every civilization. Moral force governs the world, directs the course of history. Religion lies at the foundation of the great movements of society. Christianity, Mohammedanism and Brahminism, are means of civilization. Asiatic civilization is as good as Brahminism can make it. If society ever advances there, the East must have a new religion. The Turks and Arabs can never advance until they lose their reverence for the Prophet and accept a better faith. The civilization of Europe and the United States, is the best in the world, because it is the growth of the holiest religion. In those kingdoms and states where society has advanced most, we are sure to find the best form of Christianity.

Now the great fact of any civilization is the rivalry of two classes of men, those who teach the doctrines of the prevailing religion, and the active spirits who pretend to judge these doctrines, that part of the clergy who would perpetuate authority and the free-thinkers. In the first centuries after the establishment of a religion, there are many of the first class and few of the second. The regular clergy will be, for the most part, instruments of authority. Philosophers will be few in numbers and the objects of persecution. In the course of time, free thought will claim its lawful dominion, and will throw off the yoke of authority. Reason will question faith, and examine the basis upon which it rests. The first meeting of reason and faith is usually hostile. They are the ideas that animate contending parties in church or state. Reason is radical, faith is conservative. One is impatient of the past; the other fears the future. The former relies upon the intuitions of the soul, the other clings to sacred books.

They are both right and both wrong. In time they learn to recognize each other as mutual helpers, but their first meeting is bloody. The great civil wars of history are the obstinate encounters of these two ideas.

A false religion cannot stand the test of this encounter of reason and faith. Christianity has calmly met the questionings of philosophy, without losing anything in dignity or power. Men of the largest minds are the readiest to accept the teachings of Christ. When a man or a church fears to meet reason face to face, we may be sure that there is a consciousness of weakness. He whose house is built upon a rock does not fear the rains and the floods. Reason is the best friend of Christianity, and constructs for her a sys-

tem of evidences out of the material which she fur-
nishes.

Abelard used his own mind as a test of truth, and
thus unconsciously became a champion of free thought.
With him and William of Champeaux commenced a
long battle between reason and faith, which has not
ended yet. There had, no doubt, been some skirmish-
ing in the previous centuries, but in the episcopal
school of Paris commenced the real struggle, that has
already lasted many centuries, and will last many
more. We can here prophesy, without any fear, that
Abelard will encounter opposition from every champion of authority, in Mother Church, that he may meet
during his whole life. We are far from wishing
wholly to vindicate Abelard, but he was the first decided
Protestant on the continent of Europe. He has been
followed by the unfortunate Albigenses, by Philip le
Bel, Huss, Luther, Calvin, Cranmer, and others.

If we could look deep enough into things, perhaps
we might find more significance in the quarrel of a hot-
headed Breton youth with his master at Paris, than
in any battle of modern times. " Above all," says a
lynx-eyed critic, " it is ever to be kept in mind, that
not by material, but by moral power, are men and
their actions governed. How noiseless is thought !
No rolling of drums, no tramp of baggage-wagons, at-
tends its movements : in what obscure and sequestered
places may the head be meditating, which is one day

to be crowned with more than imperial authority; for Kings and Emperors will be among its ministering servants; it will not rule over but *in* all heads, and with these its solitary combinations of ideas, as with magic formulas, bend the world to its will! The time may come, when Napoleon will be better known for his laws than for his battles; and the victory of Waterloo prove less momentous than the opening of the first Mechanics' Institute."

Soon after Abelard went to Corbeil, his bodily powers were overcome by excess of work. His strength was not sufficient for the labors that he undertook, and disease was the result. Even in his sickness, he impressed those who attended him with the greatness of his talent and the profundity of his erudition. *Hic solus scivit scibile quicquid erat,** " He alone knew whatever was knowable," was the great and laconic eulogy of Cœcilius Frey a physician of the Faculty of Paris.

Time alone can restore strength and health to his worn body. His philosophic adventures, his studies, his quarrels, the excitement of starting his new school, his lectures, his anxiety, have exhausted his vital energy, and caused a debility of the whole nervous system. What will he do? His physician advises him to breathe the fresh air of the country, and to rest. He

---

* Essay Historique, par M. et Mᵐᵉ Guizot, p. 14.

is in the midst of strangers, and flatttery will not satisfy his hungry heart.   Ambition, "powerful source of
good and ill," is for a moment forgotten, and memory
of home returns.   What magic there is in the word
home !   It unlocks the heart that refuses to yield to
any other key.   The place where one was born, is
above all others a consecrated spot for him upon earth.
When sickness comes, our thoughts wander to the
scenes of our childhood, and we remember the hand
that rocked us in the hour of helplessness.   When old
age overtakes us we wish to return to our birth-place
to die; and do we not call heaven a *home !*

Abelard, thy father will welcome thee to his mansion in the little burgh of Pallet, and thou hast there
a mother, and a sister, whose care and sympathy will
be for thee full of healing.   Follow the promptings
of thy heart; go by all means ; a few years of rest
will give to thy pale cheek the hue of health.   Paris
will not forget thee; fame and misfortune will come
sufficiently soon.

IX.

ARGENTEUIL.—A FAIR PUPIL OF THE NUNS.

LET us pass on to the year 1107. Abelard is gain-
ing strength in his native country, and is doing nothing of particular interest to us. He may now and
then have a dialectic tilt with some pugnacious brother
Breton, he may visit Roscelin again ; but we have a
new character to introduce, and must leave him until
he returns to the capital of France.

The good sisters of Argenteuil have under their
care a little girl, now six years of age, that is destined
to become the most renowned of her sex. Her name
in the far-off centuries, shall be enrolled with those of
Aspasia, the Countess Matilda, Joan of Arc, and St.
Theresa herself. Above all others she shall be celebrated for her learning, her love, her self-sacrificing
spirit, and the eloquence of her letters.

But who is she ? what is the land of her birth ? who
are her parents ? how came she here among the nuns
of Argenteuil ?

We are not altogether certain about her name. The
daughters of the convent will not allow us to question

them too closely.* A learned and famous lover will pretend that her name is derived from the Hebrew word *Heloim*, which is one of the names of the Deity ; but lovers always say and do insane things, and we are not in the least inclined to favor such a presumptuous etymology. She shall be known by the name of Heloise, and it matters not what the nuns call her now.

Paris is her birth-place. As near as we can ascertain, she was born in 1101, the next year after Abelard's arrival.

There seems to be an impenetrable mystery hanging over her parentage. It is generally admitted that Fulbert, the canon of the Cathedral of Paris, is her uncle. Her mother's name is Hersenda, but the name of her father must remain unknown. The general impression is that noble blood flows in her veins, and this impression is doubtless correct. There are certain whispers about the family of the Montmorencys, but if Heloise is in any way connected with those feudal, fervent loyalists, it is probably on her mother's side. Some silly gossips say that Fulbert is her father, but we would wager the kingdom of France, that the high-souled Heloise is not the daughter of such a piece of stupidity. We will not, however, trouble ourselves about a question that cannot be decided.

---

* Vie d'Abelard, p. 46.

The little girl is an orphan, and poor, and we will love her for the sake of her childish grace, beauty, activity and brightness. The nuns—have they not the hearts of women?—gently kiss her high-arched brow, and her little, thin, half-quivering lips.

Uncle Fulbert, the Canon of Notre-Dame, has given orders that she be instructed in the best possible manner. Argenteuil is not far from Paris, the canon can easily watch the progress of his niece, and, moreover, his authority is weighty with the sisters at the convent. They need no watching and admonition, however, for woman is by nature faithful to her trust, and it is a pleasure, rather than a task, to teach so bright a pupil. In the little girl's mystic eye, there is a nameless power that fascinates her teachers. Every nerve seems to be surcharged with vitality, and her touch is magnetic. She is as restless as the breeze of summer, but in every wayward motion or act there is a sweetness and a grace that disarm reproof. She learns without effort what other girls of her age cannot comprehend at all. A gleam of light at times seems to pass over her fair face, and she utters words whose depth of meaning astonishes the nuns and fills them with awe. There are those of lofty spirit, whose presence interprets for us the deep words of Novalis, "There is but one temple in the world, and that is the body of Man. Nothing is holier than this high form. Bending before men is a reverence done to

3*

this Revelation in the flesh. We touch Heaven, when we lay our hand on a human body." Woe to the heaven-defying, sacrilegious man that shall undertake the robbery of such a temple! There are things that may not be forgiven; there are gifts for the accepted worshipper that must not be touched by the hands of the profane. Yet, O mysterious Life, how shall we fathom thy meaning! Solemn words of toleration admonish us to pause: "Judge not, that ye be not judged."

The significance of these half mystic words will appear in due season; for the present, we will leave the dear little innocent Heloise in the care of the pious sisters of Argenteuil. To look beyond the place where earth and sky meet is impossible; with us, as we go, the visible horizon will move. The end of the rainbow, it is said, dips in a vase of gold, but the treasure always recedes when we seek it. The avaricious old Fulbert will act foolishly enough, but, like Judas, he will be an instrument in the hands of an over-ruling Power, and play the part destined for him in the general progress of things.

X.

THE CONDITION OF WOMAN AT THE BEGINNING OF THE TWELFTH CENTURY.

THE state of society may always be determined by ascertaining the condition of woman. When she is the companion of man, and her relation to him that of equality, then we may be sure that a high point of rational and moral development has been attained. The tardiness of civilization has always been chided by the complaints of woman. She represents the higher sentiments, disinterested love, the benevolent affections, religion, and delicate sensibility, the divinest part of humanity, that part of our nature, advance towards the realization of which in practical life, constitutes true progress. The treatment of woman indicates in what estimation man holds the most beautiful portion of his own being. When men are brutes, women will be slaves. The lords of creation may declare that the daughters of Eve are inferior to themselves, but such a declaration only shows their own weakness and defects. He who places a light estimate upon things of highest worth, proclaims his own igno-

rance and want of judgment. Man through the frailty of woman publishes his low estimate of all that is
holiest in the relations of life. Strike out from existence all that is suggested by the words, mother,
daughter, sister, wife, and no man would care to live.
One half of humanity is man ; another, yet equal half,
is woman. He who speaks lightly of woman; curses
the hand that supported him in the hour of helplessness, pronounces a malediction upon the fair young
being that with mingled reverence and trust calls him
father, utters blasphemy against the Being who has
filled with disinterested affection the bosom of her
whose heart beats with blood kindred to his own, and
returns hatred for love to her who has bestowed upon
him a greater gift than all wealth can buy. He who
knows woman in all of these relations, however, rarely
speaks evil of her.

In the eleventh century, the Holy Roman Empire
was overthrown by the Holy Roman Pontificate, and
woman was cursed.

The feudal world corrupted the church, and the
church was reformed by the monks. The empire was
the highest type of the feudal world, which sleeps its
everlasting sleep with the house of Suabia. The
church, once reformed, was not contented until she destroyed her corrupter.

Under feudalism, the eldest son inherited the estate,
or rather the estate inherited him. The only dower

of the daughter was the chaplet of roses and her
mother's kiss. All but the eldest inherited—the wide
realms of beggary. " Their bed is the threshold of
their father's house, from which, shivering and a-hun-
gered, they can look upon their elder brother sitting
alone by the hearth, where they, too, have sat in the
happy days of their childhood, and perhaps, he will
order a few morsels to be flung to them, notwithstanding his dogs do growl. Down dogs, down, they are
my brothers; they must have something as well as you."*

There is no asylum for these unfortunates, except
in the church. " Every provident father secures a
bishopric, or an abbey, for his younger sons. They
make their serfs elect their infant children to the
greatest ecclesiastical sees. An archbishop, only six
years of age, mounts a table, stammers out a word or
two of his catechism, is elected, takes upon him the
cure of souls, and governs an ecclesiastical province.
The father sells the benefices in his name, receives the
tithes, and the price of masses, though forgetting to
cause them to be said. He drives his vassals to
confession, and compelling them to make their wills
and leave their property, will ye, nill ye, gathers the inheritance. He smites the people with the spiritual sword
as well as with the arm of the flesh, and alternately fights
and excommunicates, slays and damns, at pleasure.

* Histoire de France, l. 4, c. ii.

"Only one thing was wanting to this system—that these noble and valiant priests should no longer purchase the enjoyment of the goods of the church by the pains of celibacy; that they should combine sacerdotal splendor and saintly dignity with the consolations of marriage; that they should enliven their family meals with the sacrificial wine, and gorge their little ones with consecrated bread. Sweet and holy hopes, these little ones, God to aid, will grow up! They will succeed, quite naturally, to their fathers' abbeys and bishoprics. It would be hard to deprive them of the palaces and churches; for the church is theirs, their rightful fief. Thus the elective principle is succeeded by that of inheritance, and merit gives place to birth. The church imitates feudalism, and goes beyond it. More than once it has given females a share of the spoil, and a daughter has been dowered by a bishopric. The priest's wife takes place by him, close to the altar ; and the bishop's disputes precedency with the count's."[*]

Thus writes one who is disposed to defend the celibacy of the priesthood, who believes that the church could never have reared the ceiling of the choir of Cologne cathedral, or the arrowy spire of that of Strasbourg ; could never have brought forth the soul of St. Bernard, or the penetrating genius of St. Thomas,

* Histoire de France, l. 4, c. ii.

if her soaring aspirations had been checked by the marriage of her clergy. We will not even condescend to defend a divine institution, since Paul, a higher authority than the successor of St. Peter, has recommended that a bishop be the husband of one wife, and will persist in attributing to feudalism and the spirit of the times the abuses that stain the history of the church. The courtesan, Theodora, raised to the popedom her lover, John XI., and her infamous daughter Marozia, did as much for Sergius III. Let the defenders of the Holy Catholic Church remember these and a thousand other things.

A monk reformed the church, and laid the axe at the root of feudalism. The greatest man of the eleventh century was the Tuscan, Hildebrand.* He must be ranked with those rare and mighty spirits who by strong will, clear insight, and untamable energy, effect successful revolutions. Under Gregory VII. (Hildebrand), the papal power first reached the point of sovereignty.

· The bold monk commenced the work of reform by declaring against the marriage of the priests. " Already, and during the power of the two popes who had preceded him in the pontificate, he had given out that a married priest was no priest ; and great agitation had ensued. An active correspondence com-

---

* See the excellent history of M. Villemain.

menced, leading to a common effort on the part of the
priests; when, emboldened by their numbers, they
loudly declare that they will keep their wives. 'We
prefer,' they said, ' abandoning our bishoprics, abbeys
and cures : let him keep his benefices.' The reformer did not blench. The carpenter's son * did not hes-
itate to let loose the people on the priests. In all directions, the multidude declared against the married
pastors, and tore them from the altar. The people
once given the rein, a brutally levelling instinct made
them delight in outraging all they had adored, in
trampling under foot those whose feet they had kissed,
in tearing the alb, and dashing to pieces the mitre.
The priests were beaten, cuffed, and mutilated in
their own cathedrals; their consecrated wine was
drunk, and the host scattered about. The monks
pushed on, and preached. The people became im-
pregned with a bold mysticism, and habituated to despise form and dash it to bits, as if to set the spirit free.
This revolutionary purification of the church shook it
to the foundation. The means resorted to were atro-
cious. . . . . . The wild anchoret, Pietro Damiani,
traversed Italy with curses and maledictions, careless
of life, and stripping bare, with pious cynicism, the
turpitude of the church. This was to mark out the
married priests for death. Manegold, the theologian,

* Hildebrand was the son of a carpenter.

taught that the opponents of reform might be slain
without compunction. . . . . . The church, armed
with a fierce purity, resembled the sanguinary virgins of Druidical Gaul, or of the Tauric Chersonesus."*

Thus did man curse his own nature in the person
of woman. Strange to say, the noblest female of the
age, the chaste and high-souled Countess Matilda, was
the friend and helper of Hildebrand. Such friendship as that which existed between these two celebrated personages, is worthy of our profoundest admiration,
but we may safely say, that God has not designed
that a whole generation of anchorites should bring the
race to a close. " In the same manner as the middle
age repulsed Jews, and buffeted them as the murder-
ers of Jesus Christ, woman was held in disgrace as
the murderess of mankind. Poor Eve still paid for
the apple. She was looked upon as the Pandora, who
had let loose woes upon the earth."

It would be interesting to trace the contest between
Hildebrand and the Emperor, between the reformed
church and the temporal power, but such a digression
would lead us too far beyond the limits of our subject.

We see, then, what was the condition of woman at
the close of the eleventh century, and consequently at
the beginning of the twelfth. Poor little Heloise!
thou dost little know what trials await thee. A few

---

* Michelet, l. 4, c. ii.

years more, and thou shalt encounter the world's temptations, and feel the heavy weight of its curse.   The
tears that sometimes flow to thy large eyes, while thy
head is lying upon the bosom of the mother abbess,
are mystic prophets of long years of sorrow, but in
thy blood there is an inborn heroism that shall defy
the maledictions of the age, and proclaim the "good
time coming," when the queenly heart of woman shall
reign in harmony with the kingly brain of man.

XI.

AN UNWELCOME AUDITOR, LISTENS TO AN OLD MASTER IN A NEW PLACE.

NOT far from the ancient city of Paris, on the southeast, near the place where the royal botanical garden now is, there was buried the remains of a recluse, who had been noted for his piety. Thither, William of Champeaux, assuming monastic habit, retired, in the year 1108. He was followed by several of his disciples, and around him there was formed a kind of voluntary congregation of regular clerks. This place afterwards became the site of the abbey of Saint Victor.*

What the archdeacon's motives were for leaving an elevated post in the church of Paris, is more than we can tell. His chances for a still more elevated place in the church were greater than those of any other man. His position as head of the cathedral school, it is said, was nearly equivalent to the first rank in

* Vie d'Abelard, p. 17.

the palace of the king.   Perhaps he wished to commence a life of peace and piety.   It may be that he
hoped to find a shelter against the storms which he had
sufficient sagacity to foresee.   This step made him very
popular with the clergy, for they admired the devotion
and humility of a man who was willing to leave a place
of emolument and honor for the solitude of a cloister.
The proud and ambitious William may have chosen
that route to the episcopacy.   A candidate for office
likes to grasp the hands of mechanics just before the
election, and human nature is the same at all times and
in all places.

Hoc vere philosopari est.   " This is truly acting
the part of a philosopher," wrote Hildebert, the celebrated bishop of Manse, afterwards the more celebrated archbishop of Tours.   He exhorted William
not to renounce his lectures, and the new recluse
followed the advice of his distinguished correspond-
ent.   Thus was commenced the great school of
Saint Victor, which has played an important part,
especially in the teaching of theology.

William was soon surrounded with pupils,* and his
life again became tranquil.   Destiny, however, has
denied him repose; he belongs to the cause of the
past, and the world moves on.   All of a sudden, in
the midst of one of his lectures, Abelard reappears

* Epistola Abælardi, in the Guizot edition, p. 8.

among his pupils. The young Breton looks older, and stronger; the glow of health is on the cheek that a few years since was so pale; there is new fire in his thought-illumined eye; he seems conscious of his power, and his face wears an expression of one knows not what settled design. Be careful, William, or thy pupils will observe in thee an uneasy look of apprehension; and their confidence will be changed to distrust. What does the belligerent Abelard want here in this peaceful retreat, in this place consecrated by the buried bones of a saint? The master is lecturing on rhetoric, and he wishes to receive instruction. It is a modest and flattering request, and he cannot be denied. Abelard is a man now, and may not be so uncourteous as to dispute his master. Perhaps he will be contented to play a subordinate part; and will thus reconcile to himself, a teacher that he once so deeply offended. " The boy is father of the man," and no such thing must be looked for.

The pretended pupil soon found an opportunity to question the master. As we have already seen, William of Champeaux was a realist, that is, he attributed to *universals* a positive reality. When one uses the word book in its general, or universal sense, it is evident that he does not mean any book in particular; and the question comes up, Does this word stand for a substance, or for a mere idea, for something *real*, or something *nominal?* William of

Champeaux contended that it stood for something real, and Abelard contended that it was used in a merely nominal sense. This question of nominalism and realism, unimportant as it may now seem, was then the dominant question in dialectics, and, as it were, the touchstone of masters and schools.* Abelard, as might have been expected, came off conqueror. His opponent was driven to the wall, and acknowledged himself conquered by striking out from his formula a word of the greatest importance to his system. Such a retraction was a deathblow to William's reputation as a teacher of philosophy. His pupils deserted him, and his spirit forsook him. Abelard was the victor; he destroyed the reputation of his antagonist, deprived the proud master of his pupils, and triumphed over an enemy.

It may be remarked, in passing, that nominalism and realism are now regarded as both true and both false. Some general words stand for things, others are mere names. Abelard was right in combating the exclusive realism of William of Champeaux, and he was also right in combating the exclusive nominalism of Roscelin, the canon of Compiegne. In proposing conceptualism as a substitute for both, he took a step in advance, and showed the fertility of his genius.†

The archdeacon, in leaving the metropolitan

* Ouvr. ined. d'Abelard, *De Gener. et Spec.*, p. 513.
† See M. Cousin's *Fragments de Philosophie Scholastique.*

school, appointed a successor. The new master, for some cause which is not clearly ascertained, gave his chair to Abelard, and took his place among the pupils. According to the rules of the establishment, no one could teach without being authorized by a recognized master. Abelard was therefore only a delegate of the new chief. The only mode of removing him was through the master of the school. Consequently William attacked his own successor, accusing him of many things, without avowing the real cause of hostility, which, without doubt, was his deference to Abelard. The new teacher was removed, and a tool of the defeated and embittered foe of Abelard was put in his place.

The decisive battle has been fought, the real victory has been won, but the new hero cannot yet take peaceful possession of the conquered territory. There is a hostile master in the great school of Paris, who is protected by the laws pertaining to instruction, and in addition to this, it is regarded as an act of rashness and almost as an offence, to teach in the city, save in the authorized manner. William of Champeaux has been unhorsed, but many things are yet to be done ere Abelard can reach the object of his ambition. He has experience, skill, learning, energy, eloquence, boldness, youth, perseverance, and unconquerable determination, and we may predict for him the most brilliant success.

XII.

SIEGE OF PARIS.

Si quæritis hujus
Fortunam pugnæ, non sum superatus ab illo.

"If you ask me what was the fortune of the combat, I was not vanquished by him."

Ovid, Metam. l. xiii.

ABELARD found it necessary to return to Melun, and there to commence his lectures again.

William of Champeaux was not benefited in the least by the temporary flight of his enemy. He lacked energy of character, and skill to repel an attack. Above all, he was conscious of weakness and defeat. The disinterestedness of his piety in seeking a retreat being called in question, he was forced to retire some distance from the city into the country; the congregation which he had formed, and a few remaining disciples followed him.*

Abelard left Melun. He put his army of disciples on the march for Paris. The city was closed against him, that is, the cathedral school, to the mastership of which he was entitled by his genius and learning, was in the hands of another. He encamped outside

* Brucker, Hist. Crit. Phil. t. iii. p. 733.

of the wall, on the heights of Saint Genevieve. It is said that he even occupied the cloister of the church dedicated to the patron saint of the besieged city. Every thing is lawful in war. Paris should have opened her great school to a philosopher, if she did not wish to have one of her sacred suburban temples defiled by the teaching of dialectics.

Saint Genevieve has since become the Sinai, as a Frenchman says, of university instruction. It was then regarded as an asylum for those who were imbued with the spirit of independence. From time to time, private schools were established there, for such as could not find admission to the crowded schools of the city, and for such as were not satisfied with the regular instruction. These schools were tolerated, rather than authorized, by the chancellor of the Church of Paris.

Among all of these teachers, Abelard was the recognized superior. Even his enemies spoke of his "sublime eloquence," of his "science that bore every test." His originality and boldness seduced the crowd, and confounded his rivals. A head and shoulders above the rest, clad in an impenetrable logical coat of mail, he provoked those around him to combat, by his novel and daring assertions, and then put them to flight by the first stroke of his terrible dialectic lance. He was swift as Achilles, strong as Ajax; woe to the unlucky man who entered the lists against him.

4

While besieging Paris, Abelard became in reality, if not in name, the master of the schools. The successor of William was no better than a phantom, terrifying a few timid souls into submission by the ghostly voice of authority.

William heard, from his retreat in the country, of the danger of his successor, and marched to his aid.* He collected around him his old partisans, vainly hoping to raise the siege. This movement was unfortunate, for the few remaining pupils of the cathedral school returned to William of Champeaux at Saint Victor. The master abandoned his chair. Philosophic famine had wasted the besieged. The two old combatants were again pitted against each other. Skirmishes took place daily between detachments from the two hostile armies of disciples. The pupils of William, who had once been beaten in single combat, lacked confidence in their master, and were generally repulsed.

In Abelard the cause of the future triumphed over the cause of the past in William. The old master fought to the last, and yielded like a hero, in obedience to a stern necessity. "If you ask me," said Abelard, quoting Ovid, "what was the fortune of the combat, I shall respond to you like Ajax—He did not conquer me." †

* Vie d'Abelard, p. 27.   † The first letter, p. 14.

XIII.

ABELARD RETURNS TO PALLET TO PART WITH HIS MOTHER.

SCARCELY had Abelard gained a final triumph over his opposers, when he was summoned * to Brittany by his mother.

He who has no love for the one that bore him, that nourished him in infancy, is not capable of any human affection. Abelard forgot his ambition, forgot his triumphs, and obeyed the summons of his mother.

But what did she want of her son at such a moment, when he had just reached the object of his ambition, when he had just grasped the prize for which he had been contending so long and so well?

Her husband had been converted, as it was said; had embraced a religious life. Beranger, who had received just enough literary culture to make him discontented with a rude military life, who had probably become disgusted with the world, for whom the " times were out of joint,"—who perhaps was earnestly seek-

* Dûm verò hæc agerentur, charissima mihi mater mea Lucia reputriare me compulit. First letter, p. 14.

ing the salvation of his soul, had sought an asylum in
a convent. The great tide of life might roar madly
on without; but as for him, he would cherish among
the religious the hope of a more blessed existence
hereafter, and strive by every recognized method to
attain it.

According to the custom of the times, his wife,
Lucie, was about to imitate his example. Before
bidding adieu to the world, she wished to see and embrace her son—her first-born !

Many were those in the middle age, who, like the
father and mother of Abelard, sought a resting-place
under the shadow of the church. Man loves repose;
he shrinks from the rude conflict with nature, by
which he compels her to yield fruits for the nourishment of his body; he dreads antagonism with his fel-
low-man; he would escape from the limitations of
external existence, and live wholly in the spirit;
therefore he builds for himself a retreat, where he
may enjoy, far from the profane, a higher, holier fellowship with kindred spirits, and realize a life that is
wholly devoted to noble ends. Asceticism, whatever
form it may take, has its root in the human heart. It
equally points to the defects of the actual, and to the
perennial beauty of the ideal. When men are happy
in society, they will not build a monastery, nor attempt
to found a new *community*.

In the Middle Age, monastic institutions flourished,

for society was profoundly unhappy. Especially at
the beginning of the eleventh century, existence
seemed to be for each one, at best, a calamity. Notwithstanding the promise of her priests, that Christianity should do away with all suffering upon earth,
still life was full of sorrow, and the strong man in the
midst of his loved ones watered the hearth-stone of
his habitation with tears. The belief had been
handed down from generation to generation, that the
world would come to an end in the thousandth year
from the nativity. As the appointed time drew nigh,
each one seemed to listen for the blast of the last
trump, and to watch for the bursting forth of flames
from the bosom of the earth. Famine and pestilence
were let loose, like angels of retribution, to punish a
sin-darkened world. Highways were strown with the
dead, and places of pilgrimage were packed with the
victims of a desolating disease. Famine seized many
that were spared by the pestilence. The stronger
killed and eat the weaker. Forty-eight were massacred and devoured by a single wretch in the forest
of Mâçon. In one place, human flesh was publicly
exposed for sale in the market-place. The beasts of
the forests visited the habitations of men, for their
daily food.*

In the general despair of the times, every body
sought refuge in the church. The abbots had to exer-

* Histoire de France, L iv., c. 1.

cise their authority to keep all kings and nobles from turning monks. The Emperor Henry II., entering an abbey, exclaimed with the Psalmist: "This is my rest for ever; here will I dwell, for I have desired it." He was accepted on a vow of obedience, and sent back to his empire.

The year one thousand, however, passed by, and a period of intense suffering was followed by a period of deep superstition. Monastic institutions greatly flourished in the eleventh century. The church, as we have already seen, increased in splendor, and was corrupted by the spirit of the feudal world; but by the monks, with Hildebrand at their head, she was reformed.

The course of Beranger and Lucie is, therefore, a common one. They are acting like multitudes of others in their times. Abelard has done well in going to receive the adieus of his mother. She claims a mother's right; and with the sage instinct of a true-hearted woman, gives him counsel that is better than any precepts of philosophy.—When was a mother ever insincere to a son?—He will not follow her advice, however, and calamities shall come as the avengers of his misdeeds. He shall follow the course of his father and mother to escape the multiplying ills of an unfortunate life, but shall find that no retreat can give quiet to a disturbed mind, and rest to a bur-thened heart. The soul of man must find peace in some other asylum than that of a convent.

'

XIV.

ANSELM OF LAON.

WHEN Abelard returned to Paris no one hindered him from taking possession of the school that was his by right of conquest. William of Champeaux, abandoning his retreat, as well as the school of Saint Victor, had been made bishop of Chalons-Sur-Marne. The two hostile philosophers will not meet again, but their enmity has not ceased. William will fulfil with sufficient dignity the office of bishop, but he lacks magnanimity, even generosity, and will prejudice, some time during the few more years that remain to him on earth, the good St. Bernard against Abelard. His hatred shall be felt by his conquering pupil, even when the turf lies cold above him.

Abelard is now the dictator of intellectual Paris. He has no rival in the schools, and his authority is supreme. He is in philosophy all that Napoleon will be in arms, and rules by the force of genius alone.

He is not contented, for his warlike nature is not satisfied with peace. The conqueror droops when there are no more enemies to be subdued. When the

business man retires, his days are listless and weary-
ing, and he wonders that happiness should have forsa-
ken him at the moment when he renounced care and
toil. Satisfaction is found only in *doing*. Alexander
wept when he had done conquering the world, for the
same reason that the merchant feels sad when he closes
for the last time the old familiar counting-room.
When one leaves scenes of activity for the purpose of
enjoying repose, he soon finds himself a victim of
ennui, and strong must be his virtue, or he will yield
to the excitement of sinful pleasures.

Abelard, moved perhaps by a desire to obtain a
position in the church, like that of William of Champeaux, for the purpose, it might be, of adding a knowledge of theology to his other acquirements, or im-
pelled, possibly, by his restless nature, to seek new adventures, left Paris for the school of Anselm at Laon.

Anselm of Laon, who must not be confounded with
Anselm, the Archbishop of Canterbury, was the most
distinguished teacher of theology in his times. He
began his teaching in Paris, and William of Champeaux had been his pupil. His reputation was such,
that pupils were attracted to Laon from all parts of
Europe. His method was simple, but his elocution
was remarkably fine. His lectures contained little
else than a commentary on the text of Scripture, but
a fine delivery charmed his auditors.

Abelard was not at all pleased with his new master. "From a distance," said the restless pupil, "he was a beautiful tree loaded with foliage; near by, he was a tree without fruit, or resembled the arid tree that was cursed by Christ. When he kindled his fire he produced smoke, but no light."* We may easily believe that he did not "long lie at ease under the shade of that tree." At first he manifested his low estimate of Anselm by neglecting his lectures. Those pupils who thought most of their teacher, were of course offended by such an exhibition of indifference. One of his fellow students asked him one day what he thought of the instruction in sacred things, hinting to him, at the same time, that his studies thus far had been confined to natural sciences. The response of Abelard was quite characteristic, and somewhat provoking. He regarded as most salutary the science that gives one a knowledge of his own soul, but thought that men of science needed nothing but a single commentary, in order to understand the sacred books. He added that such were in no need of a master. This response was not very flattering to the self-love of those who were zealous pupils, and the presumptuous young Breton, who openly neglected the instruction of the great Anselm, was made the

---

* Epistola Abælardi (*Historia Calamitatum*), p. 16. With reference to Anselm Abelard quotes from Lucan:

"   .   .   .   Stat magni nominis umbra,
Qualis frugifero quercus sublimis in agro."

4*

object of their ridicule. He coolly answered their
jeering, by saying that he was ready for them if they
wished to test the matter. The Prophecy of Ezekiel
was accordingly chosen as the most obscure and most
difficult to explain. An accompanying commentary
was given to Abelard, and he invited them to attend
his lecture the next day. Some that professed friendship, advised him not to undertake an enterprise of
such magnitude, and to remember his want of experience in such high matters. With his usual self-reliance, he replied to them that he was in the habit of
obeying his own spirit instead of following custom.

At the first lecture he had but few auditors. It
seemed to most of the students, many of whom belonged to the regular clergy, that a lecture upon the
most difficult portion of the Scriptures by a new-comer,
by one who had received no instruction in sacred science, who had never been initiated into the mysteries
of theology, was a thing too ridiculous to be counte-
nanced, too rash to be encouraged, too irreverent to be
tolerated. The few, however, that did attend, were
greatly charmed. The notes which they took
were transcribed by the others, and their eulogies
made all eager to attend the next lecture.

A new chair was thus erected by the side of that
of Anselm. A rash young man not only seemed to
despise the most distinguished of European teachers
of theology, but threatened to eclipse him among his

own pupils. The old man was astonished and enraged. A fate like that of William of Champeaux seemed to await him. Two* of his most distinguished pupils, however, came to his assistance, and recommended the old man to exercise his authority, and put a stop to the lectures of Abelard. Anselm announced to his pupils, by way of excuse for his course, that he feared lest through the inexperience of Abelard, some error concerning doctrine might escape him ; but they were not satisfied with such a pretext, and attributed to jealousy the real motives of the master for silencing so brilliant a lecturer.†

Abelard returned to Paris, having despoiled the old theologian of much of his honor. It is an established law, that every man must give place to a superior. The wisest and the best is the lawful governor of the world.

---

* Alberic of Rheims, and Lotulfus of Navarre, with whom Abelard subsequently came in contact.

† See Abelard's account in the *Historia Calamitatum*

XV.

FULBERT AND HIS NIECE.

WHEN the curious traveller goes to Paris, he not only visits the splendid constructions of modern times, but also looks after those things that are monumental of earlier ages.

When in going about that part of the city which is most ancient, the part situated on the island in the Seine, we descend by a flight of stairs from the quai Napoleon into the rue des Chantres, above the door of the first house on the left, we read this inscription :

HÉLOÏSE, ABÉLARD HABITÈRENT CES LIEUX, DES SINCÈRES AMANS
MODÈLES PRÉCIEUX.   L'AN 1118.

" Here dwelt Heloise and Abelard, precious models of sincere lovers. The year 1118."

If we go in we shall find fitted into the wall a double medallion, bearing the profile of a man and the profile of a woman. The stupid people about the place will try to make us believe that these profiles are those of Abelard and Heloise, but we had better be a little incredulous. The medallion is probably the work of a blundering restorer, who, some time in the fifteenth or sixteenth century, put it in the place of one more authentic and ancient.*

We are not certain that Abelard and Heloise ever dwelt in this house, which does not seem to be seven or eight hundred years old; but unquestionably the dwelling of Fulbert, the canon of Notre-Dame, was not far from this place.

The locality is nearly north from the cathedral. Between the house and the river there is now a wharf, but in the year 1116 or 1117, there must have been a sloping bank from the foot of the street to the running waters below. The street is narrow and winding. For centuries past it has been frequented by those connected with the metropolitan church. The different costumes of the various orders of these savers of souls according to the grace of Rome, give to the street a peculiar interest. On the bank of the river opposite, we may now see the splendid Hotel de Ville. In the early years of the twelfth century, the place where that splendid palace now stands, was a wide unoccupied shore.

In the year 1117, Heloise lived here with her uncle. She had left the convent of Argenteuil, one

* Remusat: *Vie de Abelard,* p. 51.

knows not when.   The nuns there, most likely gave
her all the instruction that they had to impart, which
in the Middle Age was more than we boasting mod-
erns are apt to think.   The education of females in
the convents had its excellencies as well as its defects.
It was too subtile and poetic, not sufficiently prosy
and practical.   Christian girls were instructed in the
literature and philosophy of antiquity, and other things
were neglected.   The imagination was developed more
than the understanding, therefore the heart was endangered.   Marriage was regarded by the church as
at least a venial sin, and the budding maiden was not
taught to look forward to a sanctified relationship in
which she might find a home for her affections.   Bun-
glers attempted to mend the work of God; confusion
was introduced, and many a one innocent as Iphige-
nia or the daughter of Jephtha, went as a victim to an
altar erected by the sightless, as a bride to the shadowy arms of death.

Heloise was then about seventeen years of age.
Although so young, her name was known, not only in
Paris, but throughout the kingdom.   Her talents and
acquirements were extraordinary; she was by nature
a queen, and took the intellectual throne, like one who
has a perfect right to rule.   Her aristocracy was
somewhat deeper than that of the cut and color of the
dress; it was that elder aristocracy of vital force and
blood, of brain and heart.   A wooden head is good

enough in its place, but is rather ridiculous when thrust inside of a crown.

Fulbert was entirely of the earth, earthy. To eat dinners, acquire money, and get notoriety of the better kind, was, for him, to live. That such a piece of flesh as he, should have been placed in the ancient city of Paris, as a spiritual guide to a numerous flock, is one of the strange things which time has to record against humanity.

It is sad to see such a child of genius as Heloise given up to the guidance of such a stolid man. One sometimes has to pay a dear penalty for being related to certain persons. Fulbert has no love for his niece of the beautiful and spiritual kind. She is admired by every body, and he likes her for the fame that she brings his house. He prides himself on being the uncle of such a queen of learning. A man who has made money, sometimes purchases for an immense sum a great work of art, and as its possessor, appropriates to himself a portion of the praises that are bestowed upon a production of genius; he cannot appreciate the noble picture or the statue which he owns, he does not love it for its beauty and intrinsic worth, but prizes it for some accidental and entirely outward value: such is the regard of Fulbert for Heloise. He cannot appreciate her endowments; in his dull eye a gifted soul has no deep, divine significance, he boasts of having a wonderful niece, as King Admetus might have boasted of having an excellent shepherd.

There are melancholy hours in which Heloise feels the oppression of solitude. The soul continually seeks for fellowship; it is happy when it finds an interpretation of its own moods in the expressed experience of another; alone, it is restless and sad. The house of Fulbert is to Heloise a prison, for among its inmates there is not one, with whom she can hold any communion of higher sentiment and thought. She is not indifferent to fame, but the approbation of the great, thoughtless, noisy world without, cannot satisfy the silent aspirations of her spirit. She is no longer a child; her heart has become the home of longings that are strange and new. A mystic tear now and then forces itself to her eye, and thoughts visit the soul, that seem like prophetic interpretations of life's future years.

Dear Heloise! one of the gods might love thee; Apollo himself might be satisfied with thy most precious of hearts; thou hast no guides, and art without experience; the serpent lurks near thee; I fear thou wilt accept the apple, which will turn to bitter ashes upon thy sweet lips!

XVI.

"THE OBSERVED OF ALL OBSERVERS."

WHEN Abelard returned to Paris, after his quarrel with Anselm at Laon, he found an unoccupied field; the schools were all opened to him. His old enemies were silent, and he took his place at the head of public instruction.

It is said, and it is probably true, that Abelard was made canon of Paris, as well as rector of the schools. There is no evidence, however, that he became a priest until afterwards; but unquestionably he was looking for advancement in the church.

In Paris, Abelard went on with his exegesis of Ezekiel, which had been begun and suspended at Laon. He was as successful in theology as in philosophy. In fact he was the first one who applied, to any extent, philosophy to the teaching of theology, and thus founded scholasticism, properly so called.

Abelard soon became the most noted man of all France, and his fame spread to distant nations. From Germany, from England, from Italy—from every civilized country, pupils flocked to Paris, attracted by the report of his learning and eloquence. Picts, Gascons, Iberians, Normans, Flemings, Teutons, Swedes, as well as the children of Rome, went to be instructed by Abelard. In a year or two after his return to Paris, the number of his pupils amounted to more than five thousand. Greatly gifted must have been the man who, in the rude Middle Age, could thus charm all Europe by the eloquent exposition of the abstract doctrines of philosophy.

The noblest young men of the whole civilized world were among the five thousand pupils that daily listened to the voice of Abelard. What is the influence of a king compared with that of such a teacher? *Quis custodiet custodes?* somewhere asks Juvenal; "Who shall keep the keepers?" He who instructs the rulers of society is a keeper of the keepers. Among those pupils there was one destined to become a pope (Celestin II.); there were nineteen destined to become cardinals; more than a hundred destined to become bishops or archbishops of France, England, and Germany. There were also many who afterwards became distinguished in the political world, who bore a conspicuous part in the affairs of the times, and left a name in history.*

"In the midst of this attentive and obedient mul-

---

* The enemies, as well as the friends of Abelard, testify to the number of his pupils. Fabulous as it seems, all authorities agree that there is no exaggeration.

titude," says Charles de Remusat,* "was often seen
passing a man with a large forehead, with a vivid and
fiery look, with a noble bearing, whose beauty still
preserved the brilliancy of youth, while taking the
more marked traits and the deeper hues of full viri-
lity. His grave and elegant dress; the severe luxury
of his person; the simple elegance of his manners,
which were by turns affable and haughty; an attitude
imposing, gracious, and not without that indolent
negligence which follows confidence in success, and
the habitual exercise of power; the respect of those
who followed in his train, who were arrogant to all
except him; the eager curiosity of the multitude :—
all, when he went to his lectures or returned to his
dwelling, followed by his disciples, still charmed by
his speech, — all announced a master the most
powerful in the schools, the most renowned in the
world, the most loved in the cité. The crowd in
the streets stopped to gaze at him as he passed by;
in order to see him, the people rushed to the doors of
their houses, and females gazed at him from their
windows. Paris had adopted him as her child, as her
ornament and her light. Paris was proud of Abelard,
and celebrated the name of which, after seven centuries, the city of all glories and oblivions has preserved
the popular memory."

* Vie d'Abelard, p. 43.

Such is the position of Abelard about the year 1117; but the conqueror shall soon be conquered; he has been sufficiently mighty to take a city; but he will not be equal to the ruling of his own spirit.

XVII.

A PAIR OF RENOWNED LOVERS.

"Thou know'st how guiltless first I met thy flame,
When love approached me under friendship's name;
My fancy formed thee of angelic kind,
Some emanation of th' all-beauteous mind.
Those smiling eyes, attemp'ring ev'ry ray!
Shone sweetly lambent with celestial day.
Guiltless I gazed; heav'n listen'd while you sung;
And truths divine came mended from that tongue.
From lips like those what precept failed to move?
Too soon they taught me 'twas no sin to love:
Back through the paths of pleasing sense I ran,
Nor wished an Angel whom I loved a Man.
Dim and remote the joys of saints I see;
Nor envy them that heav'n I lose for thee."

POPE's *"Eloïsa to Abelard."*

" THE more spirit one has," says Pascal, " the greater
his passions are, because the passions being only sentiments and thoughts which purely pertain to the
spirit, although they are occasioned by the body, it is
clear that they are still only the spirit itself, and that
thus they fulfil its entire capacity."*

* *Des Pensées de Pascal,* par M. Victor Cousin, second
edition, p. 397.

The youth and early manhood of Abelard were
pure. Philosophy was his mistress, and he served
her with all the ardor of his intense nature. His
fiery passions spent their energy in study and in dialectic war with the most renowned masters of his
times. At length the whole circle of science was completed, and every foe that appeared on the battle-field
of argumentation was conquered. His spirit would
not be at rest; it is not in the nature of man to be
satisfied without the love of woman.

What can Abelard do? He is already a canon,
and is looking for advancement in the church. Rome
has cursed woman, and will not allow any of her
priests to marry. Concubines they may have, but
wives are unlawful. He that ministers in sacred
things may say his prayers in the arms of a courtesan,
but he must not taste the sweets of wedded love.
The wicked layman may enjoy the pleasures of domestic life, but the immaculate priest is permitted to
look for sympathy and solace only among the daughters
of sin.

Abelard, then, can abandon his idea of becoming
a priest, and marry; or he can adhere to his ambition
of preferment in the church, and seek a mistress.
The latter course is chosen, and becomes the occasion
of many misfortunes.

For Abelard we do not claim saintship, yet Rome
was in part to blame for his fall. The church was at

war with nature and revelation in demanding celibacy for her priesthood. Abelard, if we judge him by the highest standard, should have abandoned the church, or in aspiring to the priesthood should have been willing to fulfil the vows which it imposes. The lax morality of the times and the habits of the clergy may soften our judgment, yet they are not sufficient excuses for his crime.

In all Paris, the niece of Fulbert, the young, the accomplished, the beautiful Heloise, was regarded as the most worthy object of his attention. Such were his renown, his manly beauty, his grace of manner and eloquence of conversation, that, in those lax times, any woman in France would have considered herself honored by his proposals. He chose the one best fitted by her studies and by the strength of her mind to become his companion, who might have been the blessed wife of his bosom until the hour of his death, had not Mother Church interposed a barrier to such a sacred union, had not ambition tempted him beyond his strength.

It is not known when Abelard and Heloise first met. Two such persons could not long remain, even in the largest city, unknown to each other. They seemed to be placed there for each other—to bless each other ; but their meeting was the occasion of sorrow instead of lasting joy.

The cunning brain of the philosopher soon contrived a plan to get access to the object of his passion. Mutual friends propose to Fulbert that he shall take the great master into his house. The residence of Fulbert is so convenient to the school; Abelard finds the cares of keeping a house so troublesome; he is absorbed in deep study, and the servants waste his income. Fulbert loves money, and is tempted with the price offered. He loves his niece, too, and thinks it is a good opportunity to complete her education under the private instruction of the most renowned teacher. Foolish old Fulbert! if a wife had been allowed thee, her eye would have seen what entirely escaped thy obtuse vision, and Heloise would not have been exposed to a danger that she was unable to withstand.

We cannot help cursing Abelard, notwithstanding all the extenuating circumstances of his times, for his sin was a deliberate act, as appears from his own confession.

"There existed at Paris," he says,* "a young lady, named Heloise, niece of a certain canon, who was called Fulbert, who in his love for her, had neglected nothing in order to give her the most complete and brilliant education. She was far from being the lowest in beauty, and was certainly the highest in literary attainments. Such knowledge of literature

---

* Abelard Op., ep. i., p. 10.

the more highly commended a young girl because it
is so rare in women, and had made her the most noted
in the whole kingdom.

" Therefore observing that she was endowed with
all those charms that are wont to attract lovers, I regarded her as a more proper person to engage in an
enterprise of love with me, and believed that I could
easily accomplish my purpose. My name was then
so great, the graces of youth and the perfection of
form gave me a superiority so unquestionable, that
from whatever female I might have honored with my
love I should have feared no repulse.

" I persuaded myself the more easily that the
young lady would consent to my desires, because I
knew the extent of her knowledge and her zeal for
learning, and because I knew that more daring things
would be written than spoken, and that thus pleasant
intercourse could always be maintained.

[" Wholly inflamed with love for this young girl, I
sought an occasion to approach her, to familiarize her
with myself in daily conversation, and thus lead her
the more easily to yield her consent. In order to
succeed in this, I employed the intervention of some
friends with the uncle of the girl, that they might
induce him to receive me into ₄his house, which
was very near to my school, at whatever price. I
pretended that my studies were very much impeded
by domestic cares, and that keeping open a house

5

burthened me with too heavy an expense. He was
very avaricious, and eager to facilitate the progress
of his niece in literature. By flattering these two
passions I soon gained his consent, and thus obtained
what I desired; for he was intent upon gain, and
believed his niece would profit by my presence for her
instruction. In regard to this he pressed me with
the most earnest solicitations, acceding to my wishes
more readily than I had dared to hope, and thus
serving himself my love; for he committed Heloise
wholly to my direction, praying me to devote to her
instruction all the time, either day or night, unoccupied in my school; and, if I found her negligent, to
chastise her severely.

"In regard to this, if I wondered at the simplicity of the canon, on the other hand, in thinking of
myself, I was not less astonished than if he had been
confiding a tender lamb to a famished wolf. In giving up Heloise to me, not only to teach, but even to
chastise severely, he was doing nothing else than
granting full license to my desires, and, even if we
were not thus disposed, to offer occasion of triumph;
for should I not be able to accomplish my purpose
with blandishments, I might bend her to my will with
threats and blows. But two considerations closed
the mind of Fulbert against any suspicion, love of
his niece, and my long-standing reputation for continence. To say all in a word; at first we were united

in one house, then in mind. ⌈Under the pretext of study, we were wholly free for love, and the retirement which love sought, zeal for reading offered. The books opened, there were more words of love than of reading: more kisses than precepts; love was reflected in each other's eyes oftener than the purpose of reading directed them to the written page. In order to keep off suspicion, blows were given, but in love and not in rage, in tenderness and not in anger,—blows that transcended the sweetness of all balms!⌉ What then? We passed through all the phases and degrees of love; all its inventions were put under requisition; no refinement was left untried. We were the more ardent in the enjoyment of these pleasures, because they were new to us, and we experienced no satiety. It was very tedious for me to go to my lessons, and it was equally laborious, for the hours of the night were given to love, and those of the day to study. I gave my lectures with negligence and tedium, for my mind produced nothing; I spoke only from habit and memory; I was only a reciter of ancient inventions; and, if I chanced to compose some verses, they were songs of love and not the secrets of philosophy. Most of these verses, as you know, have become popular, and are sung in many regions, especially by those whose life has been charmed by a similar experience."

We weep for thee, fallen Heloise! Thy spirit

has found the sympathy for which it longed, but delirium flows swiftly in thy blood, and paints upon thy youthful cheek the crimson of sin. The tongue whose eloquence charms thee is half false; in the gaze that thy lover bends on thee lurks insincerity; there is a wave of scorn in the smile that gives thee such deep joy; there is a tone of hollowness in the heart that beats against thy reclining head; thou art cursed with passion and not blessed with love. These days of intoxicating pleasure are swiftly passing; the Eden in the midst of which thou art standing shall soon be metamorphosed; its bright colors shall fade, its music shall cease, the warmth of its atmosphere shall turn to chilliness, its rich fruits shall vanish, and around thee on every side shall be desolation as far as the eye can reach. We pity thee, but cannot greatly blame; the earth is cursed beneath thee, but heaven, with its mercy, is above thee still!

XVIII.

CONFUSION ON EVERY SIDE.

GREAT was the desolation among the pupils of Abelard when they perceived the pre-occupation of their
master. A vast army of them, five thousand in number, had come together from every quarter of the
civilized world, attracted by Abelard's reputation for
eloquence and wisdom; from day to day they had
been charmed by his ingenious and brilliant lectures;
and when in their famous teacher languor took the
place of animation,—when commonplace traditions
were given instead of original and striking thoughts,—
when they perceived that his cheek was growing pale
and his eye losing his fire,—when they saw that his
love had been transferred from philosophy to another
object, they were sorely grieved, and some could not
refrain from tears at the sight of that which none
could behold without pain.

Such was the laxness of manners in the Middle
Age, or such was the infatuation of Abelard, that he
took no pains to conceal the cause of his pre-occupa-

tion. Every one in Paris knew it, except the one most interested to know it,—the uncle of Heloise. Every body spoke of his adventure; the songs which he composed and sung for his mistress were scattered abroad and sung in the streets.

The undoubting Fulbert, for a long time, saw not within his house what all Paris saw from without. So stupid was the old canon that at first he would not believe those who informed him of the wrong that Abelard was inflicting upon his family. At length his heavy eyes were opened, and the lovers were consequently separated.

The unhappy pair were overwhelmed with grief and shame. They grieved for each other more than for themselves. "How great," says Abelard, "was the grief of the lovers in their separation! How great was my shame and confusion! How great was my contrition on beholding the affliction of this dear girl! What tides of regret overwhelmed her spirit when she saw my dishonor! Each, while grieving for the other, forgot self. Each deplored a single misfortune, that of the other."*

* It has seemed to us that Abelard's regard for Heloise began in passion and ended in love. It was not the highest kind of love, and is not to be compared with that of Heloise; but we must remember that he was very-busy with the world, while she was wholly occupied with sentiment—with thoughts of her lover.

Separation only inflamed their love. Regardless of every thing but their passion for each other, they sought interviews that were all the sweeter for being stolen. When the cup of shame has once been drunk to the dregs, scandal no longer restrains us. What did the two mad lovers care for the reproach of the world, while they were to each other all in all?*

Heloise with the highest exultation soon informed her lover of the delicacy of her situation, and asked him what was to be done. Every consideration forbade her longer stay in the house of Fulbert. To remove her was a hazardous enterprise, for she was watched by her guardian with great vigilance. One night, in the absence of the uncle, Abelard entered the house by stealth, removed Heloise in the disguise of a nun, and secretly conducted her to Brittany, his native country.

* Actum itaque in nobis est quod in Marte et Venere deprehensis poetica narrat fabula.—Ep. i., p. 13.

XIX.

SECRET MARRIAGE.

" How oft, when pressed to marriage, have I said,
  Curse on all laws but those which love has made ?
  Love, free as air, at sight of human ties,
  Spreads his light wings, and in a moment flies.
  Let wealth, let honor, wait the wedded dame,
  August her deed, and sacred be her fame ;
  Before true passion all those views remove,
  Fame, wealth, and honor ! what are you to Love ?
  The jealous god, when we profane his fires,
  Those restless passions in revenge inspires,
  And bids them make mistaken mortals groan,
  Who seek in love for aught but love alone.
  Should at my feet the world's great master fall,
  Himself, his throne, his world, I'd scorn 'em all :
  Not Cæsar's empress would I deign to prove,
  No ! make me mistress to the man I love ;
  If there be yet another name more free,
  More fond than mistress, make me that to thee !
  Oh ! happy state ! when souls each other draw,
  When love is liberty, and nature law :
  All then is full, possessing, and possess'd !
  No craving void left aching in the breast :
  Ev'n thought meets thought, ere from the lips it part,
  And each warm wish springs mutual from the heart,
  This sure is bliss (if bliss on earth there be),
  And once the lot of Abelard and me."

POPE's " Eloisa to Abelard."

Fulbert, as may well be supposed, was enraged beyond measure, when he found that his niece had escaped. At first he had been overwhelmed with grief on account of the disgrace that had been brought upon his family, and severely reproached himself with being the unwitting instrument of the meeting of Abelard and Heloise ; but when the perfidious philosopher took advantage of his temporary absence to remove the object of his care and solicitation, anger alone took possession of his heart. But he knew not how to take vengeance on Abelard ; he knew not what plots to prepare for him, or what injury to do him. If he killed the seducer, or severely wounded him, he feared that his cherished niece might be the victim of vengeance in the hands of Abelard's friends. As to making himself master of his enemy's person by force, it was an impracticable thing, for he was on his guard, and prepared for resistance, if it became necessary to defend himself.

Finally, touched with compassion on account of the canon's grief, and accusing himself of treachery, Abelard sought the old man with supplications and promises, offering to make any reparation that might be demanded. He reminded Fulbert that his conduct ought to surprise no one who had experienced the power of love, or who was aware what misfortunes had from the beginning of the world befallen the greatest of men through the instrumentality of women.

5*

And in order to appease him the more, he offered the canon a satisfaction which surpassed all his hopes, in proposing to marry her whom he had seduced, provided that the marriage should be kept a secret, so as not to injure his reputation. Fulbert consented; he engaged his own faith, and that of his friends.

In the mean time, Heloise, who was sequestered with a sister of Abelard in Brittany,* had given birth to a son, which she called Pierre Astrolabus. When he returned, therefore, he found a living tie established between himself and the object of his —— which shall we call it, passion or love? She was cheerful, for, inasmuch as her reason had been seduced with sophistry, she was without self-reproach, and her eyes were blessed with the sight of a first-born son.

"I have returned," said Abelard, "to take you back to Paris, and marry† you."

Heloise smiled, for she supposed that he was speaking in jest—an unusual thing with him.

"Your uncle," he continues, "I have seen, and have promised to marry you. Do not smile, I am in earnest; and this promise has reconciled him to me."

"It becomes me then," she responded in a firm

---

* Epistola Abælardi, p. 34.

† Epistola Abælardi, p. 38.—Heloise complains in one of her letters, that Abelard has not mentioned some of the objections which she urged to their marriage.

tone, "to be also serious. I tell you, my Abelard, frankly, that I cannot consent to become your wife.",

"Your refusal," he said, "is pronounced in a decisive manner, and I must have your reasons."

"My reasons you shall certainly have," she said, "if you will accept them in the unpremeditated form in which I am able to give them."

He gravely bowed an assent, with the air of one about to engage in a philosophic disputation, and she proceeded :—

"If you suppose that this step will satisfy my uncle to the extent of appeasing his anger, you are greatly deceived. I know him thoroughly, and, you may depend upon it, he is implacable. If it be your object to save my honor, you are surely mistaken in the means you propose. Will your disgrace exalt me? From the world, from the church, from the schools of philosophy, what reproaches should I merit, if I were to take from them their brightest star. And shall a single woman dare to take to herself that man whom nature meant to be the ornament and benefactor of the race? No, Abelard! I am not yet so selfish and shameless. Then think of the state of matrimony itself. With its petty troubles and its cares, how inconsistent it is with the dignity of a wise man !"

She then fortifies her position by quotations from the Apostle Paul, from St. Jerome, and from the philosopher Cicero, and thus continues :—

"To pass by the impediments which a woman would bring to your study of philosophy, think of the situation in which a lawful alliance would place you. What relation, tell me, can there be between schools and domestics, writing-desks and cradles, books and distaffs, pens and spindles? Who, in fine, that is devoted to religious or philosophic meditations, could endure the crying of children, the lullaby of nurses trying to still them, and the turbulent bustling of disorderly servants? Who could bear the care and trouble of children at an age when they are entirely dependent? These inconveniences, you say, can be avoided in the houses of the rich. That is true, for the opulent do not mind expense, and they are not tormented with daily anxieties. But the condition of philosophers is not the same as that of the rich; and those who are seeking fortune, or whose life is devoted to worldly affairs, have no time to study philosophy and divinity. Hence, the renowned philosophers of former times have contemned the world, have shunned rather than abandoned mundane pursuits, have interdicted themselves all pleasures, in order that they might repose in the arms of philosophy alone.

"One of the greatest of these says, in his instructions to Lucilius: * 'Philosophy demands any thing

---

* Seneca.

else but leisure : all things are to be neglected that
we may devote ourselves to that for which no time
is sufficiently great. It makes little difference whether
you omit philosophy or intermit it ; for it does not
remain, when it is interrupted. Occupations are to
be resisted; they are not to be managed, but put
away ! '

"What with us the monks, who are worthy of
bearing the name, do for the love of God, the philosophers who have been renowned among the Gentiles,
have done for the love of philosophy. For among all
the peoples of the earth, whether Gentile, Jewish, or
Christian, some have always been found pre-eminent
above others in faith or purity of manners, and distinguished from the crowd by some peculiarity of
continence or abstinence.

"Among the Jews in ancient times, such were
the Nazarenes, who devoted themselves to the service
of the Lord in conformity to the law, who, according
to the testimony of St. Jerome, are represented in
the Old Testament as monks; at a later period, the
three philosophic sects, which Josephus in the eigh-
teenth book of his Antiquities, calls Pharisees, Sad-
ducees, and Essenes; among us, the monks, who
imitate the common life of the apostles, or the primitive and solitary life of John ; finally, among the
Gentiles, those who are called philosophers, for they
applied the term wisdom, or philosophy, not so much

to an acquaintance with science as to sanctity of life, as we may be easily convinced by the etymology of the word and the testimony of the saints themselves. Such is, among others, that of St. Augustine, in Book XVIII. of the de Civitate Dei, in which he points out the distinction between philosophic sects: 'The Italian school had for its founder Pythagoras of Samos, from whom it is said the name of philosophy took its rise. Previous to him, those men were called sages, who seemed to excel others by a kind of life worthy of laudation; but he, when interrogated one day in regard to his profession, responded that he was a philosopher,—that is, a seeker or lover of wisdom, inasmuch as he seemed to be extremely arrogant, who made a profession of being wise.'" *

* What a speech for an injured girl to make to her lover who hoped to mend all by marriage! In her the most astonishing erudition and sagacity are combined. She continues her quotation of authorities; but of the rest of the speech we give a paraphrase rather than a translation. Like every noble woman, she would be loved wholly for her own sake. Her lover must adhere to her, because he loves her, not because he is bound by any laws, human or divine. Any fault she can pardon, but the one fault of being indifferent towards her. Her love is so intense that binding it with any outward chain of marriage seems superfluous, and like mockery. Few, like Heloise, can fulfil the law of marriage by being above the law. Church and State, then, must not cease to demand public vows from those who would enter into the conjugal relation.

"From this passage it is evident that the sages of antiquity were called philosophers, not so much on account of their superior knowledge, as on account of their goodness. As to their continence and sobriety, I shall not attempt to collect the proofs ; I should appear like one attempting to instruct the goddess of wisdom herself. But if laymen and gentiles have lived thus, although they were free from all religious vows, you, who are a clerk, and bound to the duties of a canon, ought not to prefer shameless pleasures to your sacred ministry; to precipitate yourself into an ingulfing Charybdis, and, braving every shame, plunge irrevocably into an abyss of impurity. If the prerogatives of the church weigh lightly with you, maintain at least the dignity of philosophy. If you have no religious scruples, let the sentiment of de-cency temper your rashness. Remember that Socrates was a married man, and how bitterly he expiated such an offence to philosophy; others, warned by his example, should be made more cautious."

She also represented to Abelard the danger that would await him on his return to Paris, and, with un-paralleled generosity, declared to him that the title of lover would be more precious to her and more honorable to him than that of wife ; that she wished to retain him through his tenderness for her, and not to hold him enchained in the bonds of matrimony. Would not their meetings, after momentary separations, be the more charming, because more rare? Finally, perceiving that her efforts to convince Abelard and change his resolution were unavailing, sighing deeply and weeping, she terminated her speech in these prophetic* words : "It is the only thing that remains for us to do in order to destroy ourselves, and bring upon ourselves a misery as deep as the love that preceded it."

Recommending their young child to the sister of Abelard, they returned secretly to Paris. A few days later, having passed the night in celebrating vigils in a certain church, at the dawn of morning they received the nuptial benediction in the presence of Fulbert and several of his friends and theirs.†

---

* The instinctive judgment of woman, that results from quickness of perception and fineness of organization, that she cannot clearly express, because it is intuitive; that sometimes makes her seem obstinate because her conviction lies deeper than the understanding, and is therefore to herself inexplicable,—this instinctive judgment is often better than the articulate judgment of man, that loses in penetration more than it gains in clearness of form.

† Nocte secretis orationum vigiliis in quâdam ecclesiâ celebratis, ibidem summo manè, avunculo ejus atque quibusdam nostris vel ipsius amicis assentibus, nuptiali benedictione confæderamur.—*Epistola Abœlardi*, p. 48.

XX.

RETRIBUTION.

Alas how changed! what sudden horrors rise!
A naked Lover bound and bleeding lies!
Where, where was Eloise? her voice, her hand,
Her poniard, had opposed the dire command.
Barbarian, stay! that bloody stroke restrain;
The crime was common, common be the pain.
I can no more; by shame, by rage suppressed,
Let tears and burning blushes speak the rest.

POPE'S "*Eloise to Abelard.*"

AFTER their marriage, Heloise returned to the house of her uncle, and Abelard went to his own habitation. He saw her but seldom, and then in some disguise, or in the most secret manner. Every precaution was taken to keep his marriage with the niece of Fulbert a secret.

Concealment is impossible; "murder will out;" "every hidden thing shall be revealed." It soon began to be rumored that the great philosopher had been shorn of his locks by a fair Delilah, who, after depriving him of his strength, had entangled him in the net of matrimony. Officious friends of Fulbert declared that the only way to retrieve the honor of his

house was to make public the marriage of his niece
with her seducer.   Perhaps the canon never intended
to keep his promise ; perhaps he was influenced by his
friends; at all events, his sworn faith was broken.
Every opportunity was embraced by those connected
with his house, to make known the secret marriage of
Heloise and Abelard.

The friends of the philosopher grieved over his
folly in relinquishing his chances of preferment in the
church by espousing his mistress.   How foolish to lay
his hand on the distaff, when the crosier was within
his reach, and the mitre was not beyond his ambitious
hopes !

Far otherwise was it with the friends of Heloise.
Her honor had been retrieved, and every thing had
been attained that even ambition could desire.   Many
a noble lady would have considered herself honored
by the offered hand of Abelard; how great, then, was
the fortune of the obscure niece of Fulbert, in obtaining him for a husband ! Her marriage was soon made
the subject of conversation in every house in Paris;
and many, moved by envy, comforted themselves by
recounting the dishonorable and unpleasant circumstances that attended it.

Abelard and Heloise, however, strenuously denied *
their marriage.   Who should know so well as they ?

* Epistola Abælardi, p. 50.

Fulbert was telling a falsehood, in the vain hope of saving the honor of his house. Heloise, with consummate art, looked wholly ignorant of their meaning, when her friends began to congratulate her on her new dignity; she laughed at the ridiculous story, and solemnly protested that it was false. Abelard returned to his scholars, and again rejoiced their hearts with his devotion to philosophy, and charmed them anew with his brilliant and eloquent lectures. How absurd to suppose that such a master of learning, such a miracle of genius, such a princely professor, whose fame reached to the ends of the civilized world, for whom the beautiful and the high-born were sighing, would surrender dignities, and relinquish all hope of advancement, by uniting himself in the bonds of wedlock with a poor girl! The story was soon discredited, and the efforts of Fulbert were counteracted.

When the old man found that he had not only failed, in his endeavor to make public the secret marriage, but was also bearing himself the imputation of falsehood, he was greatly exasperated. The full sense of his injury returned, and his rage vented itself on the hapless Heloise. Was she not a senseless ingrate, careless of her own reputation, and regardless of the honor of her protector and benefactor? Heloise had a husband, and, like every woman that greatly loves, was ready to sacrifice every thing for the sake of the beloved. She bore ill-treatment in patience, until she feared that she might be deprived of the occasional visits of Abelard; she then made known to him the unpleasantness of her situation. Again he removed her by night, in the habit of a nun. The nuns of Argenteuil, with whom, as we have already seen, she had spent the years of her childhood, received with joy their ancient pupil. At the request of Abelard, they permitted Heloise to assume, with the exception of the veil, the dress of the convent.

Fulbert and his friends supposed that Abelard had removed Heloise to the convent, in order to get rid of her. A plan of vengeance was soon agreed upon. Four hired assassins, with directions to maim, but not to kill, proceeded by night to the house of the philosopher. One of his servants had been bribed, and showed them the way to his sleeping apartment.*

The perpetrators of the deed fled. Two of them were caught, and, with the treacherous servant, were severely punished.†

---

* "Undè vehementer indignati, et adversùm me conjurati, nocte quâdam quiescentem me atque dormientem in secretâ hospitii mei camerâ, quodam mihi servientem per pecuniam corrupto, crudelissimâ et pudentissimâ ultione punierunt, et quam summâ admiratione mundus excepit; eis videlicet corporis mei partibus amputatis quibus id, quod plangebant, commiseram."—*Epistola Abælardi*, p. 50.

† "Quibus mox in fugam conversis, duo, qui comprehendi potuerunt, oculis et gentialibus privati sunt. Quorum alter ille fuit suprá dictus serviens qui, cùm in obsequio meo mecum maneret, cupiditate ad proditionem ductus est."

"When the morning came," says Abelard,* "the whole city was assembled around my dwelling. How much they were stunned with astonishment—how much they afflicted themselves with lamentations—how much they vexed me with their clamor—how much they disturbed me with complaints, it is difficult, even impossible to express. The churchmen chiefly, and especially my disciples, crucified me with their insupportable cries of lamentation, so that their compassion was more cruel than the pain of my wound, so that I felt shame more keenly than bodily torture. I thought of the glory which had been lost in a moment, of the just judgment of God that had overtaken me, of the treachery for treachery which had been rendered me by Fulbert, of the triumph that awaited my enemies, of the grief that my parents and friends would feel;—I thought how the public would be occupied with my infamy—how I could appear abroad, when I should be a monstrous spectacle to all, pointed at by every finger, and spoken of by every tongue."

We pity thee, Abelard; yet it seems to be the hand of eternal justice that is laid upon thee. Words of solemn import were unheeded by thee—words written by the finger of the Infinite,—pride goeth before destruction, and a haughty spirit before a fall.

---

* Epistola Abælardi, p. 52.

This is but the beginning of calamities—torture of
soul, far more insupportable than torture of body,
awaits thee. No hero, no martyr art thou, suffering
for obedience to the just and the true ; but a violator
of the high law of brotherhood, bearing the penalty of
misdeeds. We must remind thee that the universe is
constructed on a basis of rectitude, and resign thee to
thy fate.*

* Many will charge us with severity towards Abelard;
but we cannot, in conscience, address him otherwise. We
believe in driving money-changers out of the temple of
God, in crying "woe" into the ears of Scribes and Pharisees,
in laying the rod upon the back of fools. Mercy should
always temper justice; but we open wide the flood-gates of
evil, and are most unmerciful when we dethrone justice, and
shield the criminal from the penalty of his crime. Our times
are cursed with a kind of nerveless sentimentality, that whines
over the scoundrel, and has no pity for society that the
scoundrel scourges beyond measure. Would to heaven that
the punishment which overtook Abelard, might be sternly
visited, by legislative enactment, upon every lawless breaker
of the household gods!

XXI.

THE VEIL AND THE COWL.

Canst thou forget that sad, that solemn day,
When victims at yon altar's foot we lay!
Canst thou forget what tears that moment fell,
When, warm in youth, I bade the world farewell?
As with cold lips I kissed the sacred veil,
The shrines all trembled, and the lamps grew pale;
Heav'n scarce believed the conquest it surveyed,
And Saints with wonder heard the vows I made:
Yet then, to those dread altars as I drew,
Not on the Cross my eyes were fixed, but you!
Not grace, or zeal, love only was my call,
And if I lose thy love, I lose my all.

POPE's "Eloisa to Abelard."

ABELARD had no courage left to encounter the world. His philosophy could not heal his wounded heart. His bruised spirit was bowed with recollections of deeds that conscience condemned, and there was remaining within him no strength to withstand the ridicule of his enemies. The convent alone promised him refuge from those that laughed at his misfortunes, and an asylum where he could hope to find any peace for his agitated mind and troubled soul.

His resolution was conveyed to Heloise, and he
proposed that she should follow his example. She
was then but nineteen years of age—just in the bloom
of youth. She loved Abelard, and him alone; her
heart had chosen him for "better or for worse." It
was hard to give up the world, but she had no power,
no wish to resist the will of him to whom she had already yielded whatever is most precious within the
gift of woman. A generous man, it would seem to
us, ought to have been contented with her assurance
of abiding affection, with a proposal to live the life of
a voluntary recluse, without obliging her to take
upon herself the obligation of eternal vows, but the
jealous Abelard did not wish to leave any chance for
others to possess that which he could not enjoy. He
demanded her compliance, and she, of course, having
no will, in the excess of her love, but his will, was
obedient. " At your command," said she, long afterwards, " I changed my habit as well as my inclination,
in order to show you that you were the only master
of my heart."

Even this was not enough to satisfy him. He re-
quired her not only to take the veil, but to take it
previously to his bowing his own head to receive the
cowl. Abelard could go no further; there was
nothing more that he could ask, nothing more that she
could give. " When you were hastening to devote
yourself to God," she said, " I followed you; yes, I

preceded you. For, as if mindful of the wife of Lot, who looked behind her, in the sacred habit and monastic profession, you bound me to God before you bound yourself. In that one instance, I confess, I grieved and blushed for your mistrust of me; but I, God knows, should not have hesitated to follow you at your command, if you had been hastening to perdition."

The day soon came when Heloise was to take the veil, and for ever relinquish the world. Great was the crowd that gathered at Argenteuil. The Bishop of Paris officiated. The holy veil was blessed and laid upon the altar. The gates of the cloister were opened, and Heloise appeared. Her features still bore the impress of lofty intelligence and heroism, but grief had added a softness and a sweetness all its own. She wore a look of resignation to her fate, rather than of high religious enthusiasm and eagerness to leave the world. The crowd was at first silent, but soon every heart throbbed with compassion for the fair young Heloise, who was about to take upon herself vows that may not be broken, at the command of an ungenerous lover. The passage to the altar was impeded; friends spoke to her of her charms and urged her not to proceed. Her bosom was convulsed with sobs, tears showered down her cheeks, yet her thoughts were only of him whom she loved too well. She was heard to utter, at a moment when her soul should have been

6

occupied with thoughts of God, the apostrophe of Cornelia in Lucan : " O my husband, greatest of men, who didst deserve a far happier bride than I. Fate had thus much power over thy illustrious head ! Why, wretch that I am, did I marry thee to thy undoing ? Now art thou avenged ; willingly do I sacrifice myself to expiate my crime." *

The crowd gave way before her ; she mounted the altar, covered her face with the consecrated veil, and, with a firm voice, pronounced the vows that released her from all things human, that in the language of the church, made her the spouse of Christ.

A few days after Heloise had taken the veil at Argenteuil, Abelard entered the Abbey of Saint Denis. It was rather his object to escape the gaze of men, than to find a place sacred to religious meditation, and the worship of God.† He takes with him his pride and his restless spirit ; foes will multiply on every hand, in contention with whom the best of his life must be wasted. Heloise, through long years of silent sorrow, will think much of God, but more of him whose image is constantly before her, whom her great heart so profoundly loves.

* O maxime conjux!
O thalamis indigne meis ! hoc juris habebat
In tantum fortuna caput ! Cur impio nupsi,
Si miserum factura fui ! Nunc accipe poenas,
Sed quas sponte luam.   LUCAN, L viii.
† Epistola Abælardi, p. 54.

XXII.

NO OBJECT AND NO REST: A MONODRAMA.

AT the Abbey of St. Denis, meditations of vengeance,* at first, wholly occupied the mind of Abelard. He imagined that the bishop of Paris and the canons had united in a plot to destroy him, and it was with diffi- culty that he was restrained from undertaking a jour- ney to Rome, in order to accuse them before the Pope. Men are prone to impute to the machinations of others the calamities that follow their own mis- deeds.

The clerks, and the Abbé of St. Denis, urged the new comer to resume his lectures, to instruct the poor and humble servants of God, with the same zeal that he had displayed in teaching the noble and the rich. Abelard hesitated. He was seeking retirement from the world, and wished to shun the sight of men. They expected, on their part, from the acquisition of the illustrious philosopher, new renown for the abbey that had been, since its foundation by Dagobert, a pet of

* Vie d'Abelard, p. 70.

the kings of France, and was one of the institutions of the monarchy. The new monk, who had been accustomed to rule, complained of the irregular life of the brothers, and accused the abbé himself of grave disorders.* His imprudent reproaches soon made him obnoxious to the whole fraternity, and they, in hopes of getting rid of him, urged him to yield to the importunities of his disciples, and commence again the work of instruction. With much reluctance he complied with the request of friends and foes, and, in 1120, established himself in the priory of Maisoncelle, which was situated on the lands of the Count of Champagne.

An auditory of three thousand students, it is said, soon collected to listen to the lectures of the renowned master. That obscure place could not supply them with lodgings or food. Misfortune had saddened the heart of Abelard, and his teaching was more deeply tinged with religion than it had ever been before. Like Origen, however, he explained every thing; he philosophized theology, thus to speak, and placed reason above faith.† Other schools were drained of their pupils, and the masters were made hostile by jealousy towards a successful rival. His right to teach was questioned, and the substance of his teaching was declared to be unsound. The clergy, of every

---

* Ep. Abelard, p. 58.   † Ep. Abælardi, p. 60

rank and order, was stirred up against him. Surrounded by grateful and obedient disciples, and long since accustomed to despise his enemies, Abelard thought to brave the storm and risk the combined opposition of teachers and ecclesiastics, without taking any pains to defend himself against their machinations.

In the mean time he wrote his work entitled *Introduction to Theology*, which was a kind of *résumé*, in some sort a digest, of his lectures. Its success was great, and called forth many attacks from the ecclesiastics. In answer to them, he published a biting invective against those ignorant of dialectics, who took his *dogmas for sophisms*.

Elsewhere, however, two ancient foes of Abelard were quietly plotting his destruction. Alberic and Lotalphus,* who had been his fellow pupils at the school of Anselm of Laon, were at the head of the schools of Rheims, and had not forgotten the vanquisher of their ancient teacher. Alberic was archdeacon of the cathedral, prior of St. Sixtus, and was in high credit with Raoul, his archbishop. The two professors prevailed upon the archbishop to come to an understanding with the bishop of Palestrina, who was then fulfilling the functions of a legate of the Holy See in the states of Gaul, to convoke, under the

---

* Vie d'Abelard, p. 78.—Ep. Abælardi, p. 62.

name of a council or provincial synod, a conventicle
at Soissons, for the purpose of trying Abelard. He
was accused of applying the principles of nominalism
to the dogma of the Trinity. It was in the year 1121,
when the philosopher repaired to Soissons, perfectly
willing to engage in any public discussion on the topic.
The clergy and people of that place had been preju-
diced against him, and some of his disciples came
near being stoned. The philosopher put his book in
the hands of the legate, deferring to his judgment,
and expressing, beforehand, his willingness to retract
any thing that might be at variance with the Catholic
faith. The embarrassed legate returned the book,
and referred him to the archbishop and his counsel-
lors. They did not seem to find any thing heretical,
and deferred judgment until the close of the council.

The public, moved perhaps by mere curiosity,
wished to see Abelard, and he appeared day after day,
exposing his doctrines and winning admiration. " He
harangues the public," it was said, "and no one an-
swers him ! The council draws to a close, a council
assembled chiefly on his account; and in regard to
him no question is raised ! Will the judges acknowledge that the error was on their side ?"

Alberic, with some of his followers,* called on
Abelard one day, and after paying him some empty

---

* Vie d'Abelard, p. 87.—Ep. Abælardi, p. 64.

compliments, finally expressed his astonishment at a certain doctrine which he had found in the philosopher's book.

"If you wish," replied Abelard, "I will give you a reason for it."

"We make no account," said Alberic, "of human reasons, as well as of our sense in such matters; we ask the words of authority."

Abelard opened the book, and showed him that the doctrine in question had been substantiated by a citation from St. Augustine, a recognized authority in the church.

Alberic's disciples were surprised and confused, and he answered that "it was necessary to understand the passage rightly."

"Fine news!" instantly replied Abelard; "but you demand a text and not sense. If you wish sense and reason, I am ready to give them."

Alberic, highly enraged, responded that, in this affair, neither authorities nor reasons should serve him, thus intimating, perhaps, that they were plotting against him in secret, and that they were quite sure of success in effecting his destruction.

The last day of the council arrived, and nothing decisive, as yet, had been done touching Abelard and his book. The bishop of Chartres, who was friendly to Abelard, perceiving their embarrassment, took advantage of it, and exhorted to moderation. He reminded them of the high position and great talents of Abelard, and advised that the accused should be allowed to respond. This counsel was received with murmurs, for no one could hope for any success in a debate with the subtle dialectician. It was then recommended that the philosopher should be conducted back to St. Denis by the abbé, who was then present, and that he should be tried, at some subsequent period, by a larger council. The legate assented to this advice, and all seemed to concur. The enemies of Abelard, however, who perceived that thus he would be placed beyond their influence, persuaded the archbishop to bring the affair to an issue at once. The accused was called, and appeared before the council. It was alleged that he was guilty of the heresy of Sabellius, that is, of having denied or weakened the reality of three persons in the Trinity. He was judged without discussion, and condemned without examination. He was compelled to throw his book, with his own hand, into the flames. After a day of suffering and humiliation, Abelard was placed in the keeping of the abbé of Saint Medard, and conducted by him, as a prisoner, to his convent.

The brothers of Saint Medard treated the condemned philosopher more like a guest than a prisoner. They showed him every attention, and were uniformly kind. Nothing, however, could console him. His despair reached such a pitch of madness, that he accused God himself of having abandoned him.* Strangely were the heroes of thought treated in the twelfth century; strangely have they been treated in every age.

The judgment of the council, however, did not meet with general approbation. Many disavowed their own vote, and the legate publicly attributed the affair to the jealousy of the French; repenting of the whole proceeding, he finally returned Abelard to his own convent.

At St. Denis fresh trials awaited the restless and disappointed monk. He had not been forgotten in the mean time by his old enemies in the abbey. Reading, one day, in the commentary of Bede the Venerable upon the Acts of the Apostles, that Denis, the Areopagite, had been bishop of Corinth, and not bishop of Athens, he was imprudent enough to express a doubt that the one whom the monks regarded as the founder of their abbey, had ever set foot in Gaul.† This at once raised a storm. When questioned by the indignant brothers, he was rash enough to defend the authority of Bede against that of Hilduin, whose testimony was quoted in opposition to him. Touching this legend, was questioning the religion of the crown, and the indignant fraternity refused to accept any reparation. In full assembly

---

* Ep. Abælardi, p. 78.   † Ep. Abælardi, p. 80.

6*

the abbé threatened to send him to the King, who
would demand a signal reparation for an offence so
monstrous, and ordered that, in the mean time, he
should be strictly watched.   Abelard fled by night,
and gained the territory of Thibauld, the Count of
Champagne.   He wrote back to the abbé of St.
Denis, and to his congregation, making concessions,
but they were of no use.   The Count interfered in
vain to effect a reconciliation.   The fugitive, who was
enjoying great hospitality at Provence, in the priory
of St. Agoul, was threatened with excommunication.

The aspect of affairs was fortunately changed by
the death of the abbé of St. Denis.   His successor
was more of a politician than an ecclesiastic, and
things took a favorable turn.   Abelard asked permission to separate himself from the abbey.   The new
abbé consented that he might live in any retreat that
he chose, but demanded that he should join no other
community.   The condition was accepted, and every
thing was ratified in the presence of the King and his
council.

Abelard retired to a wilderness place, on the
banks of the Ardusson, in the territory of Troyes.*
He was accompanied by a single clerk.   With the
permission of the bishop of Troyes, he constructed

* Ep. Ab. p. 88.

an oratory out of the branches of trees, which he dedicated to the Trinity. His retreat was soon known,
and a new generation of scholars flocked to hear the
renowned master. He expressed his desire to remain
alone, but they importuned him for lessons, which at
length he consented to give. Eager students constructed in the forest huts like the cell of their master. At the end of the first year he was surrounded
in the wilderness with six hundred disciples. No fee
was demanded for his lectures, but the necessities of
life were supplied by those to whom he freely gave
the treasures of his mind.

The number of his students increased, and it became necessary to enlarge their place of worship. A
respectable building was erected, which was solemnly
dedicated to the Comforter, to the *Paraclete*. Such
a dedication was an innovation that could not be tolerated in one already suspected. New enemies arose,
more formidable than the old, who were representa-
tives of the principle of authority, and instinctively
hated the representative of the principle of reason.

Chief among these enemies were St. Norbert and
St. Bernard.

Norbert,* who sprang from a distinguished family,
who had spent his youth in pleasures, became a priest
in 1116   He was an ardent missionary of faith and

---

* Vie d'Abelard, p. 115.

penitence. In 1120, he laid the foundation of a regular order of monks, and at the end of four years
found himself at the head of nine flourishing abbeys.
In 1126, he became archbishop of Magdebourg.
" Powerful and revered in the church," says M. De
Remusat, "protected by great princes, he joined to
an indefatigable activity a singular faith in his own
inspiration, in a sort of personal revelation, which led
him to undertake prophecies and miracles. Persuaded of the speedy coming of Antichrist, he pursued
with redoubtable zeal every one who seemed to him
to menace faith and unity." Abelard numbers Norbert among his persecutors, and such was the mystic
character of the zealot's mind, that he must have been
incapable of excusing and appreciating the wholly intellectual Christianity of the great theological dialectician.

Abelard's greatest antagonist was St. Bernard.
" Like Abelard, he was of noble birth. Originally
from Upper Burgundy, from the country of Bossuet
and Buffon, he had been brought up in that powerful
abbey of Citeaux, the sister and rival of Cluny, which
sent forth such a host of illustrious preachers, and
which, fifty years later, originated the crusade against
the Albigeois. But Citeaux was too splendid and too
wealthy for St. Bernard; and he descended into the
poorer region of Champagne,* and founded the mo-

---

* Not very far from the *Paraclete.*

nastery of Clairvaux in the *Valley of Wormwood.*
Here he could lead at will the life of suffering to
which he cleaved, and from which nothing could tear
him, for he would never hear of being any other than
a monk, when he might have been archbishop or pope.
Forced to reply to the various monarchs who consult-
ed him, he found himself all-powerful in his own de-
spite, and condemned to govern Europe. It was a
letter of St. Bernard's, which caused the King of
France to withdraw his army from Champagne; and
when the simultaneous elevation of Innocent II. and
of Anaclete to the Papal throne, had given rise to a
schism, the French church referred the decision to
St. Bernard, and he decided in favor of Innocent.
England and Italy opposed his choice: the abbot of
Clairvaux wrote to the King of England; then, taking
the pope by the hand, led him through all the cities
of Italy, which received him on bended knee. The
people rushed to touch the saint, and would struggle
with each other but for a thread drawn out of his
gown. His whole road was marked by miracles.

" But, as we learn from his letters, these things
were not his chief business. He lent, but did not
give himself to the world—his heart and treasure
were elsewhere. He would write ten lines to the
King of England, and ten pages to a poor monk.
Abstracting himself from all outward concerns—a
man of prayer and sacrifice, no one knew better how

to be alone, though surrounded by others; his senses took no note of external objects. Having, his biographer tells us, walked the whole day along the lake of Lausanne, he inquired in the evening whereabouts the lake might be. He would mistake oil for water, and coagulated blood for butter. Almost every thing he took his stomach rejected. He quenched his hunger with the Bible, his thirst with the Gospel. He could scarcely stand upright; yet found strength to preach the crusade to a hundred thousand men. He seemed rather a being of another world than mortal, when he presented himself to the multitude with his white and red beard, his white and fair hair, meagre and weak, hardly a tinge of life on his cheeks, and with that singular transparency of complexion so admired in Byron. So overpowering was the effect of his preaching, that mothers kept their sons from hearing him, wives their husbands; or all would have turned monks. As for him, when he had breathed the breath of life into the multitude, he would hasten back to Clairvaux, rebuild his hut of boughs and leaves, and soothe in studies of the Song of Songs, the interpretation of which was the occupation of his life, his love-sick soul.

"Think with what grief such a man must have learned the success of Abelard, and the encroachments of logic on religion, the prosaic victory of reason over faith, and the extinguishment of the flame of sacrifice in the world—it was tearing his God from him."*

These two men preached against Abelard, throwing doubts upon his faith and suspicions upon his life.† The abbé of Clairvaux was not, it is probable, at this period, acquainted with the enemy of faith, and champion of reason, but had heard of his adventures, and knew of his logical duels with schoolmen and ecclesiastics. It must be remembered, too, that the *Valley of Wormwood* and the Paraclete were not far distant from each other, so that the two abbeys may be regarded as having been rivals. It is certain that the philosopher was in fear of the saint. During the last days of his stay at the place of his retreat, he constantly expected to be dragged before a council as a heretic. Such was the state of his mind, caused by apprehension, that he even thought of seeking refuge on infidel ground, among the enemies of Christ.†

About the year 1125, the abbey of Saint Gildas lost its head, and, after the consent of the abbé and monks of Saint Denis had been obtained, the vacant post was offered to Abelard. He accepted the offer, comparing himself, in escaping from the enmity of France, to St. Jerome, fleeing from the injustice of Rome.

* Michelet. † Ep. Ab. p. 96.
‡ Ep. Ab. p. 102.—Inter inimicos Christi Christianè vivere.

Saint Gildas* was in Brittany, situated on the summit of a promontory, overlooking the ocean, whose waves broke mournfully on the rocks beneath. The eloquent professor, the learned philosopher, the accomplished lover, who was withal a poet and a charming singer, went among an irregular, disorderly, violent, ferocious tribe of monks and savages, who could understand nothing, who knew not how to obey. Abelard became the subject of a tyrannical king, and the head of an abbey that had allowed itself to be despoiled to purchase venality for its misconduct. Surrounded by barbarians, he was powerless. No wonder that he became melancholy, and poured out his sadness in songs as plaintive as the wild winds that howled around his habitation.†

* Vie D'Abelard, p. 120.

† Six of these elegiac songs, *Odæ flebiles*, in which the author breathes out his own sorrows under the transparent veil of biblical fictions, have been found in the library of the Vatican at Rome.

XXIII.

HELOISE AGAIN.—THE MONODRAMA CONTINUES.

" Ah, think at least thy flock deserves thy care,
Plants of thy hand, and children of thy prayer.
From the false world in early youth they fled,
By thee to mountains, wilds, and deserts led.
You raised these hallowed walls; the desert smiled,
And Paradise was opened in the Wild.
No weeping orphan saw his father's stores
Our shrines irradiate, or emblaze the floors;
No silver saints, by dying misers giv'n,
Here bribed the rage of ill-requited heav'n;
But such plain roofs as Piety could raise,
And only vocal with the Maker's praise."

POPE'S " Eloisa to Abelard."

IN the mean time, Heloise, it would seem, had been
almost forgotten by her wandering spouse. We have
found no mention of her name, in tracing his life thus
far, since he entered the abbey of St. Denis. Her
memory, however, may have been buried in his heart
during these years of persecution and sorrow, and
cherished there in faithfulness and silence.

At the convent of Argenteuil, the character and
energy of Heloise soon placed her in the highest

rank. She was made prioress, and the church spoke
of her with respect. But she was not destined to
remain there a long time in quiet possession of her
authority, and in the enjoyment of her honors.

It was found, by an examination of the ancient
charters, that the monks of St. Denis could lay claim
to Argenteuil. The history of these charters it is
not necessary to trace. The legal right was with the
monks, and, in order to make sure the claim, the
abbé of St. Dennis accused the nuns of Argenteuil of
grave irregularities. At his instance, a bull was
obtained, in 1127, by which the nuns were dispos-
sessed. The next year they were violently ejected.
Some of the sisterhood entered the abbey of Notre-
Dame-des-Bois, on the banks of the Marne; others,
among whom was Heloise, sought, here and there, an
asylum.*

News of this reached Abelard at St. Gildas.
Already, in the midst of his sorrows, had he felt
remorse for leaving the Paraclete,—for abandoning his
followers,—for deserting his last friends. Immediately on receiving information that the prioress of
Argenteuil was wandering in search of a religious
home, he returned to the country of Champagne, and
invited her to occupy his abandoned oratory. The
invitation was accepted, and to Heloise and her com-

* Vie d'Abelard, p. 126.

panions he made a perpetual and irrevocable cession of all the property belonging to the deserted Paraclete. This donation was approved by the bishop of Troyes, in whose diocese the abbey was located; less than two years afterwards, was approved by the pope, and declared inviolable under penalty of excommunication.

This approval was given by the new pope, Innocent II., the successful rival of Anaclete. When the two were elected to fill the papal chair, Innocent, not finding sufficient support in Italy, found it necessary to seek an asylum in France. He disembarked with his cardinals at the port of St. Gildas, and was supported by Abelard, as well as by St. Bernard. When he was firmly seated on the papal throne, he did not forget one of the most distinguished abbés of France, who had been his friend in the hour of need, and granted every thing that was requested, in regard to transferring the abbey of Paraclete to Heloise and her followers.

Heloise was twenty-nine years of age when she took possession of that celebrated institution. Her title, at first, was that of prioress, but a bull, bearing the date of 1136, designated her as abbess.

At first, the abbess and her sisters had to endure many privations, but their resources were soon aug-

* Vie d'Abelard, p. 128.

mented, through the respect and affection of the neighboring people.* "God knows," says Abelard, "they have been more enriched, I think, in a single year, than I should have been in a hundred years, if I had continued to dwell at Paraclete; for if their sex is weaker, the poverty of females is more touching, and more easily moves the heart; and their virtue is more pleasing to God and men. And, then, the Lord awarded to the eyes of all so visible a grace in this woman, my sister, who was at their head, that the bishops loved her as their daughter, the abbés as their sister, the laymen as a mother; and all equally admired her piety, her prudence, and in all things an incomparable sweetness of patience."†

Abelard returned to the government of his savage subjects at St. Gildas; but, now and then, visited the nuns at Paraclete, giving them his counsel and support, preaching to them, and affording them at times temporal as well as spiritual aid. He saw Heloise but rarely, and spoke with her but little. Continu-

---

* "Abelard," says M. Michelet, "had nothing but his genius. Born noble, rich, eldest of his family, he left every thing to his brothers. Nevertheless he did not wish to receive any thing from lords and kings for the purpose of building the house of Heloise. His disciples ran to his aid. Simple priests, indigent scholars, mendicants of science, they found treasures for their master. 'Soon,' said the spouse of Abelard, 'we knew not what to do with the offerings.' "— *Mémoire sur l'Education des Femmes au Moyen Age.*

† Ab. Op., ep. i., p. 34.

ally watched and suspected, by some he was blamed for neglecting the new sisterhood, and by others for visiting them at all.

In addition to the "heart-ache," caused by ungrounded suspicions, fresh troubles arose for him at the abbey. Misfortunes "come not single spies but in fierce battalions." His life was in danger. He feared to travel, for he believed that assassins were lying in wait for him. He celebrated mass with precaution, apprehensive of poison in the communion cup. He went to Nantes, to visit the count, who was sick, and lodged at the house of one of the brothers, that dwelt in that city. A monk, who accompanied him, ate of food that he did not dare to touch himself, and was poisoned. He even left the abbey with a few faithful brothers, and lived in isolation.

In the mean time, a severe fall from a horse seriously impaired his already declining health. Excommunication was at length resorted to, and some of the refractory monks were expelled from the abbey, but order was not restored. Fearing assassination, he gained the sea by a subterranean passage, and escaped, it is said, under the conduct of one of the lords of the country. From the asylum which he reached, he wrote, for the consolation of an unfortunate friend, that celebrated letter, which is entitled, *Historia Calamitatum*,—history of his misfortunes.

The *Historia Calamitatum* is a romantic autobiography, in which the author not only narrates the principal events of his external life, but also recounts the adventures of his mind and the emotions of his heart.   It marks an epoch in the life of Abelard. With it ends that fulness of biographic detail which thus far has not been wanting.   The history of his calamities fell, by chance, into the hands of Heloise, and called forth the first of those celebrated letters, that have been eagerly read by so many generations; that have not lost their freshness and charm during the tumultuous changes of nearly eight hundred years.

These letters, so rich in romantic interest, will form, in their chronologic order, several of the subsequent chapters.

XXIV.

LETTER OF HELOISE TO ABELARD.

"Soon as thy letters trembling I unclose,
That well-known name awakens all my woes;
Oh, name for ever sad! for ever dear!
Still breath'd in sighs, still usher'd with a tear.
I tremble too, where'er my own I find,
Some dire misfortune follows close behind.
Line after line my gushing eyes o'erflow,
Led through a sad variety of woe:
Now warm with love, now with'ring with my bloom,
Lost in a convent's solitary gloom!
There stern religion quench'd th' unwilling flame,
There died the best of passions, Love and Fame.
  "Yet write, oh write me all, that I may join
Grief to thy griefs, and echo sighs to thine.
Nor foes nor fortune take this power away;
And is my Abelard less kind than they?
Tears still are mine, and those I need not spare,
Love but demands what else were shed in pray'r;
No happier task these faded eyes pursue;
To read and weep is all they now can do.
  "Then share thy pain, allow that sad relief;
Ah, more than share it, give me all thy grief.
Heav'n first taught letters for some wretch's aid,
Some banish'd lover, or some captive maid;

They live, they speak, they breathe what love inspires,
Warm from the soul, and faithful to its fires,
The virgin's wish without her fears impart,
Excuse the blush, and pour out all the heart,
Speed the soft intercourse from soul to soul,
And waft a sigh from Indus to the pole."

POPE's *" Eloisa to Abelard."*

To her lord,—yes, to her father ; to her husband,—yes, to her brother ; his servant,—yes, his daughter ; his wife,—yes, his sister.

HELOISE TO ABELARD.

THE letter, dearest, which you recently sent to a friend of yours, for the purpose of consoling him, has by chance fallen into my hands. From a glance at the superscription I recognized it as yours, and began to read it with so much the more avidity as the more ardently I cherish the writer himself. I wished at least to reproduce from his words the image of the one that I have lost. Full of gall and wormwood, I remember, was that letter which related the lamentable history of our conversion, and of your continual afflictions.

You amply fulfilled the promise made to that friend at the commencement of your letter, that, in comparison with yours, he should regard his misfortunes as nothing, or as of little account. Having exposed the persecutions directed against you by your masters, and the treachery to which you were a

victim (*in corpus tuum summæ proditionis injuria*),
you proceeded to a recital of the execrable envy and
the excessive hatred of your disciples, Albericus of
Rheims, and Lotulphus of Lombardy.

You did not forget to mention that, by their sug-
gestions, your glorious work on theology was committed to the flames ; that you yourself were condemned, as it were, to a prison.   Then follows an
account of the machinations of your abbé, and of your
false brethren ; an account of the calumnies, from
which you had most to suffer, of those pseudo-apos-
tles, moved against you by envy ; and an account of
the scandal every where raised by the name Paraclete
given, contrary to custom, to your oratory : finally,
an account of those insufferable and hitherto unre-
mitted persecutions of your life, by that most cruel
tyrant, and those execrable monks, whom you call
your children, closes this sad history.

No one, I think, could either read or listen to
these things without tears.   How must it be, then,
with me !   The very fidelity of your narrative has the
more fully renewed my sorrows.   These sorrows have
been deepened, too, on account of your perils, which
you represent as continually increasing.   We are all
compelled to despair of your life, and daily our trembling hearts and agitated bosoms expect, as the last
news, the report of your death.

In the name of Christ, who hitherto has protected
7

you for his service, whose humble servants we are, and thine, we beseech you to write us frequently, informing us by what perils you are surrounded; since we alone remain to you, to participate in your grief or in your joy. Those who condole with us usually afford some consolation to our sorrowing hearts, and a burden laid upon several is more easily borne, or seems more light. If the tempest should subside a little, then hasten your letters, for they will be messengers of joy. Whatever may be the subject of your letters, they will afford us not a little comfort; they will at least prove that you are mindful of us.

How pleasant the letters of absent friends are, Seneca himself teaches us, by an appropriate example, writing thus in a certain place to his friend Lucilius: "I thank you for writing to me often; for you show yourself to me in the only way you are able. As soon as I receive your letter we are together." If the pictures of absent friends are pleasant to us, which renew their remembrance, which lighten the pain of absence with a vain phantom of consolation, how much more pleasant are the letters which bring to us the true signs of an absent friend!

Thanks to God, no envy can prohibit, no difficulty can prevent you from giving us your presence in this manner; let no delay, I beseech you, come from your negligence.

You have written to a friend a long letter of consolation. in view of his misfortunes, it is true, but really touching your own. In narrating these with diligence, for the purpose of consoling him, you have greatly added to our desolation, and while you desired to heal his wounds, you have inflicted new wounds of grief upon us, and have deepened those already existing. Cure, I pray you—you who are anxious to cure the wounds which others have made—cure those which you have made yourself. You have calmed the pains of a friend, and a companion, and have thus paid the debt due to friendship and intimacy; but to us, who should be called worshippers, rather than friends, daughters rather than companions, or by any other name, if there be one still more sweet and holy, —to us, you are bound by a more sacred obligation.

As to the importance of the debt which obligates you to us, it is not necessary to rest upon arguments and testimonies, as though a doubtful thing were to be proved, and if all were silent, the facts speak for themselves. You, after God, are the sole founder of this place, the sole constructor of this oratory, the sole builder of this congregation; you have built nothing here upon a foreign foundation. All that is here is your creation. This solitude, frequented only by wild beasts and robbers, had known no habitation of men, had never possessed a single dwelling. Among the dens of wild beasts, among the retreats of robbers, where the name of God was never called upon, you erected a divine tabernacle, and dedicated a temple to the Holy Spirit. Nothing for this work did you receive from the riches of kings or princes, although you might have demanded and obtained every thing; in order that whatever was done might be attributed to yourself alone. Clerks or scholars, coming in a crowd to listen to your instruction, furnished you with all necessary things ; and those who were living on ecclesiastical benefices, who had been accustomed to receive rather than to present offerings, and who, previously, had possessed hands for taking and not for giving, here became importunate and prodigal in presenting offerings.

Yours, therefore, truly yours, is this new plantation in the field of the Lord, and frequent watering is still necessary for its young plants, in order that they may flourish. Feeble enough, from the very nature of the female sex, is this plantation; it is infirm, though it were not new. Therefore it demands more diligent and assiduous culture ; according to the word of the Apostle: " I have planted, Apollos watered; but God gave the increase." The Apostle had planted and founded in faith, through the doctrine of his preaching, the Corinthians, to whom he was writing. Apollos, a disciple of the Apostle himself, had watered them by his holy exhortations, and thus the divine grace bestowed upon them an increase of virtues. Uselessly do you cultivate by your admonitions and sacred exhortations a foreign vine, which you have not planted, and which is changed for you into bitterness. Remember what you owe to your own—you, who are so careful of another's. You teach and admonish rebels, but meet with no success. In vain you scatter before swine the pearls of divine eloquence. Consider what you owe to the obedient—you who are exhausting yourself for the disobedient. Remember what you owe to your daughters—you who are wasting so much upon enemies. And, omitting others, think how much you are indebted to me; that the common debt which you owe to all the women who have devoted themselves to God, you may pay to her who has devoted herself wholly to you.

How many and how important treatises, and with what diligence, the holy Fathers have composed, to teach, exhort, or even to console religious women, you, with your abundant knowledge, know better than I with my little store of learning. Therefore, with no ordinary astonishment have I remarked your long oblivion in regard to the tender commencements of our conversion, because, moved neither by reverence for God, nor love for us, nor by the example of the holy Fathers, you did not try to console me, while fluctuating in my faith, and worn down with unabating grief, either by coming to rejoice my ear with the sound of your voice, or by sending a letter to comfort my heart.

You knew that your obligations to me were the stronger for our having been united in the sacrament of marriage; and the immoderate love which, as every one knows, I have always borne for you, has increased your indebtedness to me.

You know, dearest, all know, how much I lost in losing you. An infamous and hitherto unheard of crime, in depriving you of my love, tore me from myself. Incomparably greater is the grief caused by the manner of the loss, than that caused by the loss itself. The greater the cause of grieving is, so much the greater remedies for the purpose of consolation must be applied. I expect consolation from no other, for you, who alone have caused me to grieve, can alone console me. You alone are able to sadden me, to make me joyous, or to comfort me. And you alone are under obligations to comfort me, for so far did I comply with your wishes, that, in order not to offend you in any thing, I had the courage to destroy myself in obedience to your command. I went even farther, and, strange to say, my love for you rose to such a height of delirium that it sacrificed, without hope of regaining it, the sole object of its desire. At your command I changed my habit as well as my inclination, in order to show you that you were the only master of my heart.

God knows I never sought any thing in you except yourself; you, you alone, not your possessions did I desire. Neither the rights of matrimony, nor any dowry have I expected; neither my own pleasures nor my own wishes, but yours, as you yourself know, have I studied to fulfil.

Although the name of wife seems more holy and more valid, another has always been sweeter to me, that of friend; or, if you will not be shocked, that of concubine or mistress. The more I humbled myself before you, the more, as I thought, should I elevate myself in your favor, and thus injure the less the glory of your excellence.

I thank you for not having wholly forgotten my sentiments, in this regard, in the letter addressed to your friend for his consolation. You did not disdain to mention some of the reasons by which I endeavored to dissuade you from our marriage, from inauspicious nuptials: but you passed over in silence most of the reasons which caused me to prefer love to marriage, liberty to chains. I call God to witness that if Augustus, supreme master of the world, had offered me the royal honor of his alliance, I should have accepted with more joy and pride the name of your mistress than that of his empress. Neither riches nor power constitute the superiority of a man: riches and power are the gift of fortune, while merit alone establishes the claim to superiority.

The woman who more willingly marries a rich than a poor man, and who seeks in a husband posses-

sions rather than himself, surely has a venal soul.
Surely to her who is induced to marry from such considerations, a reward rather than love is owed.   Certain it is that she is in pursuit of fortune, and not in
pursuit of a husband, and that, had it been possible,
she would have prostituted herself to a richer.   We
find the clearest proof of this truth in the words of
Aspasia, as reported by Æschines, the disciple of Soc
rates.   This feminine philosopher, wishing to reconcile Xenophon and his wife, ends her exhortations by
the reasoning which follows : " As soon as you have
realized that there exists not upon earth a better man
or a more amiable woman, you will know how to recognize and enjoy the good fortune which has happened to you in common, that the husband has the
best of women, and the wife the best of men."

This sentiment, which seems to be almost the result of inspiration, must be the utterance of wisdom
herself rather than of philosophy.   It is a divine
error, and a happy fallacy in the married, when perfect satisfaction and sympathy protects against any
violation the ties of matrimony, not so much by the
continence of their bodies as by the chastity of their
souls.

But that which error confers upon others, a manifest truth conferred upon me.   But those qualities,
which none but a wife can discover in her husband,
were so conspicuous in you, that the whole world did

not so much believe as know that they existed. My love was then so much the more true, as it was the farther from resting upon error. For who among kings, who among philosophers, could equal you in fame? What country, what city, what village did not ardently desire to see you? Who, I ask, when you appeared in public, did not hasten to look at you, and follow you at your departure with eager eyes?

But you possessed two things, by which you were able to entice the minds of any females; I mean a charming voice in singing, and a fascinating manner in conversation. We know that other philosophers have excelled least of all in these accomplishments. As though it were a pastime, for the purpose of re-creation, after the stern labors of philosophy, you composed a multitude of verses and amorous songs, the poetic thoughts and musical graces of which were every where responded to; so that the sweetness of the melody did not permit even the illiterate to be unmindful of you. Especially on this account were women sighing for you in love. And since the greater part of these verses chanted our loves, my name was soon made known in many regions, and many females were inflamed with jealousy against me.

What endowment of mind or body did not adorn your youth? What woman, then envying me, does not my misfortune now compel to pity me, when I am deprived of so many pleasures? What man, or what

woman, although at first my enemy, does not due compassion now soften toward me?

And I am indeed innocent, as you know. Crime
is not in the act, but in the intention. Justice does
not regard the things that are done, but the intention
with which they are done. What my feelings have
always been toward you, you alone, who have proved
them, can judge. To your examination I commit
all things, upon your testimony I rest my cause.

Tell me one thing, if you are able, why, since our
entrance upon a religious life, which you resolved
upon without consulting me, you have so neglected
me, so forgotten me, that you have never come to encourage me with your words, nor in your absence
have consoled me with a letter : tell me, I say, if you
are able, or I will say what I think, what indeed all
suspect. It was desire rather than friendship that
drew you to me, passion rather than love. When,
therefore, that ceased which was the object of your
desire, every thing else which you exhibited on account
of it, equally vanished.

This conjecture, dearest, is not so much mine as
that of all, not so much special as common, not so
much private as public. Would that it seemed so to
me alone, and that your love might find some defenders, by whom my grief might be somewhat calmed!
O that I might be able to imagine reasons for excu-

sing you, and persuading myself that to you I am still an object of interest !

Attend, I pray you, to that which I request, and it will seem small and very easy for you. Since your presence is denied me, give me words of which you possess such an abundance, and thus afford me at least the sweetness of your image. In vain shall I expect to find you bountiful in things, if I find you avaricious in words. Hitherto I have believed that I have merited many things from you, having complied with every thing for your sake, and persevering still in absolute submission to you. When I was in the bloom of youth, it was not religious devotion, but your command, that drew me to the asperity of monastic life. If for this I have merited nothing in your eyes, how vain has been my labor. No reward for this must be expected by me from God, out of love to whom it is evident that I have as yet done nothing.

When you were hastening to God I followed you, yes I preceded you. For, as if mindful of the wife of Lot, who looked behind her, in the sacred habit and the monastic profession you bound me to God before you bound yourself. In that one instance, I confess, I grieved and blushed for your mistrust of me. But God knows I should not have hesitated to follow you, at your command, if you had been hastening to perdition. For my heart was not with me, but with you. But now, more than ever, if it is not with you it is nowhere, since it cannot exist without you. Deal with it gently, I beseech you. But gently you will have dealt with it, propitious it will have found you, if you return favor for favor, little for much, words for things. Oh that your love were less sure of me, that it might be more solicitous! The more secure I have made you, the more have I encouraged your neg-ligence. Remember, I beseech you, what I have done; and recollect how much you are indebted to me.

While I was enjoying the delights of love with you, it was regarded by most as uncertain whether I was following the impulse of my heart or the instinct of pleasure. But now the end explains the begin-ning. I have denied myself all joys that I might be obedient to your wish. I have reserved to myself nothing, unless it be the hope that thereby I might become more completely yours. What then must be your iniquity, if, as my sacrifices increase, your grati-tude decreases; if, when I sacrifice every thing, you entirely forget your obligations—especially when the demand made is so small, and for you so easy to be complied with.

Therefore, by the God to whom you have conse-:rated yourself, I beseech you to give me your pres-ence in the manner which is possible to you, that is, by writing to me some consolation. If for no other reason, do it for this end, that, thus reanimated, I may devote myself with more alacrity to the service of God. Formerly, when you sought me for earthly pleasures, you visited me with frequent letters, and by your frequent songs you placed Heloise in the mouths of all. Every place, every house, resounded with my name. How much more rightly might you now excite me toward God, than you did then towards earthly pleasures. Remember, I beseech you, what you owe to me, consider what I ask; and I terminate this long letter by a short ending:

Adieu, my only beloved!

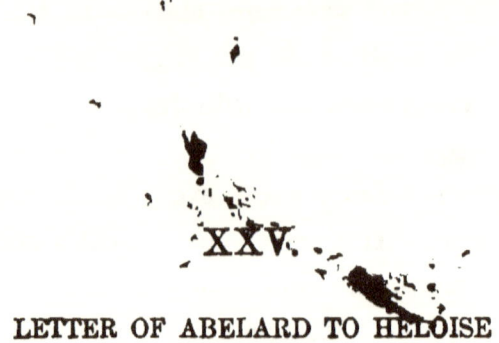

XXV.

LETTER OF ABELARD TO HELOISE

To Heloise, his dearest sister in Christ, Abelard, her brother in the same.

INASMUCH as, since our conversion from the world to God, I have not written you, as yet, any thing by way of consolation or exhortation, it must not be imputed to my negligence, but to your wisdom, in which I always have the greatest confidence. For I have not believed that she was in need of such aids, to whom Heaven has abundantly distributed its best gifts—who, by words as well as by example, is able to teach the erring, to sustain the weak, to encourage the timid.

You were, long since, accustomed to do these things, when you were only a prioress under an abbess. If you now bestow the same care upon your daughters that you then bestowed upon your sisters, I believe it is a sufficient reason why I should regard any instruction or exhortation on my part as superfluous. But if it seems otherwise to you in your humility, and you are in need of my direction and teaching in regard to those things that pertain to God, inform me upon what subject you wish me to write, that I may answer you upon that point, as the Lord shall give me ability.

But, thanks to God, who, breathing into your heart solicitude on account of the weighty and imminent perils to which I am exposed, has made you partaker of my affliction; so that by the intercession of your prayers, the divine compassion may protect me, and shortly put Satan under my feet. Especially for this end, I have hastened to send the form of prayer which you, my sister, once dear to me in the world, now most dear to me in Christ, earnestly solicited from me. By repeating this, you will give to the Lord a sacrifice of prayer, in order to expiate my great and manifold transgressions, and to avert the perils which continually threaten me.

But as to the favor which the prayers of the faithful obtain with God and his saints, especially of women, for those that are dear to them, and of wives for their husbands, many testimonies and examples occur to me. Convinced of their efficacy, the apostle admonishes us to pray without ceasing. We read that the Lord said to Moses: " Let me alone, that my wrath may wax hot." And to Jeremiah : " Therefore pray not thou for this people, neither lift up cry nor prayer for them, neither make intercession to me."

By these words, God himself clearly shows that the prayers of saints put upon his own anger a rein which checks it, and hinders him from inflicting upon the wicked the punishment they deserve. He whom justice naturally conducts to vengeance, is turned by the supplications of his servants, and, as if by a certain force, is as it were involuntarily restrained. So to him that is praying, or about to pray, it is said: "Let me alone, and do not make intercession to me." The Lord commands us not to pray for the impious. The just man prays, notwithstanding the prohibition of the Lord, and obtains from him what he asks for, and changes the sentence of the angry judge. So to the supplication of Moses is subjoined the words: "And the Lord repented of the evil which he thought to do unto his people."

It is written elsewhere, concerning the universal works of God: "He commanded, and they were created." But in this place it is to be remembered that he said his people had merited affliction, and that, prevented by the virtue of prayer, he did not fulfil what he had said. Learn, then, how great is the efficacy of prayer, if we pray as we are commanded; since what the Lord had commanded him not to pray for, the prophet nevertheless obtained by praying, and turned the Lord from what he had said. Another prophet again says to him: "In wrath remember mercy."

Let those princes of the earth hear this and be instructed, who pursue with more obstinacy than justice
the infractions of their decrees, and blush at seeming
remiss if they become compassionate, and wicked if
they change an edict, or do not fulfil the tenor of an
imprudent law, although they might amend words by
deeds. They might be compared to Jephtha, who
made a foolish vow, and more foolishly fulfilled it, by
sacrificing his only daughter.

He who wishes to become a member of the Eternal
says with the Psalmist: " I will sing of mercy and
judgment: unto thee, O Lord, will I sing." " Mercy,
as it is written, exalteth judgment." In regard to
which the Scripture elsewhere declares: " For he
shall have judgment without mercy that showed no
mercy."

The Psalmist himself, observing this sentiment,
overcome by the supplications of the wife of Nabal
the Carmelite, for the sake of mercy, broke the oath,
which on account of justice he had made, to destroy
her husband and his whole household. David, therefore, preferred prayer to justice; and the supplication
of the wife effaced the crime of her husband.

Let this example, my sister, encourage your tenderness, and be for it a pledge of security; for if the
prayer of this woman obtained so much from a man,
do not doubt that God will hear your prayer in my
behalf. Surely God, who is our Father, loves his

children more than David loved a supplicating woman. And he indeed was esteemed a pious and merciful man; but piety itself and mercy itself is God. And the woman who supplicated David belonged to the profane world, and the sanctity of the religious profession had not made her the spouse of God.

If indeed your intercession cannot deliver me, the holy community of virgins and widows who are with you will obtain that which might not be awarded to your prayers alone. In fact, he who is truth itself has said to his disciples: "Where two or three are gathered together in my name, there am I in the midst of them." And again: "If two of you shall agree on earth, as touching any thing that they shall ask, it shall be done for them of my Father which is in heaven." Who cannot see how much the frequent prayers of a pious congregation may avail with God? If, as St. James affirms, "the effectual fervent prayer of a righteous man availeth much," what may not be hoped for from the multitude of a holy congregation?

You know, dearest sister, from the thirty-eighth homily of St. Gregory, the marvellous effects which the prayers of certain men produced upon their brother, in spite of his resistance and incredulity. What is there carefully written down concerning the extreme bodily peril of this man, concerning the most miserable anxiety of his soul, and the despair and weariness of his life, has not escaped your attention. And oh that this might invite you, and the assembly of your sisters, more confidently to pray that he may keep me alive for you, through whom, according to the testimony of Paul, women received their dead raised to life again!

For if you turn over the pages of both testaments, you will find that the great miracles of resuscitation were exhibited only, or by preference, to women, and that, either for them or upon them, these miracles were performed. The Old Testament mentions that two dead persons were revived on account of maternal prayers—one by Elijah, the other by Elisha. The New Testament contains an account of the resuscitation of three persons by the Lord, which, being exhibited to women, most especially confirm the language of the apostle which we quoted: "Women recovered their dead raised to life again."

Indeed, at the gate of the city of Nain, he resuscitated and returned to his mother the son of a widow, touched with pity for her. He also raised Lazarus, his friend, from the dead, at the earnest supplications of his sisters, Mary and Martha. When he accorded the same favor to the master of the synagogue, in answer to the prayer of her father, "Women received their dead raised to life again;" since, being resuscitated, she had received her own body again, as the others had received the bodies of their relatives. Few persons indeed interceded with their prayers, yet these resuscitations were granted. The manifold prayers of your devotion will easily obtain the preservation of my life.

Your abstinence as well as continence, which is, as it were, a sacrifice to God, will find him so much the more propitious as it is regarded by him with the more grace. And perhaps the greater part of those who were restored to life were not faithful. We are not told that the widow, for whom the Lord revived her son without her asking it, was faithful. But we indeed are not only bound to the faith by integrity, but we are also united by the same religious vows.

I will now omit your monastic congregation, in which very many virgins and widows bear devotedly the yoke of the Lord; to you alone will I go—to you, whose sanctity I know is very powerful with God, whose succor is due to me first of all, especially in the midst of the adversities which overwhelm me. Remember, therefore, always in your prayers him who is especially thine, and persevere in your prayer with the more confidence on account of the justice of your petition, which will render it the more acceptable to God, to whom we must pray. Hear, I beseech you, with the ear of the heart, what you have frequently heard with the outward ear. It is written in Proverbs: "A virtuous woman is a crown to her husband." And again: "Whoso findeth a wife, findeth a good thing, and obtaineth favor of the Lord." And in another place: "Houses and riches are the inheritance of fathers: and a prudent wife is from the Lord." And in Ecclesiastes [Apocrypha]:

"Blessed is the man that hath a virtuous wife."

And a few lines after:

"A good wife is a good portion."

And according to apostolic authority:

"The unbelieving husband is sanctified by the wife."

The divine grace has permitted our country of France to experience this truth, since, by the prayer of his wife Clotilda, rather than by the preaching of saints, King Clovis, being converted to the faith of Christ, the whole kingdom was so subjected to the divine law, that, by the example of the higher classes, the lower classes were invited to perseverance in prayer. This perseverance is especially recommended to us in the parable of the Lord:

"Which of you shall have a friend, and shall go unto him at midnight, and say unto him, Friend, lend me three loaves; for a friend of mine in his journey is come to me, and I have nothing to set before him? And he from within shall answer and say, Trouble me not; the door is now shut, and my children are with me in bed; I cannot rise and give thee. I say unto you, Though he will not rise and give him, because he is his friend, yet because of his importunity he will rise and give him as many as he needeth."

By this importunity of prayer, thus to speak, Moses, as I mentioned above, softened the severity of divine justice, and changed its sentence.

You know, dearest, how much affection your convent heretofore was accustomed to show me in prayer, when I was present. At the close of the canonical hours, the sisters were accustomed to offer for me a special supplication to the Lord. After the psalmody of the anthem and the response, they added the following prayers and collect:

" *Responsum.*—Forsake me not, withdraw not thyself from me, O Lord."

" *Versus.*—Be thou, O Lord, always ready to defend me."

" *Preces.*—Preserve thy servant, my God, who putteth his trust in thee. O Lord, hear my prayer, and let my cry come unto thee."

" *Oratio.*—O God, who, through the least of thy servants, hast been pleased to gather together in thy name thy handmaidens, we beseech thee to grant unto him, as well as us, to persevere in thy will. Through our Lord Jesus Christ," etc.

But now in my absence from you, I have the more need of your prayers, since I am overwhelmed with anxiety on account of increasing peril. I supplicate and beseech you, and beseech and supplicate you, that I may experience now in my absence the sincerity of the tenderness which you exhibited to me when I was with you, by your adding at the end of the canonical hours this formula of prayer :

"*Responsum.*—Forsake me not, O Lord, the Father and Governor of my life, lest I fall before my adversaries, and mine enemy rejoice over me."

"*Versus.*—Take thy arms and thy shield, and arise in my defence, lest he rejoice."

"*Preces.*—Preserve thy servant, my God, who putteth his trust in thee. Send unto him, O Lord, the help of thy Holy One; and from Sion protect him. Be to him, O Lord, a tower of fortitude in the presence of his enemies. O Lord, hear my prayer, and let my cry come unto thee."

"*Oratio.*—O God, who through thy servant hast been pleased to gather together thy handmaidens, we beseech thee to protect him from all adversity, and to return him safe to thy handmaidens. Through our Lord Jesus Christ," etc.

If the Lord should deliver me into the hands of my enemies, and they prevailing over me, should destroy me, or, by any fortune whatever, should I, absent from you, go the way of all flesh, I beseech you to transfer my body, whether it may have been buried or may lie exposed, to your cemetery, where our daughters, yes, our sisters in Christ, more frequently beholding my tomb, may be invited to pour forth their prayers for me to the Lord. I suppose that no place can be safer and more salutary for a contrite and penitent soul, than that which is appropriately consecrated to the true Paraclete, that is, to the Comforter; and is especially adorned with that name. Neither do I believe that there is a more appropriate place for Christian burial, among the faithful, than the cloisters of females devoted to Christ. It was women who were solicitous concerning the burial of the Lord Christ Jesus, who, both before and after his burial, used precious ointments, who faithfully kept watch at the sepulchre, and wept the loss of their spouse. They also were first consoled by the appearance and the words of the angel that announced the resurrection of Christ, and soon after they merited to taste the joys of his resurrection, to see him twice appear, and to touch him with their hands.

Finally, above all things, I ask you, who are now too solicitous on account of the perils to which my body is exposed, to be especially solicitous in regard to the safety of my soul, to exhibit to me when I am dead how much you have loved me during my life, by awarding to me the special and particular benefit of your prayers.

Live, you and your sisters—live, and remember me in Christ.*

---

* In the original, a couplet:

> "Vive, vale, vivantque tuæ, valeantque sorores,
> Vivite, sed Christo, quæso, mei memores."

XXVI.

LETTER OF HELOISE TO ABELARD.

"Ah wretch! believed the spouse of God in vain,
Confess'd within the slave of love and man.
Assist me, heav'n! but whence arose that pray'r?
Sprung it from piety, or from despair?
Ev'n here, where frozen chastity retires,
Love finds an altar for forbidden fires.
I ought to grieve; but cannot what I ought;
I mourn the lover, not lament the fault;
I view my crime, but kindle at the view,
Repent old pleasures, and solicit new;
Now turned to heav'n, I weep my past offence,
Now think of thee, and curse my innocence.
Of all afflictions taught a lover yet,
'Tis sure the hardest science to forget!
How shall I lose the sin, yet keep the sense,
And love th' offender, yet detest th' offence?
How the dear object from the crime remove,
Or how distinguish penitence from love?
Unequal task! a passion to resign,
For hearts so touched, so pierced, so lost as mine.
Ere such a soul regains its peaceful state,
How often must it love, how often hate!
How often hope, despair, resent, regret,
Conceal, disdain,—do all things but forget.

8

But let heaven seize it, all at once 'tis fired ;
Not touch'd, but rapt; not waken'd, but inspired !
Oh come! oh teach me nature to subdue,
Renounce my love, my life, myself—and you.
Fill my fond heart with God alone, for he
Alone can rival, can succeed to thee."

POPE's "Eloisa to Abelard."

To her only one after Christ,—his only one in Christ.

TO ABELARD HELOISE.

I am astonished, dearest, that, transcending the custom of epistles, even contrary to the natural course of things, in the address of your letter, you have placed me before yourself;—a woman before a man, a wife before her husband, a handmaid before her lord, a nun before a monk, a deaconess before an abbé.   Surely it is the right and becoming order, when we write to superiors or to equals, to place their names before our own.   But if we are writing to inferiors, the order of names must follow the order of dignity.

We have also been not a little astonished that you should increase the desolation of those to whom you ought to have offered the remedy of consolation, and that you should excite the tears which you ought to have wiped away.   For who of us could read without weeping what you wrote near the end of your letter: "If the Lord should deliver me into the hands of my enemies, and they, prevailing over me should destroy me . . . . ? &c." O dearest! how could your heart conceive such a thing, and how could your lips endure to speak it? Never may the Lord so forget his poor servants as to make them survivors of thee! Never may he grant us a life, which would be more insupportable than every species of death! It belongs to you to celebrate our obsequies, to commend our souls to God, and to send before you to him those that you have assembled in his name, that you may no longer be solicitous concerning them, and that you may follow us with the more joy on account of your greater security in regard to our safety.

Spare, I beseech you, my lord, spare such words, by which you make those that are already miserable, most miserable; and do not rob us before death of that little of life which remains to us. Sufficient unto the day is the evil thereof; and that day, full of bitterness, will bring anguish enough with it to all whom it shall find. "For why is it necessary," says Seneca, "to anticipate evils, and to lose life before death?"

You ask, my only one, should any accident shorten your days, while you are absent from us, that we may cause your body to be removed to our cemetery, in order that you may receive the greater benefit of our prayers, which will be constantly called forth by memory of you. But how, indeed, could

you suppose us capable of forgetting you? But
what time will be fit for prayer, when the highest per-
turbation shall permit no quiet?—when neither the
soul shall retain the sense of reason, nor the tongue
the use of speech?—when the mind insane, thus to
speak, towards God himself, having already irritated
rather than appeased him, shall not appease him by
prayers so much as it shall irritate him by complaints? Then nothing will remain for us unfortunates but to weep; it will not be permitted us to
pray, and it will be necessary for us to follow rather
than to bury you; and we shall be in a condition to
be interred instead of being able to inter another.
We, who will have lost our life in you, shall in no
way be able to live, when you are gone. And oh that
we may not be able to live so long! The mention of
your death is a kind of death to us. But what must
be the reality of your death, if it shall find us still
living? May God never permit that, as your survivors, we may pay the debt to you, or that to you we
may leave the patrimony, which from you we expect!
Oh that, in this, we may precede, and not follow you!

Spare us, then, I beseech you; spare at least thy
only one, by omitting to use such words, which pierce
our souls like swords of death, which render the anti-
cipation of death more terrible than death itself.

The soul that is overwhelmed with grief is not
quiet, neither is the mind that is filled with perturba-

tions open to divine influences. Be unwilling, I beseech you, to hinder us from serving God, to whom
you have devoted our lives. It is to be desired that an
inevitable event, which, when it comes, brings deep sorrow with it, may come unexpectedly, lest that which
no human foresight can turn aside, may torment us
long beforehand with useless fear. Full of this
thought the poet thus prays to God:

"Sit subitum quodcumque paras, sit cæca futuri,
  Mens hominum fati. Liceat sperari timenti."*

But if you were lost, what hope would there be
left to me ? or what cause would there be for remaining in this pilgrimage of life, where I have no remedy
for its ills but you, and no remedy in you except the
fact that you live ? All other pleasures from you are
denied me. Your presence, which could sometimes
return me to myself, it is not permitted me to enjoy.

Oh ! if I may say it, Heaven has been cruel to me
beyond all conception. O inclement clemency ! O unfortunate fortune ! she has so far consumed her weapons
against me, that she has none left for others against
whom she rages ! Against me she has exhausted her
full quiver, so that others in vain fear her resentment.

---

* "May whatever thou preparest be unexpected, may the
mind of men be blind to future fate. May it be permitted to
him who fears to hope." These lines are from Lucan.

Neither would she find a place in me for another wound, if she had a single arrow left. Among so many wounds she fears to inflict one more, lest my punishments be ended with death. And although she does not cease to work at my destruction, yet she fears the death which she hastens.

O I am the most miserable of the miserable, the most unhappy of the unhappy! I was elevated by your love above all women; but thrown down thence, my fall in my person and yours, has been proportioned to my elevation. The greater the elevation is, the more terrible is the ruin! Among noble and powerful women, whom has fortune been able to place before me, or to make equal to me? Whom has she so cast down and overwhelmed with grief? What glory did she confer on me in you! In you what ruin did she bring upon me! How she has carried to extremes both favor and disgrace, so that she has observed moderation neither in good nor in evil! She made me beforehand more fortunate than all, in order that she might make me the most miserable of all; that, when meditating upon the extent of my loss, lamentations might consume me, equal to the griefs that had oppressed me; that a bitterness on account of things lost might succeed, equal to the love of things possessed which had preceded; and that the joy of the highest pleasure might terminate with the deepest sorrow and pain.

And, in order that more indignation should spring
from the injury, all the rights of equity have been vi-
olated in regard to us. For while we were enjoying
the pleasures of a solicitous love,* we were spared the
vengeance of heaven. But when we corrected unlawful relations with those lawful, and covered the baseness of fornication with the honor of marriage, the
angry hand of the Lord was laid heavily upon us, and
the conjugal couch could not procure pardon for its
chaste pleasures from him who had so long tolerated
pleasures that were impure.

A man caught in any act of adultery would sufficiently expiate his crime by the punishment which you
have endured. What others incur by adultery, you
have incurred by the marriage by which you were expecting to make satisfaction for all injuries. What
adulterous females bring upon their paramours, your
own wife brought upon you. Neither was this when
we were wholly abandoned to our earliest pleasures,
but when, separated for a time, we were living more
chastely; you at Paris, presiding over the schools,
I at Argenteuil, by your order, in the company of
the nuns. This separation should have protected
us, for we had imposed it on ourselves; you, in order
to devote yourself more studiously to your pupils, I, in
order to devote myself more freely to prayer or medita-

* "Ut turpiore, sed expressione vocabulo utar, fornicatio
vacaremur."

tion of Holy Scripture; and while we were living so
much the more holy as we were the more chaste, you
alone expiated with your blood the crime which was
common to us both.   You alone bore the punishment;
both were in fault; you were the least culpable, and
you bore all the pain.

In lowering yourself, and elevating me and all of
my family to the honor of your alliance, you rendered
sufficient satisfaction to God and men, not to deserve
the chastisement which those traitors inflicted upon
you.   O how unfortunate I am, that I should have
been born to be the cause of so great a crime!   O fatal sex!   It will always be the destruction of the
greatest men!   Hence it is written in Proverbs, concerning the shunning of women: "Hearken unto me,
therefore, O ye children, and attend to the words
of my mouth.   Let not thine heart incline to her
ways, go not astray in her paths.   For she hath cast
down many wounded: yea, many strong men have
been slain by her.   Her house is the way to hell, going down to the chambers of death."   And in Ecclesiastes: "And I find more bitter than death the
woman whose heart is snares and nets, and her hands
as bands: whoso pleaseth God shall escape from her,
but the sinner shall be taken by her."

At the beginning, the first woman seduced man,
and was the cause of his being driven out of paradise:
she who had been created by the Lord as an aid to

him, became the means of his destruction. That
bravest Nazarite, the man of the Lord, whose conception had been announced by an angel, was overcome
by Delilah alone, and, delivered up to his enemies, and
deprived of his eyes, was driven by her to such an
extent of grief, that he destroyed himself, in a common ruin with his enemies. Solomon, the wisest of
men, was so infatuated with a single woman that he
had espoused, and was driven by her to such a state
of insanity, that he whom the Lord had chosen for
building his temple,—his father, David, notwithstanding his justice, having been found unworthy of doing
this,—was plunged by her into idolatry until the end
of his life, abandoning the worship of the true God,
whose glory he had celebrated, whose commandments
he had taught, with the words of his mouth and his
writings. The saintly Job experienced his last and
sorest trial in his wife, who excited him to curse God.
The subtle tempter knew well, for he had often
proved it, that the easiest ruin for men is found in
their wives.

Extending his ordinary malice to us, you, whom
he had not been able to destroy by fornication, he
tried with marriage; he found in good the instrument
of destruction which he had not been able to find in
evil.

I thank God for one thing at least, that I do not at
all resemble the women that I have cited; that the

8*

tempter has not made me consent to the fault, for the
commission of which, nevertheless, I was made the
cause. Although I am justified by the purity of my
intentions, I have in no way incurred the penalty of
consenting to this crime; nevertheless I have committed many sins, which do not allow me to believe
myself entirely innocent of it. Inasmuch as I served
the pleasures of carnal delights, I therefore have deserved what I now suffer, and the consequences of my
previous sins have justly become punishments.

O that I could do penance worthy of this crime,
that the length of my expiation might in some sort
balance the pains of your punishment; and that what
you have suffered for a moment in body I might suffer
during my whole life in contrition of mind, and that
this might satisfy you at least, if not God!

To confess to you the infirmity of my most
wretched mind, I find no penance with which I am
able to appease God, whom I am always accusing
of the greatest cruelty, on account of this injury;
and, opposed to his dispensation, I offend him more
with my indignation, than I appease him with the
satisfaction of my penance. It cannot be said that
penance has been made for him, however great may
be the bodily affliction, if the mind still retains a willingness to sin, and is still swayed by its primitive
desires. It is easy to confess our faults, to accuse
ourselves of them, or even to afflict our bodies with

external pains. It is extremely difficult to tear tho mind away from the desires of the highest pleasures. This is the reason why Job, after having said: " Therefore I will not refrain my mouth,"—that is, I will loose my tongue, and open my mouth in confession, that it may accuse me of my sins,—immediately added: " I will speak in the anguish of my spirit." Gregory, in an exposition of this passage, says: " There are some who confess faults with an open mouth, but they know not how to confess with contrite hearts, and rejoice while saying things to be bewailed." It is not sufficient to avow our faults, it is necessary to avow them in bitterness of soul, in order that this very bitterness may punish us for whatever the tongue accuses us, through the judgment of the mind.

But this bitterness of true repentance is very rare, as St. Ambrose has remarked: " I have found more who have preserved innocence, than who have truly repented." But those pleasures of love, which we enjoyed together, were so sweet to me, that they can neither displease me, nor glide from my memory. Wherever I go, they present themselves to my eyes, with all their allurements. Neither are their illusions wanting to me in my dreams.

During the solemnity of divine service, when prayer ought to be the more pure, the enticing phantoms of those pleasures so take possession of my most

miserable soul, that I am occupied with those base
delights, rather than with my prayer. When I ought
to be grieving for the commission of sins, I am rather
sighing for the return of pleasures that are lost. Not
only the things which we did, but the times and places
in which we did them, have been with your image so
fixed in my mind, that during my waking hours, all is
lived over again in imagination, and in my dreams, all
the past returns. Sometimes the cogitations of my
mind are manifested in my motions and expressions,
and words escape me which betray the irregularity of
my thoughts.

O truly miserable I am, and most worthy of that
complaining of a grieving soul! " O wretched man
that I am, who shall deliver me from the body of this
death?" And would that I could truly add what
follows: " I thank God, through Jesus Christ our
Lord."

This grace, dearest, has come to you, and a single
corporeal plague has protected you against many
plagues of soul, and God is found to be the most propitious in that wherein he is believed to be most ad-
verse to you. He is like a physician, who does not
spare pain, provided he can save the life of his patient.*

---

* His autem in me stimulos carnis, hæc incentiva libidinis,
ipse juvenilis fervor ætatis, et jucundissimarum experientia
voluptatum, plurimùm accedunt, et tantò ampliùs suâ me im-
pugnatione opprimunt, quantò infirmior est natura quam
oppugnant.

I am called chaste, because it has not been perceived that I am a hypocrite. Purity of the flesh is
taken for virtue, as though virtue belonged to the
body instead of the soul. I am praised by men, but
I have no merit with God, who proves the heart and
reins, and sees in secret.

I am praised for being religious in these times,
when there is only a small part of religion that is not
hypocrisy; when he is most extolled who does not
offend the judgment of men. Doubtless, it is in some
manner laudable, and in some manner appears acceptable to God, not to scandalize the church by the bad
example of an outward act, whatever the motive may
be; for thus we do not give infidels an occasion of
blaspheming the name of the Lord, and carnal men
an occasion of defaming the order to which we belong.
And this, too, is a gift of divine grace which gives
not only the power to do good, but also the power to
abstain from evil. But the latter precedes in vain,
when the former does not succeed, as it is written:
"Abhor that which is evil, cleave to that which is
good." And in vain is either done, if it is not done
through the love of God.

But in every stage of my life, God knows that I
have feared more to offend you than to offend him,—
that I have sought more to please you than to please
him. Thy command, and not the love of God, led
me to assume religious habit. See how unhappy a

life is mine—a life more wretched than all others, if
here I endure so many things in vain, without the expectation of any reward in the future.   Thus far my
simulation has deceived you, as well as others; you
have regarded that as religion which was nothing but
hypocrisy; so commending yourself to my prayers,
you ask from me what I expect from you.   •

Do not, I beseech you, put so much confidence in
me, lest you should cease to succor me with your
prayers.   Do not suppose me well, lest you should
deprive me of the pleasure of a remedy.   Do not believe that I am not needy, lest you should defer to
aid me in my necessity.   Do not suppose me strong,
lest I should fall ere you can sustain me.   Many
have been injured by flattery, and the support
which they need she has taken away.   Through the
prophet Isaiah, the Lord exclaims: "O my people,
they which lead thee cause thee to err, and destroy
the way of thy paths."   And through the mouth of
the prophet Ezekiel: "Woe to the women that sew
pillows to all arm-holes, and make kerchiefs upon the
head of every statue, to hunt souls."*   On the other
hand, it is said by Solomon: "The words of the wise
are as goads, and as nails fastened by masters of assemblies, which are given from one shepherd."

Desist, I beseech you, from praising me, lest you

---

* A figure, say the commentators, to represent the lulling
of men to sleep by deceitful predictions.

incur the known baseness of adulation, and the crime of mendacity; or, if you believe there is any thing good in me, do not praise me, lest the praise itself vanish in the breath of vanity. No skilful physician judges of an interior disease by an inspection of external appearances. Nothing that is common to reprobates and the elect, obtains any merit with God. The really just often neglect those external practices that strike the attention of all, whilst no one conforms to them with greater case than the hypocrite.

The heart of man is corrupt and ever inscrutable. Who can understand it? There are ways which seem right to men; but their issues lead to death. The judgment of men is rash in those things which are reserved solely for the examination of God. Hence it is written: "Praise no man during his lifetime." For, in praising a man, we are liable to destroy the virtue itself which makes him worthy of praise.

But your praise is so much the more perilous to me, as it is the more grateful; and I am so much the more taken and delighted with it, as I am the more studious to please you in all things. Distrust me, I beseech you, instead of confiding in me, that I may always be assisted with your solicitude. The danger is greater now than ever, for there is remaining in you no remedy for my incontinence.

Do not exhort me to virtue, do not provoke me to combat, in saying, "Virtue is perfected by trial;"

and, "He only shall be crowned, who shall have strived to the last." I do not seek the crown of victory. It is enough for me to shun peril. It is safer to shun peril than to wage war. In whatever corner of heaven God may place me, it will satisfy me. No one will there envy another, since for each one, what he obtains will be sufficient.

My position in this respect is fortified by authority. Let us hear St. Jerome: "I confess my weakness; I am unwilling to contend in hope of victory, lest in some way I may lose victory. Why should we abandon the certain, and contend for the uncertain?

XXVII.

EPISTLE OF ABELARD TO HELOISE.

To the Spouse of Christ, the Servant of the same.

TO HELOISE ABELARD.

Your last letter, I remember, is summed up in four points, into which you have disposed the vivid expression of your complaints. At first, indeed, you complain that, contrary to the custom in letters, even contrary to the natural order of things, my letter directed to you placed you before me in the salutation. In the second place, you complain that I increased your desolation, when I ought to have offered consolation, and that I excited the tears which it was my duty to wipe away, by saying: "If the Lord should deliver me into the hands of my enemies, and they prevailing over me should put me to death," etc. In the third place, comes up again that old and perpetual complaint of yours against Providence, about the mode of our conversion to God, and the cruelty of the treachery practised against me. Finally, you accuse yourself, in opposition to my praise, and earnestly supplicate me to address you no more in that manner.

I have determined to answer your objections singly, not so much for my own justification as for your instruction and encouragement; that you may assent to my commands the more freely, when you shall learn that they are reasonable; that you may listen so much the more attentively in regard to things which pertain to you, as you shall find me the less reprehensible in regard to things which pertain to myself; and that you may fear so much the more to contemn me, as you shall find me the less worthy of reprehension.

In regard to the preposterous order of my salutation, as you call it, you will recognize, by giving diligent attention to it, that I have acted in accordance with your own sentiment. For, what all can see, you have yourself said, that when we write to superiors their names must come first. You know that you became my superior, and that you began to be my mistress* from the time when you were made the spouse of my master, according to the words of St. Jerome, writing to Eustochia: "This is the reason why I write, my mistress Eustochia. Surely I ought to call the spouse of my master my mistress." It is a happy nuptial exchange, that you, at first the wife of

---

* *Domina mea esse cœpisti.* It is hardly necessary to say that the word mistress is used in its highest sense.

a wretched human creature, should be elevated to the couch of the highest king. Neither is the privilege of this honor extended to your former husband alone, but to all other servants of the same king. Be not astonished, therefore, if I commend myself to you as, living or dead, the subject of your prayers; for it is everywhere admitted that the intercession of a spouse with her lord is more powerful than that of a servant, and that the voice of a mistress has more authority than that of a slave.

As the model of these, the queen and spouse of the Sovereign King is described with care in these words of the Psalmist: "Upon thy right hand did stand the queen, in gold of Ophir." In other words, she remains familiarly by her spouse, and walks side by side with him, whilst all others keep far away, or follow at a respectful distance. Filled with the sentiment of her glory and her prerogative, the spouse in Canticles exultingly says: "I am black, but comely, O ye daughters of Jerusalem.' And again: "Look not upon me because I am black, because the sun hath looked upon me."

It is true that these words describe in general the contemplative soul, which is specially named the spouse of Christ, yet they pertain still more expressly to you, as the habit which you wear proves. .

Surely the exterior garment of black, or coarser material, like the mourning habit of good widows, who

bewail their deceased husbands whom they loved,
shows that you, according to the Apostle, are truly
widowed and desolate in this world, and ought to be
supported from the revenues of the church. The
grief of those widows, on account of the death of
their Lord, is commemorated in the Scripture, where
they are described as sitting by the sepulchre and
weeping.

The Ethiopian is black, and so far as the exterior
is concerned, appears to other women deformed; nevertheless, she does not yield to them in interior beauties, but in most respects is more beautiful and whiter. *

* Habet autem Æthiopissa exteriorem in carne nigredinem,
et quantum ad exteriora pertinet, cæteris apparet feminis deformior; cùm non sit tamen in interioribus dispar, sed in
plerisque etiam formosior, atque candidior, sicut in ossibus
seu dentibus. Quorum videlicet dentium candor in ipso etiam
commendatur sponso, cùm dicitur: "Et dentes ejus lacte can-
didores."

Nigra itaque in exterioribus, sed formosa in interioribus
est; quia in hàc vitâ crebris adversitatum tribulationibus
corporaliter afflicta quasi in carne nigrescit exteriùs, juxtà
illud Apostoli: "Omnes qui volunt piè vivere in Christo tri-
bulationem patientur." Sicut enim candido prosperum, ità
non incongruè nigro designatur adversum. Intùs autem,
quasi in ossibus, candet, quia in virtutibus ejus anima pollet,
sicut scriptum est: "Omnis gloria ejus filiæ regis ab intùs."
Ossa quippè, quæ interiora sunt, exteriori carne circumdata,
et ipsius carnis, quam gerunt, vel sustentant, robur ac fortitu-
do, sunt, benè animam exprimunt, quæ carnem ipsam, cui
inest, vivificat, sustentat, movet, atque regit, atque ei omnem
valetudinem ministrat. Cujus quidem est candor, sive decor,
ipsæ, quibus adornatur, virtutes. Nigra quoque est in exte-

Indeed this blackness, the effect of corporeal
tribulations, easily detaches the minds of the faithful
from the love of mundane things, and elevates them

rioribus, quia dùm in hâc perigrinatione adhuc exulat, vilem
et abjectam se tenet in hâc vitâ; ut in illâ sublimentur, quæ
est abscondita cum Christo in Deo, patriam jàm adepta. Sic
verò eam sol verus decolorat, quia cœlestis amor sponsi eam
sic humiliat, vel tribulationibus cruciat; ne eam scilicet pros-
peritas extollat. Decolorat eam sic, id est dissimilem eam à
cæteris facit, quæ terrenis inhiant, et sæculi quærunt gloriam;
ut sic ipsa verè lilium convallium per humilitatem efficiatur:
non lilium quidem montium, sicut illæ videlicèt fatuæ vir-
gines, quæ de munditiâ carnis, vel abstinentiâ exteriore, apud
se intumescentes, æstu tentationum aruerunt. Benè autem
filias Hierusalem, id est, imperfectiores alloquens fideles, qui
filiarum potiùs, quàm filiorum nomine digni sunt, dicit: "Nolite me considerare quòd fusca sim, quia decoloravit me sol."
Ac si apertius dicat: Quòd sic me humilio, vel tàm viriliter
adversitates sustineo, non est meæ virtutis, sed ejus gratiæ
cui deservio.

Aliter solent hæretici, vel hypocritæ, quantùm ad faciem
hominum spectat, spe terrenæ gloriæ sese vehementer humil-
iare, vel multa inutiliter tolerare. De quorum hujusmodi
abjectione, vel tribulatione, quam sustinent, vehementer mirandum est; cùm sint omnibus miserabiliores hominibus, qui
nec præsentis vitæ bonis, nec futuræ fruuntur. Hoc itaque
sponsa diligenter considerans dicit: "Nolite mirari cur id
faciam." Sed de illis mirandum est, qui inutiliter terrenæ
laudis desiderio æstuantes terrenis se privant commodis, tàm
hîc quàm in futuro miseri. Qualis quidem fatuarum virgi-
num continentia est, quæ à januâ sunt exclusæ.

Bené etiam, quia nigra est, ut diximus, et formosa, dilec-
tam, et introductam se dicit in cubiculum regis, id est, in secretum vel quietem contemplationis, et lectulum illum, de

*

to the desires of eternal life, and frequently draws
them from the tumultuous life of the world to the secret of contemplation.   This is what happened to
Paul at the beginning of that kind of life which we
have embraced, that is, the monastic life, as St. Jerome writes.   This poverty of habit seeks solitude
rather than the world, and is the surest safeguard of
that denial of and that retreat from the world, which
most especially become our profession.   For rich dress,
most of all things, excites us to appear in public,
which is sought by no one except for the gratification
of vanity, and the pomp of the world, as St. Gregory
has shown in these words : " No one thinks of adorn-

quo eadem alibi dicit: "In lectulo meo per noctes quæsivi
quem diligit anima mea."   Ipsa quippè nigredinis deformitas
occultum potiùs quàm manifestum, et secretum magis quàm
publicum amat.   Et quæ talis est uxor, secreta potiùs viri
gaudia quàm manifesta desiderat, et in lecto magis vult
sentiri quàm in mensâ videri.   Et frequenter accidit, ut nig-
rarum caro feminarum, quantò est in aspectu deformior, tantò
sit in tactu suavior : atque ideò earum voluptas secretis gau-
diis quàm publicis gratior sit et convenientior, et earum viri,
ut illis oblectentur, magis eas in cubiculum introducunt, quàm
ad publicum educunt.

Secundùm quam quidem metaphoram benè spiritualis
sponsa cùm præmisisset: "Nigra sum, sed formosa," statim
adjunxit: "Ideò dilexit me rex, et introduxit me in cubiculum suum," singula videlicèt singulis reddens.   Hoc est, quia
formosa, dilexit, quia nigra, introduxit.   Formosa, ut dixi, intùs
virtutibus quas diligit sponsus: nigra exteriùs corporalium
tribulationum adversitatibus.

ing himself in a solitary place, but where he can be seen." But the chamber of which the bride speaks, is that to which the spouse himself invites us for prayer, as this passage from the Gospel testifies : " But thou, when thou prayest, enter into thy closet, and when thou hast shut thy door, pray to thy Father which is in secret." As if he had said: not in the highways and in public places, like the hypocrites. He calls the closet a place secret from the tumult and observation of the world, where it is possible to pray more quietly and more purely. Such are the secret places of monastic solitudes, where we are commanded to shut the door, that is, to obstruct every passage, lest for some reason the purity of prayer be obstructed, and the eye trespass upon the unhappy soul. We are grieved to see still, among the people of our habit, so many despisers of this counsel, or rather of this divine precept, who, when they are celebrating the divine offices, the choirs and chancels being thrown open, impudently present themselves before the faces of women as well as men, and especially when in the solemn ceremonies they degrade the precious ornaments of the priest- hood by engaging in rivalry with men of the world to whom they show themselves. In their opinion the festival is so much the more beautiful, as it is the richer in external ornament, and the more sumptuous. In regard to their blindness, which is so deplorable

and so contrary to the religion of Christ's poor, it is
better to pass over it in silence, since it would be impossible to speak of it without shame.   Always juda-
izing, they follow their own habit as a rule, and make
the word of God a dead letter by their traditions, for
they conform to custom instead of duty.   Nevertheless, as St. Augustine remembers, the Lord has said:
"I am Truth," and not, "I am custom."   To their
prayers, those which they make with open door, whoever wishes, commends himself.   But you, who have
been introduced by himself into the chamber of the
celestial king, and are quiet in his spiritual embraces,
the door being always shut,—you are wholly devoted
to him.   As you adhere the more closely to him, and
as the Apostle says: "He that is joined unto the
Lord is one spirit," I have the more confidence in
the purity and efficacy of your prayer, and the more
ardently solicit your aid.   I trust that the dearness
of our mutual affection will increase the fervor of
your petitions in my behalf.

As to the pain which I have given you by men-
tioning the danger which threatens me, and the death
which I fear, I have in that only answered your demand, ever your prayer.   The following are the very
words of the first letter which you sent:

"In the name of Christ, who hitherto has protected you for his service, whose humble servants we
are and thine, we beseech you to write us frequently,

informing us by what perils you are surrounded; since we alone remain to you, to participate in your grief or your joy. Those who condole with us usually afford some consolation to the sorrowing, and a burden laid upon several is more easily borne, or seems more light."

Why then do you reproach me for having made you participate in my anxiety, when you have com-pelled me to do it by your supplications? In view of this desperate life which, with torture, I am living, does it become you to rejoice? Do you wish to par-ticipate in my joy only, and not in my grief? Do you wish to rejoice with the rejoicing, and not to weep with the weeping? There is no greater differ-ence between true and false friends than this, that the former are faithful in adversity, while the latter remain only so long as prosperity lasts. Leave off your reproaches, then, I beseech you, and suppress these complaints that are wholly foreign to the heart of charity.

Or if you are still pained in this respect, you must consider that, placed in such imminent peril, and in daily despair of my life, it behooves me to be solicitous in regard to the safety of my soul, and to provide for it, while it is still permitted. If you love me truly, you will not complain of this precaution. And if you have any hope of divine mercy toward me, you should even desire that I may be freed from the miseries of this life, which, as you see, are insup-

9

portable. You know well, that whosoever should free me from this life, would put an end to my torments. What pains may await me hereafter is uncertain, but from how great pains I should be delivered is certain.

The end of a wretched life is always sweet, and those who suffer with others in their misfortunes, and condole with them in their sorrows, desire that these misfortunes and sorrows may be terminated, and even to their own hurt, if they sincerely love those whom they see in trouble, and they are not mindful of an event that brings grief to themselves if it brings deliverance to their friends. So a mother who sees her child wasting away with a painful and incurable disease, desires that death may come to terminate the suffering which she cannot bear to look upon, and prefers that it should die rather than be the companion of misery. And whoever is greatly delighted with the presence of a friend, nevertheless rather wishes that he should be absent and happy, than present and miserable, for, not being able to remedy his pains, he cannot bear the sight of them.

It is not permitted you to enjoy my presence, even in misery. And when my presence would be useless to you for any purposes of pleasure, I do not see why you should prefer for me a most miserable life to a happier death. If you desire that my miseries should be prolonged for your own interest, you are evidently my enemy rather than my friend. If you shrink from seeming to be my enemy, I pray you, as I have already said, desist from your complaints.

But approve the praise which you reprobate; for in this very thing you show yourself more worthy of it; for it is written: " He that shall humble himself, shall be exalted." And Heaven grant that your thought may accord with what you have written. If such were your real sentiments, your humility is true, and will not vanish before my words. But take care, I beseech you, that you do not seek praise by seeming to shun it, and that you do not reprobate that with your lips which in heart you desire. In this regard, St. Jerome writes thus to the virgin Eustochia : " We yield ourselves freely to our adulators, and although we reply that we are undeserving, and blush, nevertheless the soul within rejoices in praise." Such a one Virgil describes in the lascivious Galathea, who sought the pleasure that she desired by appearing to fly, and incited her lover the more toward herself by feigning a repulse :

"Et fugit ad salices, et se crepit ante videri."

Flying, she desires to be seen before she conceals herself, for by this flight she is the more sure of obtaining the caresses of the youth, which she seems to shun. So when we appear to shun the praise of men, we provoke it the more, and when we pretend to wish to conceal ourselves that no one may see in us any thing to praise, we excite the more the praises of those who are not wary, for thereby we seem the more worthy of praise.

And these things I speak, because they frequently happen, not because I suspect any such thing in you, for I do not doubt your humility; but I wish to have you shun even these words, lest you may seem to those who do not know you to seek glory, as St. Jerome says, by shunning it. Never will my praise inflate you, but will always incite you to better things, and your zeal for the attainment of the virtues for which I praise you, will be earnest in proportion to your desire of pleasing me. My praise is not to you a testimony of religion, that you should thereby be inspired with pride. No one must be judged by the panegyrics of friends, nor by the vituperations of enemies.

Finally, it remains to speak to you of your old and perpetual complaint, of your presuming to accuse God on account of the mode of our conversion, instead of wishing to glorify him, as it is just. I believed that the bitterness of your soul had vanished, on account of the striking proofs of the divine mercy towards us. The more dangerous this is to you—it consumes the body as well as the soul—the more it excites my pity and my regret. If, as you profess, you study above all thing to please me, then, that you may not torture me, that you may please me supremely, reject that biterness from your heart. With this you cannot please me, nor can you with me arrive at beatitude. Could you bear that I should go thither without you—you who profess your willingness to follow me even to perdition? But seek religion for this one thing at least, that you may not be separated from me when, as you believe, I am hastening to God; and that you may seek it the more earnestly, call to mind how blessed it will be for us to set out together, and how much the sweetness of our companionship will add to our felicity. Think of what you have said; remember what you have written, that in the manner of our conversion God has showed himself, as it is manifest, so much the more propitious to me, as he is believed to have been the more averse. But in this his holy will is pleasing to me, because it is to me most salutary, and to you as well as to me, if the excess of your grief admit a reasonable judgment. Do not complain that you are the cause of so great a good, nor doubt that God predestined you to be the source of it. Weep not on account of my sufferings, for it would also be necessary for you to weep on account of the sufferings of the martyrs and the death of the Lord. Could you more easily bear what has happened to me, and would it offend you less, if it had justly happened to me? No, surely, for then it would be the more ignominious for me, and the more glorious for my enemies, since justice would procure

praise for them, and my fault contempt for me. No
one would then accuse them for their act; no one
would be moved with pity for me.

But, to assuage the bitterness of your grief, I
could show the justice as well as the utility of what has
happened to us, and I could show you that God was
more right in punishing us after marriage than when we
were living an irregular life.*

You also know that, when I transferred you into
my native country, you were clothed in the sacred

---

* "Ut tamen et hoc modo hujus amaritudinem doloris le-
niamus, tàm justè quàm utiliter id monstrabimus nobis acci-
disse, et rectiùs in conjugatos quam in fornicantes ultum
Deum fuisse. Nôsti post nostri confœderationem conjugii, cùm
Argenteoli cum sanctimonialibus in claustro conversabaris,
me die quâdam privatìm ad te visitandam venisse, et quid ibi
tecum meæ libidinis egerit intemperantia in quâdam etiam
parte ipsius refectorii, cùm quo aliàs diverteremus, non hab-
eremus. Nôsti, inquam, id impudentissimè tunc actum esse
in tàm reverendo loco et summæ Virgini consecrato. Quòd,
etsi alia cessent flagitia, multò graviore dignum sit ultione.
Quid pristinas fornicationes et impudentissimas referam pol-
lutiones quæ conjugium præcesserunt? Quid summam denique
proditionem meam, quâ de te ipsâ tuum, cum quo assiduè
in ejus domo convivebam, avunculum tàm turpiter seduxi?
Quis me ab eo justè prodi non censeat, quem tam impudenter
antè ipse prodideram? Putas ad tantorum criminum ultionem momentaneum illius plagæ dolorem sufficere? Imò tantis
malis tantum debitum esse commodum? Quam plagam di-
vinæ sufficere justitiæ credis ad tantam contaminationem, ut
diximus, sacerrimi loci suæ matris? Certè nisi vehementer
erro, non tàm illa saluberrima plaga in ultionem horum con-
versa est, quàm quæ hodiè indesinenter sustineo.

habit, that you pretended to be a nun, and by such a pretence profaned the sacred institution to which you now belong. Judge thence how properly the divine justice, or rather the divine grace, has drawn you in spite of yourself into that religious state, of which you did not fear to make a jest; it has imposed on you as a punishment that very habit whioh you daringly assumed, in order that the falsehood of pretending to be a nun might be remedied by the truth of being a nun in reality.

If to the divine justice you join the consideration of our interest, you will acknowledge God did every thing for the sake of our good, and not for the sake of his own vengeance. See, dearest, see how with the strong nets of his mercy the Lord has taken us from the depths of that sea so perilous, from what a devouring Charybdis he has delivered his creatures in distress, already wrecked in the whirlpool, and contending against the saving hand, so that either of us might utter that cry of wonder and love: " The Lord was solicitous concerning me !" Think and reflect upon the dangers which surrounded us, and whence the Lord snatched us : and unceasingly with hymns of gratitude recount how much the Lord has done for our souls ; and console by our example the transgressors who despair of his mercy, showing all what can be done by penitence and prayer, when so many benefits have been conferred on the impenitent and the hard-

cned. Observe the most exalted counsel of the Lord
in regard to us, and how he tempered his justice with
mercy; how prudently he made use of evils, and di-
vinely overcame impiety, for, by the just infliction of
a bodily punishment upon me, he saved two souls.
Compare our danger and the manner of our deliverance. Compare the disease and the remedy. Behold
the cause of so much indulgence, and admire the pity
and the love of God.*

* Nôsti quantis turpitudinibus immoderata mea libido
corpora nostra addixerat, ut nulla honestatis vel Dei reveren-
tia in ipsis etiam diebus Dominicæ passionis, vel quantarum-
cumque solemnitatum ab hujus luti volutabro me revocaret.
Sed et te nolentem, et prout poteras reluctantem et dissua-
dentem, quæ naturâ infirmior eras, sæpiùs minis ac flagellis
ad consensum trahebam. Tanto enim tibi concupiscentiæ ar-
dore copulatus eram, ut miseras illas et obscœnissimas voluptates, quas etiam nominare confundimur, tàm Deo quàm mihi
ipsi præponerem: nec tàm aliter consulere posse divina
videretur clementia, nisi has mihi voluptates sinè spe ullâ
omninò interdiceret.

Undè justissimè et clementissimè, licet cum summâ tui
avunculi proditione, ut in multis crescerem, parte illâ corporis
sum minutus, in quâ libidinis regnum erat, et tota hujus concupiscentiæ causa consistebat: ut justiè illud plecteretur
membrum, quod in nobis commiserat totum, et expiaret pa-
tiendo quod deliquerat oblectando: et ab his me spurcitiis,
quibus me totum quasi luto immerseram, tàm mente quàm
corpore circumcideret: et tantò sacris etiam altaribus
idoniorem efficeret, quantò me nulla hinc campliùs carnalium,
contagia pollutionum revocarent. Quàm clementer etiam in
eo tantùm me pati voluit membro, cujus privatio et animæ
saluti consuleret, et corpus non deturparet, nec ullam offici-
orum ministrationem præpediret; imò ad omnia quæ honestè

I merit death, and God gives me life. I am called, and I resist. I persist in my crimes, and unwill-

geruntur, tantò me promptiorem efficeret, quantò ab hoc concupiscentiæ jugo maximo ampliùs liberaret. Cùm itaque
membris his vilissimis, quæ pro summæ turpitudinis exercito
pudenda vocantur, nec proprium sustinet nomen, me divina
Gratia mundavit, potiùs quàm privavit, quid aliud egit quàm
ad puritatem munditiæ conservandam sordida removit et
vitia?

Hanc quidem munditiæ puritatem nonnullos sapientium
vehementissimè appetentes inferre etiam sibi manum audivi-
mus, ut hoc à se penitùs removerent concupiscentiæ flagitium,
pro quo etiam stimulo carnis auferendo et Apostolus perhibetur
Dominum rogâsse, nec exauditum esse. In exemplo est ille mag-
nus christianorum philosophus Origenes, qui, ut in se penitùs
incendium exstingueret, manus sibi inferre veritus non est: ac
si illos ad litteram verè beatos intelligeret, qui seipsos prop-
ter regnum cœlorum castraverunt, et tales illud veraciter im-
plere crederet, quod de membris scandalizantibus nobis
præcipit Dominus, ut ea scilicet à nobis abscindamus et proji-
ciamus, et quasi illam Isaiæ prophetiam ad historiam magis
quàm ad mysterium duceret, per quam cæteris fidelibus
eunuchos Dominus præfert, dicens: "Eunuchi si custodierint
sabbata mea, et elegerint quæ volui, dabo eis in domo meâ et
in muris meis locum, et nomen melius à filiis et filiabus. Nomen sempiternum dabo eis, quod non peribit." Culpam tamen non modicam Origenes' incurrit, dùm per pœnam corporis remedium culpæ quærit.

Zelum quippè Dei habens, sed non secundùm scientiam,
homicidi incurrit reatum inferendo sibi manum. Suggestione
diabolicâ, vel errore maximo, id ab ipso constat esse factum,
quod miseratione Dei, in me est ab alio perpetratum. Culpam
evito, non incurro. Mortem mereor, et vitam assequor. Vo-
cor, et reluctor. Insto criminibus, et ad veniam trahor invi-
tus. Orat Apostolus, nec exauditur. Precibus instat, nec
impetrat. Verè Dominus sollicitus est mei. Vadam igitur
et narrabo quanta fecit Dominus animæ meæ.

ingly am driven to pardon. The Apostle prays, and
is not heard; he persists in prayer and does not pre-
vail. Truly the Lord is solicitous concerning me. I
will go therefore and proclaim how much the Lord has
done for my soul.

Come and join me; be my inseparable companion
in one act of grace, since you have participated with
me in the fault and in the pardon. For the Lord is
not unmindful of your safety; yes, he is most especially mindful of you, for he has clearly foreordained that
you should be his by a certain divine presage, since
he designated you as Heloise from his own name which
is Elohim.

He, I say, has mercifully ordered that by one of us
both should be saved, when the devil was trying to destroy us both by one. A little while before the catastrophe, the indissoluble law of the nuptial sacrament
had bound us together, and while I desired to retain
you always to myself,—you loved by me beyond measure,—the Lord was preparing the circumstances
which should turn our thoughts toward heaven.

For if we had not been married, my retreat from
the world, or the counsel of your relatives, or the attraction of pleasure, would have retained you in the
world. Behold how much the Lord has been mindful
of us, as if he had reserved us for some great purpose,
as if he had been indignant or grieved that those talents for science and literature, which he had intrusted

to us both, were not used exclusively for the honor of his name; or as if he were in fear in regard to his most unfaithful servant, as it is written: "Women cause even the wise to apostatize." Of this, Solomon, the wisest of men, is a proof.

Your talent of prudence indeed brings daily increase to the Lord; already to the Lord you have given many spiritual daughters, whilst I have remained fruitless, and have labored in vain among the children of perdition. O what a terrible misfortune! What a lamentable loss, if, given up to the impurities of carnal pleasures, you should bear with grief a small number of children for the world, instead of bearing with joy so great a number for heaven. You would be nothing more than a woman,—you who now transcend even men, and who have exchanged the malediction of Eve for the benediction of Mary. What profanation if those sacred hands, which now are employed in turning the holy page, were condemned to the vulgar cares which are the lot of woman!

Be no longer afflicted, then, my dear sister, I beseech you; cease to accuse a father who corrects us so tenderly; attend rather to what is written: "Whom the Lord loveth, he chasteneth." And in another place: "He that spareth his rod hateth his son." This is transitory and not eternal; it purifies us, and does not destroy.

Take courage, listen to this sovereign word, that

comes from the mouth of Truth itself: "In your patience possess ye your souls." Hence Solomon has said : "He that is slow to anger is better than the mighty; and he that ruleth his spirit, than he that taketh a city."

Are you not moved to tears and bitter compassion, when you behold the only Son of God seized by the most impious, dragged away, mocked, scourged, buffeted, spit upon, crowned with thorns, hung upon the infamous cross between two thieves, finally in such a horrible and execrable manner suffering death, for your salvation and that of the world? Him, my sister, who is thy spouse and the spouse of the whole church, keep continually before your eyes, and in your heart. Gaze upon him as he goes to his crucifixion, bearing his own cross. Be one of the multitude, one of the women, who were beating their breasts and weeping, as St. Luke narrates in these words : "And there followed him a great company of people, and of women, which also bewailed and lamented him." He turned towards them with benignity, and mildly predicted to them the vengeance that should follow his death, and taught them how to guard themselves against it. " Daughters of Jerusalem, weep not for me, but weep for yourselves, and your children ; for behold the days are coming, in the which they shall say, Blessed are the barren, and the wombs that never bore, and the paps which never gave suck. Then they shall begin

to say to the mountains: Fall on us; and to the
hills: Cover us; for if they do these things in a
green tree, what shall be done in the dry?"

Sympathize with him who freely suffers for your
redemption, and participate with him in the pains of
the cross which he bears for you. Approach in spirit
his sepulchre, weep and mourn with the holy women,
who, as I have already said, were sitting at the
sepulchre, weeping their Lord. Prepare with them
perfumes for his burial; but let them be better, let
them be spiritual, instead of material; for such he
requires of you, since he was not able to receive them
from the others. Suffer for him, then, with all the ardor of your zeal, with all the strength of your devotion.

The Lord himself, by the mouth of Jeremiah, ex-
horts the faithful to participate in his sorrows: "Is
it nothing to you, all ye who pass by? Behold, and
see, if there be any sorrow like unto my sorrow." It
is as if he should say: "Is there a death worthy of
being lamented in view of that which I am suffering,
in order to expiate the crime of others, while I am
myself innocent?" But he is the way whereby the
faithful may return from exile to their native land.

This cross, from which he cries out, is the ladder
that he has erected for us. Upon this the only Son
of God was slain, he was offered as a sacrifice, because
he was willing. Learn to suffer with him, and fulfil
what the prophet Jeremiah predicted concerning de-

voted souls: " They shall mourn as for the death of an only child, and they shall weep for him as it is customary to weep for a first-born."

Behold, my sister, what profound affliction the friends of a king profess for the loss of his only and first-born son. Look upon the desolation of the family, and the grief of the whole court; but it is the spouse of this only son who is the deepest mourner, whose grief is beyond bounds.

Such, my sister, be your affliction, such be your grief for the death of that spouse, to an alliance with whom you have been fortunately elevated. He has purchased you, not with his possessions, but with himself. With his own blood he has bought you and redeemed you. Behold how much right he has to you, and how precious you are in his sight.

Thus the apostle, comparing the value of his soul, and the inestimable price of the sacrifice which was offered for its salvation, renders homage to the grandeur of the benefaction, and cries out: " God forbid that I should glory, save in the cross of our Lord Jesus Christ, by whom the world is crucified unto me, and I unto the world." You are more than heaven, more than earth, since the Creator of the world has given himself for your ransom. But what mysterious treasure has he, then, discovered in you—he to whom nothing is necessary, if, in order to possess you, he has consented to all the tortures of his agony, to all the opprobrium of his punishment? What has he sought in you, if not yourself? Behold your true lover, who desires only you, and not what belongs to you. Behold your true friend, who said in dying for you: "Greater love hath no man than this, that a man lay down his life for his friends." It was he, and not I, who truly loved you. My love, which drew us both into sin, was only desire,* it does not merit the name of love. I have, you say, suffered for you, and perhaps it is true; but I have rather suffered by you, and even against my will; not for the love of you, but by the violence that was done me; not for your safety, but for your despair. On the contrary, Christ willingly, and for your salvation, suffered for you, and by his suffering he cures all languor, removes all passion. Towards him, then, and not towards me, be directed all your devotion, all your compassion. Grieve on account of the injustice and cruelty that befall the innocent; and not that a just vengeance fell on me, for it is rather a favor for which we should both thank Heaven

You are unjust, if you do not love justice; and great is your sin, if you voluntarily oppose the divine will, and reject the gifts of grace. Bewail your Redeemer, and not your seducer,—him who has served you, and not him who ruined you,—the Lord who

---

* Miseras in te meas voluptates implebam, et hoc erat totum quod amabam.

died for you, and not the servant who still lives, and who has just been truly delivered from death.

Take care not to merit the reproach by which Pompey silenced the complaints of Cornelia :

> . . . . Vivit post prælia Magnus,
> Sed fortuna perit; quod defles illud amâsti.*

Submit, my sister, submit, I beseech you, with patience to the trials, which have mercifully befallen us. It is the rod of a Father, and not the sword of a persecutor. The father strikes to correct, lest the enemy should strike to kill. He wounds to prevent death, and not to cause it. He wounds the body and cures the soul. He ought to have put to death, and he gives life. He arrests the malady, and makes the body sound. He punishes once, not to punish for ever. By the wound which has caused one to suffer, he saves two from death. Two sin, one is punished.

This indulgence of the Lord in regard to us, is an effect of his compassion for the feebleness of your sex, but in some sort it was your due. You were more infirm by nature, but stronger in continence, and therefore less guilty. I thank the Lord, who has freed you from punishment, and has reserved you for

* "Pompey survives the battle, but his fortune has perished; what you deplore you loved."

the crown.* Although you would refuse to hear it, and would hinder me from saying it, nevertheless it is a manifest truth. The crown is the reward of one who strives continually, and he alone will obtain it who strives to the end.

There is indeed no crown remaining for me, for there is no longer any cause for striving.† Yet if there is no crown laid up for me, I still suppose it a great good for me to incur no penalty, to escape eternal punishment by temporary pain. The men who abandon themselves to the passions of this miserable life, are compared in Scripture to beasts.

I complain the less that my merit should be decreased, while I am certain that yours is increasing. We are indeed one in Christ,—one by the bond of marriage. Whatever pertains to you, I do not regard as foreign to myself; but Christ is yours, because you have been made his spouse. And now, as I mentioned above, you hold me as a servant, whom formerly you acknowledged as your lord; but a servant joined to you by spiritual love, rather than subjected to you by fear. Hence, my confidence in your

---

* Cum me unâ corporis mei passione semel ab omni æstu hujus concupiscentiæ, in quâ unâ totus per immoderatum incontinentiam occupatus eram, refrigeravit ad martyrii coronam.

† Deest materia pugnæ, cui ablatus est stimulus concupiscentiæ.

intercession is great; I can obtain that by your prayer, which I cannot obtain by my own; especially at this time, when a multitude of cares and imminent dangers distract my mind, and allow no quiet moments for prayer. I am far from imitating that messenger of Candace, queen of the Ethiopians, who went from so great a distance to Jerusalem to adore God in his temple. To him on his return the Apostle Philip was sent to convert him to the faith,—of which he was worthy, on account of his prayer and assiduous reading of the Scripture. As he was always occupied during his journey, the divine grace, notwithstanding the anathema pronounced against riches and idolaters, permitted that he should fall on a way that would furnish the Apostle the most abundant means to work his conversion.

That nothing may impede my request, or hinder it from being fulfilled, I hasten to send you a prayer which I have composed, which with uplifted hands you will offer to Heaven for us both.

PRAYER.

" O God, who, from the very beginning of the creation of man, woman having been formed out of the side of man, hast sanctioned the great sacrament of the conjugal union, and who, by thy own birth, and by thy first miracle, hast raised it to

higher honors, and hast allowed me, even in my frailty
or in my incontinence,—as it may please thee,—to
partake of the grace of this sacrament; reject not the
prayers of thy handmaid, which, a suppliant, I pour
out in the presence of thy majesty for my own sins,
and for the sins of him who is dear to me. Pardon,
O thou who art most benign,—who art benignity itself,—pardon our manifold crimes, and let the multitude of our transgressions be swallowed up in the
immensity of thy unspeakable compassion. Punish
us now, I beseech thee, for we are guilty, and spare
us hereafter; punish us in time, that we may not be
punished in eternity. Use against thy servants the
rod of correction, and not the sword of anger; chastise the flesh, but save our souls. Come as a purifier,
not as an avenger; with mercy, rather than with justice; as a pitying father, not as a severe master.

"Try us, O Lord, and measure our strength, as the
prophet requests, when he beseeches thee to examine
his power of resistance, and to proportion to it the
temptation. Through the blessed Paul, thou hast
promised to thy faithful ones that they shall not be
tempted beyond their strength.

"When it pleased thee, O Lord, and as it pleased
thee, thou didst join us, and thou didst separate us.
Now, O Lord, what thou hast mercifully begun, mercifully complete. And whom thou hast once separated in the world, eternally join together for thyself

in heaven, O thou, who art our hope, our portion, our expectation, our consolation. Blessed be thy name, O Lord, for evermore."

Farewell in Christ, spouse of Christ; in Christ farewell, and in Christ live. Amen.

XXVIII.

LETTER OF HELOISE TO ABELARD.

"Yet here for ever, ever must I stay;
Sad proof how well a lover can obey!
Death, only death, can break the lasting chain;
And here, e'en then, shall my cold dust remain,
Here all its frailties, all its flames resign,
And wait till 'tis no sin to mix with thine."

POPE's "*Eloisa to Abelard.*'

To her master,—his servant.

THAT you may have no reason for accusing me of dis-
obedience, I shall check, as you have commanded,
the language of immoderate grief. I will try to suppress, at least in writing to you, those expressions of
weakness and sorrow against which it is so difficult,
or rather impossible, to fortify myself in an interview.
For nothing is less in our power than the mind, and
this we are rather compelled to obey, than able to
command. When we are under the influence of
strong emotions, we cannot so effectually repress

them, that they may not be exhibited in action, and manifest themselves in words, which are the ready signs of the soul's passions. As it is written : " Out of the abundance of the heart the mouth speaketh." Therefore I shall not allow my hand to write those things which I could not prohibit my tongue from speaking. Oh that my heart were as able to command its grief, as my hand is to command its writing !

Some solace you are able to confer, although you cannot wholly cure my grief. One thought drives out another, and the mind, when new objects engage the attention, is forced to abandon or to suspend its haunting memories. A thought has so much the more power to occupy the mind, and turn it aside from other things, as its object is more honorable, and seems to us more essential.

We supplicate you, therefore, all of us, the servants of Christ, and your children in Christ,—we supplicate you to accord to us, in your paternal goodness, two things, which seem to us absolutely necessary :—First, to teach us the origin of the female monastic institution, the rank and authority of our profession ; Second, to frame and send to us a rule, appropriate to our sex, ——*

---

* Not another word of these letters will we translate. Heloise is here leaving herself, and nothing can tempt us to follow her. She discourses with great learning about something foreign to her own heart ; but, as dearly as we love

her, we shall not allow her, at the command of Abelard, to
fling monastic dust in our eyes. Her warm, love-laden heart,
is beating thick and fast; her soul-lit eyes are swimming in
tears ;—her spirit does not obey, if her hand does ;—we will
look at her, and not at the pale dead words that she writes.
Hitherto she has written of herself, and to translate her
burning language, has been a constant delight. With Abelard we have been on good terms, tolerating his pedantry;
and, for the sake of his many sorrows, pardoning the want
of something that the hearts of women and poets can feel,
that cannot be reduced to a formula, and construed to
thought.

Abelard's answer to this letter is a treatise on monastic
institutions, and possesses no interest for any mortal in the
nineteenth century.

XXIX.

THE CURTAIN FALLS.*

As a stone that is rolled from a mountain starts slowly, at first turned out of its way by every inequality of surface, but gathers force as it goes, at length leaping all barriers; so our narrative in the beginning shaped its course in the midst of details, but now it must touch upon here a point, and there a point, and hasten to a close.* It was pleasant to dwell with Abelard in his youth, when a noble ambition was calling forth his energy; it was pleasant to dwell with him in his early manhood, when he was conquering in heroic battle those who would silence a rising man; it was pleasant to dwell with him when he was strangely related to one of the noblest of women; there was a grave satisfaction in following him over the arid wastes of his first years of monastic life, in journeying with him through the burning sands of persecution; for we knew that there was an oasis ahead, which

---

* This figure is borrowed from "Waverley."

promised a cool shade and refreshing fountains,—a resting-place where the weary for a little season might have at least a sombre peace, a solemn hour of repose in which to recount with melancholy pleasure the joys of vanished days, and to make preparation for a " way that must once be trod by all ;" but before us now the desert again lies, stretching away as far as the eye can reach, inviting the wanderer with many a deceptive mirage. The man whose life has been so full of strange vicissitudes is entering upon it, and his next asylum will be where the wicked cease from troubling and the weary are at rest.

The most tranquil period of Abelard's life was during the few first years that followed his correspondence with Heloise. The Abbess of Paraclete sent him difficult questions in theology, which she could not understand, and he employed his time in answering them. For her he also composed a book of hymns, which are not destitute of poetic merit. He collected his sermons and dedicated them to her, and at her demand, wrote his *Hexameron*,—a commentary on the first chapter of Genesis. During this period he either wrote or finished most of his works.* Persecution for a season ceased. The enemies of reason, and the friends of authority seemed to fear the influence of Abelard. On the side of the philosopher were the prince of

* Vide *Ouvrages medits d'Abelard*, by Cousin.
10

Champagne; the duke of Brittany; and the Garlands,
who formed a dynasty of ministers under Louis le Gros
and his sons.   He was also favored by the king himself.   His opinions had spread far and wide, making
for him a multitude of friends.   Many of his old pupils, who loved and admired their master, were then
holding places of authority in the schools, in literature, and in the church.   The influence of Heloise
was great, and of course was used for the safety of
her lover.

About the year 1136, Abelard opened his school
again for a short time, on the hill of St. Genevieve,
near Paris.   How long he remained, or why he left,
is unknown.[*]

In the mean time an incident occurred at the Paraclete which revived his quarrel with the church.
Saint Bernard visited Heloise and expressed his admiration for the order of the convent, but took it upon
himself to complain of an alteration in the prayer,
made by Abelard.   The complaint of course reached
him, and he was not the man to let it pass in silence.
He wrote[*] to Saint Bernard, defending his own version,
and rebuked the saint for saying *daily bread* instead
of *supersubstantial bread*.   One was the representative of free thought, and the other of authority, in the

---

[*] Vie d'Abelard, p. 171.

[†] Ab. Op., Part ii., Ep. 5. P. Ael. ad Bern. claræv. abb.,
p. 244, et Serm. xiii., p. 858.

Middle Age, and even so small a breeze was sufficient to fan the slumbering fires of antagonism between them.

It must be remembered, too, that Abelard had made himself in many ways obnoxious to the church. He was skilled in invective, and had used it unsparingly against the ignorance and vices of the convents. Even bishops did not escape his rash criticism. The traffic in indulgencies was attacked, and some high dignitaries in the church were accused of attempting false miracles. His temper was irritable; he loved controversy, and was proud. It was easy to be seen that his doctrines, if not in themselves heretical, at least tended to innovation.

Guillaume de Saint Thierry commenced the movement on the part of the church. He wrote a common letter to the bishop of Chartres and Saint Bernard, calling attention to the heresies of Abelard. Bernard, who dedicated his passions to the service of the church, as the old chevaliers did their arms, gave a willing ear to the accusation, and the bishop of Chartres acted with him without energy, without resistance, for he had no bitter feeling toward the philosopher.

Saint Bernard had one or two friendly conferences with Abelard, which in reality amounted to nothing. While they were together they did not greatly disagree, but each carried away with him a sentiment of animosity. Conflicting ideas cannot live together in the

world at peace; they set men and nations quarrelling,
The saint preached against the doctrines and the example of the philosopher. Abelard defended himself
in a manner not the best adapted to conciliate. Bernard wrote to the pope, using his skill, his zeal, his
energy*—every art of which he was master, to preju
dice the holy see against the subtle and dangerous
champion of reason.

Abelard, when wearied with seeing himself defam-
ed in every quarter, demanded public proof of the
charges preferred against him.

At Sens, the archiepiscopal city of Champagne,
there was to be on the Octave of Pentecost, in 1140,
an exposition of the relics of the church. Louis VII,
who found great delight in relics, was to be a specta-
tor at the festival. Prelates and bishops, princes and
rulers,—dignitaries in church and state—were to be
present.

Abelard wrote to the Archbishop of Sens, asking
that those who were to assemble to witness the exposition of the relics of his church might constitute a synod, or council, before which he might respond to his adversaries and vindicate his faith. The Archbishop
consented, and wrote to Saint Bernard to appear and
make good his accusation of Abelard. The saint refused, alleging his incompetence to engage in a tour-

* Hist. de Saint Bernard, par M. l'abbé Ratisbonne, t. ii.,
c. xxix., p. 31. Vide St. Bern. Op. Ep. clxxxviii., et seq.

nament with the philosopher, who had been accustomed
to the logical saddle, and who had been trained to the
use of the dialectic lance, from his very youth. He
added that Abelard's writings were sufficient to con-
demn him. He wrote, however, to the bishops, to be
on their guard against the enemy of Christ.

When the time of the festival came, there assembled kings, archbishops, princes, bishops, distinguished masters of schools, and a great concourse of people.
Saint Bernard found it necessary to attend, if he would
not relinquish the accusation of heresy brought against
his rival and antagonist. Wherever he appeared
the masses bowed with reverence, for his appearance
was full of sanctity, and his mien was humble. On
the other hand, the crowd shrank from Abelard, for
his bearing was lofty, and his adversaries had taught
the common people to regard him as an enemy of all
that is sacred and true.

On the second day of the festival, the philosopher,
surrounded by his followers, appeared before the
waiting assembly. Saint Bernard was there, and held
in his hand the works of Abelard, out of which he had
picked seventeen passages that contained heresies, or
errors in faith. He ordered that these should be
read in a loud voice; but Abelard, interrupting the
reader, said that he would hear nothing, that he appealed to the Pontiff of Rome, and went out of the

assembly.* Every one was amazed; but order was preserved, and the passages that had been extracted from his writings were condemned as heretical.

Abelard doubtless saw condemnation written on the faces of his judges, and, knowing that he had friends at Rome, boldly appealed to the sovereign of the church. "His adversaries," says Brucker,† "could neither endure nor penetrate the clouds with which he enveloped simple truths; superstition, ignorance, hypocrisy, envy found matter for the cruel persecution of a man so worthy of better times and a better destiny. He has a right to be counted among the martyrs of philosophy."

Those who condemned the doctrines of Abelard were solicitous concerning the decision of Rome. Two letters were addressed to the pope,—one in the name of the archbishop of Sens and his suffragans, the other in the name of the archbishop of Rheims and his suffragans. Both of these were written by Saint Bernard. He also wrote to the pontiff on his own account. There was also correspondence with some of the cardinals,—with any who could be of service in defaming or in counteracting the influence of Abelard.

The persecuted philosopher set out for Rome, to plead his cause before the pope. He believed

* An account of this is contained in the 189th, 191st, and 337th epistles of Saint Bernard.
† Hist. Crit. Phil., t. iii., p. 764.

that he should not be condemned unheard; but in this
he was destined to be disappointed. He was condemned as a heretic to perpetual silence, and the order
was given that his books should be burned. And this
was not all. He and Arnauld de Brescia were to be
confined separately, in such religious houses as seemed
most convenient.

In the mean time Abelard, who was growing old,
whose health was broken, had sought rest on his
journey, at the hospitable abbey of Cluny. Peter the
Venerable had kindly received him, and was treating
him as a distinguished-guest. Although bowed with
infirmities, he was still strong in hope. The news of
the decision of Rome broke his spirit. He then let
go the phantom of ambition, to whose shadowy embrace he had abandoned himself so long, at the expense
of all that is dearest in life.

The prematurely old man was fortunately in the
hands of one who knew how to pity his misfortunes—
who knew how to pour upon the bleeding wounds of
his heart the oil and the wine of consolation—whose
authority and wisdom could procure peace for him
with his enemies. The venerable Peter, who reminds
us of the good Fenelon, wrote to the pope, and obtained permission for Abelard to spend the rest of his
days at Cluny. The philosopher wrote a confession
of faith, and the abbé of Cluny brought about a reconciliation between him and Saint Bernard. Every

effort was made to sweeten the declining years of the
far-famed knight-errant of logic, who had fought so
many battles—who had conquered so many enemies—
who had himself at length fallen beneath the heavy
hand of Rome.

At Cluny, the habits of Abelard were austere.
The monks treated him kindly, and, so far as his fast-
declining health would permit, he gave them instruction in philosophy and religion. "It was the super-
intending providence of Heaven," says* Peter the
Venerable in a letter to Heloise, "which sent him to
Cluny in the last years of his life. The present was
the richest which could have been made us. Words
will not easily express the high testimony which Cluny
bears to his humble and religious deportment within
these walls. Never did I behold abjection so lowly,
or abstemiousness so exemplary. By my express desire, he held the first place in our numerous community; but in his dress he seemed the last of us all.
When in our public processions I saw him walking
near me, collected and humble, my mind was struck;
so great a man, thought I, by self-abasement is thus
voluntarily brought low! Contrary to the practice of
many, who call themselves religious men, Abelard
seemed to take delight in penury; and the most
simple and unadorned habit pleased him most. He

---

* The Hist. of the Lives of Abelard and Heloise, by the
Rev. Joseph Berrington, p. 301.

looked no further. In his diet, in all that regarded
the care of the body, he was reserved and abstemious.
More than what was absolutely necessary, he never
sought for himself, and he condemned it in others.
His reading was almost incessant; he often prayed;
and he never interrupted his silence, unless when,
urged by the entreaties of the monks, he sometimes
conversed with them, or in public harangues explained
to them the great maxims of religion. When able, he
celebrated the sacred mysteries, offering to God the
sacrifice of the immortal Lamb; and after his reconciliation to the apostolic see, almost daily. In a word,
his mind, his tongue, his hand were ever employed in
the duties of religion, in developing the truths of
philosophy, or in the profound researches of literature."

The abbé of Cluny, observing that the health of
Abelard was rapidly declining, sent him to the priory
of Saint Marcellus, near Chalons, which, as well as
the abbey, was in Burgundy. This priory was not
far from the river Saone, and on account of its healthy
location, was regarded as the best place for the residence of an invalid. On the 21st of April, 1142, Peter
Abelard set out upon a new journey; that fiery soul
of his vanished from the earth, into the viewless
Eternity, went to those realms over which methinks
troublesome Mother Church, notwithstanding her pre-

10*

tensions, has no jurisdiction. Let him who is sure
that he is above ambition,—whom passion has never
caused to err,—who has never laid snares for an
enemy,—who has never awakened in the breast of
unsuspecting woman a love that he could not nobly
and purely return;—let such a one stand upon the
grave of Abelard and curse him; but we must let fall
for him a sincere tear. Pity him we must; and with
our pity mingles much admiration.

Peter the Venerable—blessings on the benevolent
old man!—conveyed the heavy news to Heloise, in the
kindest manner, tempering the sad narrative with the
sweetest spirit of consolation. The monks of Saint
Marcellus would not give up the body; but the good
abbé of Cluny obtained it by stealth, and took it to
its rightful owner, the abbess of Paraclete.

Heloise lived 21 years longer, and continued to
be the object of the admiration and the veneration of
her age. She died May 16, 1164. " Heloise," says
the cautious and learned Charles de Remusat, " is, I
believe, the first of women." We will at least say
this, that no woman mentioned in history has loved so
deeply as she. Every woman, before she learns to
distrust man, loves, like Heloise, with the whole soul;
but her soul was so finely tempered, her love was so
profound, that distrust itself was conquered; in her
eyes the real lover was continually clothed with her

own ideal; hence her love was eternal, like her own
creative spirit. *Procul, procul, este profani!* but let
those who know what a great and constant love means,
circle near in silence, and lay gently upon the coffin's
lid the mystic branch of perennial green.

XXX.

RETROSPECT.

O anime affannate
Venite a noi parlar.

Dante.

In order to be perfectly fair towards Abelard, we here insert the most eloquent defence of him that has ever been written.*

"Once, a long time ago, lived two personages much enamored of each other. Never were lovers more true, more beautiful, more unfortunate, etc."

In commencing his fable, the ancient chronicler seems to enter with full sails upon our subject, for he sums up in few words the entire life of Heloise and Abelard. His personages are forgotten, but all the world knows ours. The history of their misfortunes has traversed the centuries; each generation has

---

* Lettres d'Abælard et Heloise, traduits sur les manuscrits de la bibliotheque royal, par E. Oddoul: precédées d'un essai historique, par M. et. Mme. Guizot. Edition illustre par I. Gigoux. Paris: E. Houdaile, 1839. Vol. 2, at the commencement. In translating this eulogy, we have omitted certain portions that seemed less important.

hailed in their united names the glorious symbol of love. In view of these noble victims poets have been inspired, tender hearts have been touched; and in their course, at once triumphal and melancholy, the two lovers have received every homage, here a flower, there a tear.

The renown which they have acquired is not usurped. How, in fact, can we help feeling a vivid sentiment of admiration in presence of that high love which neither time nor fortune can overcome; of that ardor of passion which neither blood nor tears can extinguish, which survives hope, and which, as a last testimony, breaks the very portals of the tomb; passion so exalted and superhuman, that tradition has been able to express it only with the aid of the marvellous?

Heloise appears to us from the first with that grandeur of character which did not quit her. It is an entrance upon the stage truly heroic. Scarcely has she had time to act or speak, before you are aware that an invincible sentiment is to govern her whole life, that this sentiment is her life itself. Abelard does not take her; she does not believe that she is giving herself; one would say that she awaits him, and that she belongs to him from all eternity, that she has come into the world only to acccomplish this mission of loving beyond all verisimilitude. The antique fatality, so terrible and so majestic, is here found

again, brought back to the touching proportions of
love.   To it Heloise abandons herself with her whole
soul; and that impatience which pushes on the predestined, and which frightens us in those who must
arrive at crime, offers us in her person a ravishing
spectacle.

As soon as the star of Abelard has shone in the
clear sky of her youth, like the Magi who went to
visit Christ, she collects her richest presents, and
comes to lay at his feet her beauty, her love, her reputation—the gold, the incense, and the myrrh.   Still
she finds herself too poor! In return, she asks nothing.   If she obtains a look, a sweet word, it will
always be for her a *favor*, a *grace.*   She does not cal-
culate the duration of this unequal exchange: the
thought of protecting herself against an injurious
abandonment is far from her mind.   For a dowry,
she gloriously chooses shame, and rejects with sincere
tears the name of wife.   Eager for any self-renuncia-
tion, she only fears remaining below that task of affection which she believed she could never fulfil with all
the devotion of her heart.   Noble queen, more adorned
with her own voluntary dishonor than with a royal
wreath!   Saintly, sublime, and unaffected nature, that
touches the heaven without effort in wishing to remain
upon the earth, that increases in grandeur by all the
humility which it would impose on itself!

Still later, after her marriage, she repels the felicitations which are addressed to her. She refuses, by a magnanimous falsehood, the honor of the rank which belongs to her, and which all women are jealous to maintain. She obstinately denies herself entrance upon the world, and consents to suffer from her uncle the anger and the vengeance of his wounded pride. But, far from the dark valleys where selfishness thrives, where none but bitter fruits grow, her foot, whose trace the angels adore, treads the heights that are flooded with light, that are clothed with perennial flowers; a celestial benediction is shed upon all her sacrifices, and divine felicities spring for her from all the griefs which are laid upon her by the world. What does she now care for the murmur of men? A look of love has spread above her head a firmament, whose unalterable azure could not be obscured by the smoke of their scorn.

This complete forgetfulness of self, this generous abdication of her own personality, which places Heloise in turn in the rank of superior souls, is also a valuable index for understanding Abelard. What kind of a man must he have been who, with one word, irrevocably fixed the destiny of the first woman of her century? He shows himself, he calls her: Here I am, Heloise responds; and from her virginal sphere she descends toward him, as upon an inclined plane. If any thing can give us a just idea of his merit, it is surely the violent and enduring love with which he inspired Heloise. She would not have made an ordinary man her God. On his side, Abelard shows himself worthy of her. The terms which he uses to paint his passion prove how deeply this noble love was rooted in his soul. It seems as though one could hear his voice still trembling with all the emotions which he had previously felt.

It is known nearly in what measure they loved: an account of this love should now be rendered, each should be assigned his part in the common expenditure, and the position which they kept toward each other should be clearly designated. This question has always provoked a singular diversity of opinion.

This disagreement of minds, sometimes the most eminent, upon a point which they have examined with impartiality, is nevertheless explained in a natural manner; the question is here concerning sentiment, that is, concerning something which defies all rules and all methods.

In fact, if the events which carry with them their own demonstration, are differently judged; if they are exposed to controversy, both in the causes which produced them, and in the consequences with which they are fraught;—how will it be with thoughts, by no means translatable into acts, scarcely expressible in words, and which can therefore furnish only an uncertain datum, and a floating basis for our decisions? Destitute of the inflexibility of accomplished fact, they come to us only under a relative mode; instead of governing our appreciation by the power which is their own, they are subject to feeling. It is then that opinions are liable to be different. Our criterion is no longer in the nature of the thing itself, which is submitted to us; it is in ourselves. The only way which remains open to us is that of interpretation, and how many issues it has!

A complete latitude is therefore reserved for the personal opinion of whoever would occupy himself with a question like this. Whatever may be the authority of those who have previously resolved it, their affirmation can have only the force of conjecture.

We wish to make known the intimate thought of the lovers, as it has been revealed to us by an attentive examination of their letters. This study is not without interest. Heloise and Abelard will for an instant live again under our eyes.

The history of their good fortune is short. Two years have scarcely passed away, when the memorable vengeance of Fulbert comes to open to them a career at once so sad and so glorious.

By the order of Abelard, Heloise, as we know, entered a convent.

This circumstance has given rise to great eulogies upon Heloise, and to a grave accusation against Abelard. He has been reproached with having been *incapable of enduring that Heloise should remain free, when she ceased to belong to him.* Let us examine his conduct.

After the accident of which he was the victim, what was it necessary to do ?

Despair counselled a double death. Heloise would doubtless have consented to die with him; but he was a Christian, and did not wish to combat misfortune by crime. Separation having become necessary, the convent was an asylum, sure and sacred, where each of them might carry a thought with which could never be associated any other image than that of God. In pronouncing the same religious vows, they renounced, for heaven, their conjugal tie, which seemed broken upon earth. This was still for Abelard a kind of joy.

Abelard once in the convent, was it proper that Heloise should remain in the world ? was it not evidently to recoil before the vow of chastity ? was it not to disgrace the first epoch of their loves, and to show also that she had followed the instinct of pleasure, and not the impulsion of her own heart ? The world pardons the faults of a great passion, but it rightly brands vulgar disorders. Would not a refusal, on the part of Heloise, to embrace a religious life, have seemed like a tacit invitation to the desires of a new lover ?

Abelard did not admit the possibility of a fall; but in fine this possibility existed, and when this idea alone contained for him all the torments of the nether world, was it necessary to risk, on the vain scruples of delicacy, the sad repose which might still remain to him?

He knew also the warning of the Scripture: *He who does not shun danger, will succumb to it.* Would he have fulfilled his whole duty towards Heloise, if he had not fortified her against these temptations? Abandoned to the snares of the world, she either would succumb, and then it was necessary to render a feebleness impossible; or she would come out from them pure, and then there was nothing better to do than to render more easy for her, by the solitude of the cloister and its macerations, a victory which the world would so sharply dispute with her, and would doubtless make more difficult for her? The honor and the interest of Heloise, the love and the conscience of Abelard, all dictated the course which he took—all justified the use which he made of his authority. All that one can see in it, is a wise and noble foresight. There is a long distance between this sentiment, and a defiance equally offensive to both.

A passage in one of the letters of Heloise has served as a text for articulate reproach against Abelard. Let us not be deceived by a few words that are very vivid, and escape in the transport of passion. The letters of lovers have always been full of those

hard accusations and those deep reproaches which we
must be careful not to take as serious. This rancor
of words, this bitter and implacable style, is often
found in persons who perfectly agree. In our opinion,
then, the words of Heloise do not prove that Abelard
was jealous in the bad sense of the word, nor even
that Heloise really thought so. Between her and
him, her complaint had no other meaning than an assurance of devotion, than the protestation of a love
ready to be frightened, and which is irritated with
even the appearance of doubt and suspicion.

Let us return to Heloise at the moment in which
she took the veil at Argenteuil. No one less than I,
certainly, is disposed to rob her of eulogy. But there
are so many things to praise in this woman, that we
must not stop at secondary circumstances like this.
I know not over-well what is meant by the *liberty* of
Heloise, nor whether the consequences of this liberty
accord with the love which she had for Abelard, and
with the nobleness of sentiment of which she gave
so many proofs. She could not, during the life of
Abelard, marry a second time. Then, by what ac-
commodations could she reconcile the secret advanta-
ges of this liberty with the observance of sworn faith,
with the respect which in so high a degree she bore
for her husband ? No, indeed, Heloise does not wish
for this liberty. The world must have been for her a
real convent; she is already dead to the world. If

she made a *sacrifice*, as she herself said, by that we
must understand her resignation to the bodily austerities of the religious profession—things whose utility
was poorly enough demonstrated for her, even after
ten years of practice. Neither let us forget, although
she has not mentioned it, that the convent had
snatched her child from her arms, and thus had immolated the joys of the maternal sentiment. The natural repugnance which she felt for the convent doubtless yielded still to this other privation. Her sacrifice
was, then, great and real; but the high opinion which
we entertain of Heloise forces us to believe that it
would not be at all consistent with that species of
suicide, the idea of which is gratuitously attributed
to her.

That which we love from the first is her obedience
to her husband, that respectful and absolute confidence
of the centurion, which asks no reason, and for which
one word is sufficient: Do this, says Abelard, and she
does it.

Formerly, in order to escape marriage, she could
oppose him with her reasonings, her prayers, and her
tears: resistance was then as great a proof of love as
submission itself: now, the least hesitation would be
a revolt and a crime, for she would inflict a mortal
wound upon Abelard. He has said: Go, and she
goes. Should the fiery gulfs of the earth be opened
beneath her feet, still she will go.

Let us forget what was quite out of the ordinary course in the conversion of Heloise. Other women before, other women since, have accepted or sub mitted to the same conditions of life, whose privation would not have been remarked without the celebrity of the pleasures of which they were the consequence. The element of our admiration is not, then, in a fact whose accomplishment must be referred to its neces-sity; we find it higher, in the thoughts with which Heloise accompanies it. The more Abelard is alarmed on account of his misfortune, the more she wishes to reassure him by irrefragable proofs of devo-tion. The more the horizon presents to the eyes of Abelard sombre tints, the more does she wish to enrich it with ideal hues,—the more does she wish to display there unlooked-for splendors. Under the complaint of Cornelia appears to us the solemn en-gagement which she took in her own heart; and we see that she has already fulfilled it during a period of ten years with religious fidelity, when she expresses it in her second letter, in words which those who have read them will never forget :—

"Would that I might do penance sufficient for this crime, and that the length of my expiations might balance in some sort the pains of your punish-ment! What you have suffered for a moment in body, I would suffer all my life in the contrition of my soul: at least, after this satisfaction, if any one can still complain, it will be God, not you."

In view of such a sentiment, does it not seem that Love himself has passed before us, and that these words are a virtue gone out from the borders of his divine garment? We must here cry out with the poet :—

> O glorious trial of exceeding love,
> Illustrious evidence, example high !

Magnanimity, its radiant in crown, has not a brighter jewel.

Moreover, testimonies of this nature are not rare in the extraordinary love of Heloise and Abelard.

The unanimous opinion of contemporaries had so well established its glory, that it was traditionally maintained in all its splendor nearly five hundred years. The monument which alone could consolidate it, and render it imperishable, did not begin to be erected till 1616, under the hands of d'Amboise. He collected the letters of the two lovers, buried until then in some rare manuscripts of the thirteenth century, and thus restored to us the testament of their love and of their genius.

Unfortunately we have a deficiency to establish. A part of their correspondence is wanting to us. Those letters, written *al tempo' dei dubbiosi desiri*, at the time when each word is a hymn; when the

heart is so light in the breast, that it seems borne in
the hand of an angel; when the ear is filled with
sweet murmurs, and the soul with unknown rap-
tures; when the eyes, as far as their vision reaches,
every where meet none but pleasing views; when the
virginal crowd of hopes can admire their own beauty
in a limpid memory; when memory itself is a hope;
when, in the chalice of the infinite, our intoxicated
lips quaff a potion of flame which never slakes the
spirit's thirst; when the thought, ever the same,
with which the mind is nourished, seems to us a worship rendered to God, and each breath from the bosom
a vapor of incense which ascends to him;—those letters, like a charming echo in which all the voices of
joy are mingled,—that of the past which is the most
dreamy, that of the present which is the most loved
and the most tender, and that of the future which
unites both the others;—those letters we do not possess.

Two years have disappeared like a world en-
gulfed; like an Atlantis sunk in the midst of the
waves, with its fragrant villas, its verdant asylums
sacred to Pales, its crowns of flowers plundered of
their leaves upon the festive table. Who shall
return to us the riches of those two vessels, whose
sails were filled with sweet sighs, which were laden
with ravishing messages, and which have not been
able to land upon the shore of posterity! Irrepara-

ble loss ! Those two years left no traces,—gracious
sisters, who took for themselves all the nuptial joys,
who fell asleep in the tomb by wrapping, like Polyx-
ena, the folds of their garment around their divine
beauty, and whom their sisters have continually wept !

At an epoch wholly warmed with the divine fires
of enthusiasm, what immortal hues did not love
assume under the hand of Heloise and Abelard !
Prosperity is the true domain of love. That it may
mount its car and rejoice the heavens with its presence, it must have its crown of luminous rays, its
orient must be sown with roses, its zenith must be of
fluid gold, and it must be clothed with a crimson robe
at its setting. We have the god without his attri-
butes. His altar is saddened by the fillets consecrated to his remains, and by the sombre branches of
the cypress.

However, if of those two correspondences, produced at such different times, and under such different impressions, one was to be lost, we think that the
more precious remains to us. The first would have
charmed our eyes with sweet pictures, would have
deliciously recounted to us,—

> "Quanti dolci pensier, quanto disio
> Menò costoro al doloroso passo ;"

and, without doubt, instead of entering hastily upon
that life so arid and so wasted by suffering, it would

11

have been sweet for us to traverse the fresh shades of their short felicities. But the second appears far more important in the eyes of most. The secret of their hearts is in this, perhaps, more distinctly revealed.

Is it not also true that continued prosperity can interest us very little,—can affect us scarcely at all? Suffering attracts us more, seems nearer to our nature, and humanity is mostly found in mournful vicissitudes. Always favored by circumstances, the love of Heloise would have occupied her whole life; she would have remained enveloped in the mysterious joys of the connubial state and in the tranquil sweets of maternity. Like so many other females, she would have borne with her to the tomb the secret of that divine force which was given her, and of that admirable sentiment which *believes all, hopes all, endures all, suffers all*. A misfortune has revealed to us that secret, and that misfortune has made us admire all the treasures concealed in her soul. She has been made a queen by a crown of thorns.

Sad and bitter royalty! Admiration too dearly purchased! It is under the sackcloth of the nun that we find the ardent and passionate woman; it is only by her tears that we can judge of the graces of her smile. It was necessary that the vase should be broken that we might be permitted to breathe its celestial perfume.

Heloise does not go to seek consolation in the monastic life. No healing plant will grow for her in the barren earth of the cloister, nor in the vase of pious mortifications. For her there are but two events in her life,—the day when she knows that she is loved by Abelard, and the day when she loses him. All the rest is effaced for her eyes in a night profound. Her tears at the moment of pronouncing the religious vows are not given to fear, but to regret. Half her soul is lost, and the future has no longer for her either vague terrors or vague promises. Her past days are accursed,—accursed are her days to come; an unbroken grief equally covers them with its black wings. Let her enter, then, with indifference into those sad solitudes where nothing but sobs is heard from earth, nothing but menaces from heaven ; into that death which remembers life !

Heloise is not stoical; neither is the mysticism of hope a pillow which can put to sleep her chagrins; there is no more repose for her. What matters it that the wounded fawn has escaped to its retreat, if it carries with it the fatal dart ? With the holy words of the liturgy, her mouth, in spite of her, will mingle words profane. All illusions will hover before her eyes, and touch her with their wings of flame. By day, during the solemnity of the sacrifices, fascinated by an interior contemplation, her soul will wander into the world of sweet reveries;—hearts that leap

with joy,—looks that cannot be broken off,—words
half uttered, whose meaning is for heaven,—lips that
seek each other,—sighs that are mingled,—eternity
floating between two moments,—delicious disquiet, at
the foundation of which throbs and moans an infinite
desire,—all the dreams that issue from the ivory gate,
will come to surround her with their magic circle, and
to reconstruct for her eyes the edifice of her vanished
joys.   The night, continuing her dream, and reviving
the hours that passed too quickly away, will bring
back their light phantoms to seize her soul, and rock
it in their velvety arms; to repeat sweetly in her ear
the acclamations of the crowd, and the popular
triumphs of her lover, and also the sound of his foot-
step, as when he ascended the winding stairs of her
house on the banks of the Seine, and the longed-for
accents of his voice.

But, in the morning, the spectre of widowhood is
there awaiting her awakening, to deposit each day upon
her lips a bitterer dreg, in her eyes a more scalding
tear, in her heart a more painful regret, and upon her
face a more hopeless pallor.

Ten years of prayer, of abstinence, and of sleepless-
ness weighed upon that fiery nature without dampening
its ardor.   In vain the walls of the cloister hung over
her with their gloomy shades; in vain they enveloped
her with their sepulchral influences; in vain they gathered around her the folds of an anticipated shroud,—

the impulse and the flame still survived under the sack·
cloth. Under the vaults of the convent she breathes
the ardent atmosphere of days that are no more. She
passes and repasses there, as it were under the magnificent arches of an enchanted palace. There every
object has received something from her own soul, every
echo is filled with well-known voices that welcome her,
that retain her. A deposed queen, she marches again
into her kingdom, and the triumphant charm replaces
her a moment upon the throne she lost.

The deception is not long. Violently recalled to
the actual world, the recluse finds herself face to face
with the deplorable causes of her misfortune; then
she is soured and vexed, she accuses men and destiny,
and, swelling the voice of her grief to the tone of au-
dacious murmurs, she would, like Job, lay her request
at the feet of the Eternal, and contest the matter with
him.

Why has she been so hardly chastised ? Why is
she widowed ? Ah ! our dove was scarcely made for
the monastic languors of which Colardeau speaks, and
how different was her vocation ! If you doubt it,
look at what she utters. The vitality of youth is
poured upon those breathing and native pages, where
memory is prodigal of its honey and its gall. Her
thought vibrates with all the thrills of the flesh,—her
speech has a sex; and that shivering with which she
is electrified, and which runs over her from head to

foot, doubtless has not its origin in the cloister. The pulsations of her blood can still be counted upon the paper which she touched. (Ah! Fulbert, what have you done?) Such passages are only a paraphrase of the charming Song of Solomon.

But what a profound and pure sentiment there is under this plastic form of her love! How does it breathe over the dust of this earth a divine breath, which penetrates and ennobles it! If her pen is sister to the pencil of Rubens, we should still know not how to forget its relationship with that of Raphael. From those half-formed thoughts, whose bosom one sees rising and trembling like an appeal of voluptuousness, escapes an irradiation of modesty which covers and protects them, like that golden cloud which, upon Mount Ida, screened from the eyes of the other divinities the loves of the powerful mother of Olympus.

What delicacy also, what discretion, what respect, united with the most abandoned passion! If any word seems to go beyond the sacred limit which her heart prescribes to itself, if any complaint tempered in the fire of her sorrow seems to preserve its sharpness, that sorrow stops short, and is forgotten,—a single sentiment remains—the fear of having betrayed her love by an expression too little guarded. As soon as she returns upon herself by a recantation in those adorable circuits; behold her wholly occupied in explaining herself, and her soul grounds itself upon in-

describable endearments in order to retrieve an error
that she has never committed.

It is not in vain that we have loved the rare sub
mission of Heloise. She perseveres to the end, without ever being wearied. When we see her weeping,
groaning, heaping reproaches upon imprecations, we
ask ourselves, where will the murmuring wave of her
anger subside? One word from Abelard, and all is
calm. From the height of all that storm, she descends
in the timid silence of obedience, and the rage of her
rebellion is calmed, even to the humble posture of
supplication: "I will be silent—pardon me."

Who could think that such a woman may have
been paid with ingratitude? It is, however, what has
been pretended. Most have been severe towards
Abelard. It has been said that on his part the seduction of Heloise was a fault that had not even love for
an excuse,—that it was done coldly, with deliberate
purpose, as a pastime,—that he deceived the confidence
of Fulbert. There has been established between the
expressions of the spouses a sorry parallel for Abelard.
He has been treated as a loose pedant, a hard and
cold man, as a brute, in every way unworthy of the
love so vivid, so noble, so disinterested, of Heloise.
The charge is grave, for it has been made in history,
which increases the importance of every thing it
touches, and by hands which seem to partake with
history this privilege. We hasten to shun this charge

as a testimony that it does not belong to us to combat,—we shall be more at our ease with the opinion which it represents.

Since Boyle, it has been a habit among those who have spoken of Abelard to equip against his love a small reasoning, to put in the lists some phrases armed from head to foot, and to give them full rein against that *unfortunate*, who did not sufficiently love his wife. I like this chivalrous exaltation, and this harsh demand in favor of Heloise. We are happy to find so many people disposed to do better than Abelard. Without doubt, it is well to break a lance in favor of beauty,—the part is brilliant to play in France, and such passages at arms will always be applauded; but at the moment when the champions lower the visier, and bending upon the saddle-bows with lance in rest, await only the signal for combat . . . . hold, knights! you are tilting against justice and truth; your adversary also bears the colors of your own lady;—would you then destroy her lover out of gallantry for her? Your valor is likely to frighten Heloise; she is not the one, I fear indeed, who has put on for you your spurs.

What a fine history has been spoiled! How has that delicious legend been defloured, by making the man a roue, and the woman a duped mistress!

These are errors not very dangerous, it is true,— nevertheless, should they have no other inconvenience

than to mar the pleasures of our mind, they ought to
be removed. Say what you will of Abelard; that he
knew not the Greek, nor the sense of the law *Quin-
que Pedibus*,—pierce him in default of his theology,
wound his dialectics, bury to the hilt the sword of your
criticism in the softness of his character —it is the side
poorly defended; refuse him every other merit and
every other glory, but at least do not rob him of
his love for Heloise, do not make of him an incarnate
syllogism; let the heart of the man throb beneath the
cuirass of the philosopher.

The language of Abelard seems to us at once fit-
ting and tender. He knows the ravage caused by the
Letter to a friend, which fell into the hands of Heloise. Heloise is not strong, as she herself confesses;
if he be a moment feeble, she is lost. See also with
what nobleness and what dignity he comes to heraid!
How the exhortations of piety borrow in his mouth the
insinuating charm and the delicate persuasives of love!
He has judged her situation,—an end has been made
of earthly joys. But if there is no more hope, there
is still fear. Heloise looks to him; she questions him
as to his attitude; at the least sign of fainting on his
part, she is ready to fall into blasphemy. Let the
vulture tear his heart, it matters little, his face must
show no signs of his grief. So he is calm; at least
he forces himself to appear so. His courage is as
great as his misfortune.

11*

Without doubt, to consider only the ascetic exter-
nals of his style, we might be disposed to take the
letters of Abelard for sermons; and it may be said
that such is not the language of love in the ordinary
conditions of life. But here every thing is out of the
common course. In order to judge his letters rightly,
we must place ourselves at the right point of view.
A man broken by every misfortune, wounded in his
person and in his affections; betrayed, calumniated,
persecuted, scarcely guarding his life against the
poison of his enemies and the poniards of his foes;
bowed with infirmities, overcome by excess of labor
and austerities of every kind; macerated in body and
soul, calling death as a benefit which can alone put an
end to his intolerable punishments,—such is the man
who writes to Heloise after long years of separation;
and if he remembers his love for her, it lives also in
company with another thought,—

> One fatal remembrance—one sorrow that throws
> Its bleak shade alike o'er our joys and our woes—
> To which life nothing darker nor brighter can bring,
> For which joy hath no balm, and affliction no sting.

But must we expect from Abelard letters like
those which Mirabeau wrote to Sophie? Did the
cell of the abbé of St. Gildas conceal hopes like
those which the tower of Vincennes concealed? If
these men both polluted the sacred ground of affran-

chisement, were they not widely separated when they were writing,—one to her who had been his wife, the other to her who was his enamored still ? Shall we ask from Abelard the naive transport of a page, or the bucolic elegies of a swain ?

Abelard has not ceased to love Heloise; on the contrary, the admiration which he feels for a courage already long proved, his respect for a life devoted to the accomplishment of the most rigorous practices, his gratitude for sacrifices so generously accepted, his regrets even in view of so beautiful an existence, broken like a flower by his hands,—all increases his love, elevates and confirms it. But it is no longer altogether a worldly love. The position of the parties is an exception.

Love is no longer free, it must give up its allure- ments to imperative exigences. Its form is pre- scribed. Abelard will study it in the religious obli- gations which are imposed on them, in the care of the heart which he wishes to heal, in the effects which he ought to produce upon a soul in grief, and still sick with memories. It is there that he must find her; she will have a veil after the manner of widows. She will be melancholy ; but in that graceful and lan- guishing shade, in the morbidness of her emotions, it will be easy to guess how strong and luxuriant was the life with which the body was formerly animated.

By a fatal compromise with the duties of their

habit, will the troubled tide of impenitent memories
mingle with the lustral waters of religion ?   A
Catholic priest, on the guard against himself, not
daring to give way to the overflowing of an affection
which he fears at present like a crime, he observes
himself, he fears the dangerous contagion of too vivid
a word, and the rupture of a wound scarcely healed ;
he puts all the tenderness of the husband under the
disguise of Christian symbols and of sacred texts.

If perchance his soul, softening at a memory too
touching, lets escape the cry of its grief, all in a
fright, he changes the past instantly, he implores in
his turn, he appeals to the generosity of Heloise, to
her love and her pity ; he asks her pardon for the
frightful torture which he would experience in seeing
her so unworthily vanquished ; and the courage which
she did not possess for herself, she will find, since
Abelard has need of it.

He speaks to her of his own perils, but it is for
the purpose of giving a change to that grief which,
always falling back upon itself, frets itself, and is increased without relaxation ; it is for the purpose of
turning to the future that attention which is torn
with the memory of the past ; the past is the only
enemy which it is necessary to vanquish.   He risks
nothing in saddening the soul of Heloise with the sentiment of dangers that threaten him ; he uses fear as
an auxiliary, as a powerful diversion from despair.

Inasmuch as he makes her think about him more than about herself, he profits by the victory; he no longer lets her turn her eyes towards an epoch apparently cursed with the malediction of Heaven. He breaks every tie that still binds her to earth; he encourages her to sustain herself on the lofty and serene heights of Christianity, and by a touching artifice, placing himself at the feet of God, he calls upon her to follow him, and extends to her his arms. He is sure of making her come to him. He invites her to new nuptials in Christ, and the sweet creature yields to this other love, although she likes the old better. It shall never be said that she once disobeyed him.

Do not take his numerous theological dissertations for works of supererogation, nor his numerous citations of Scripture as useless rhapsodies; for he thus traces his journey towards heaven; he smooths all obstacles, he strews his way with green branches and with various flowers from the holy books; he marshals in an ascending series along his route the noble company of Apostles and Fathers of the Church, who encourage her with voice and gesture, who bless her, on the way, with their venerable hands, who sustain her, console her, fortify her, and accompany her with their benedictions. Moreover, does he not himself journey with her ?

No! Abelard is not for Heloise a cold pedagogue. From that tree of science whose fruits he would have her taste, there silently distils a manna of tenderness that nourishes her courage. No! he is not a rigid monk, who lets fall from his lips nothing but anthemas. He knows how to win her to the austere contemplations of duty by words that animate her dying hope, that give to that poor eager soul its food of love.

Having once placed her upon the ground of reason, he appeals to her on every side. On the side of her sense of justice: "Would she oppose the evident will of Heaven?" On the side of her pride: "Pompey is living, but his fortune has perished. Did Cornelia, then, love what she has lost?" On the side of her conscience and her responsibility: "She is an abbess, she also has charge of souls." He knows that in a soul as great as that of Heloise, justice, dignity, conscience, are not vain words; he knows that a spirit as vigorous as hers always acts in virtue of a conviction, of the head or heart, of reason or sentiment, and because he believes in truth. This is the reason why he discusses with her, why he instructs her in faith, why he lavishes upon her without measure all the lessons of resignation.

The task is difficult. Like the mother of young Arthur, Heloise is entrenched in her own grief. She has ended by loving it and complaining of it. She is ingenious in tormenting herself, and in creating new subjects for tears. Abelard is obliged to watch her with the greatest attention.

He forgets nothing, not a question remains unanswered,—each word is considered; he does not stop there; he extends and developes a sentiment scarcely expressed in the letter of Heloise; an objection is attacked and demolished ere it is raised. He searches to the bottom of her heart, and if any bitter doubts conceal there their serpent heads, he stifles them; he chases as it were from a temple all the thoughts which might profane with their presence the majesty of divine love; his prayer is imperative, and he knows how to make his authority obeyed.

We see in that something else than indifference, something else than a dry division and sub-division,— something else than a poor return for the passion of Heloise. The love of a lover, the love of a master, the love of a brother in Christ,—the love of beauty, of genius, of the soul,—all that, makes only a single love in the heart of Abelard. He loves Heloise in the past, in the present, in all time; and we applaud him with a tenderness mingled with admiration, when, feeling that earth is wanting to him, he takes her in his apostolic arms to carry her with him to heaven.

By what false preoccupation, by what untimely exigence, has Abelard been accused of coldness! It has been forgotten that he is older than Heloise, and that his infirmities double the weight of his years. All the sentiments expressed in his letters are conformed to his situation. We find in them neither the ardor of youth nor the transport so justly admired in those of Heloise, for they are there in their place; but that tender and profound pity, that complaisant and exhaustless effusion, that vigilant guard which he keeps over her, those paternal efforts of a man who suppresses his own grief in order to calm that of an adored child which pierces his soul with its cries, —is all that so *icy* ? Is it not rather indicative of the truest, the noblest, the most touching love ?

With Heloise his words are the veil and not the expression of his love. In our turn, we know the words by the meaning; we search for the caressing inflections of thought rather than for those of speech.

If we observe Abelard with care, instead of accusing him of indifference, we shall be astonished at the progress of his passion,—the catastrophe which might have destroyed it only served to inflame it. At that exile of happiness he gives hospitality in his soul to larger loves. He attracts his spouse to embraces more intimate, purer, ever enduring.

But Heloise has seen heavens so deep and so radiant, that she knows not how to prefer those that are proposed.

Pressed on all sides, she takes refuge in his love for her, as in an asylum. Love is her stronghold, it suffices for her defence. With a single word she disconcerts the already triumphant calculations of that

Christian logic: "It is not God, it is you that I wish to please." And every thing is again put in question. It is by her very love that she must be conquered. Abelard is obliged to say to her: "I make common cause with God,—love him therefore."

She capitulates, but she wishes only a small corner of paradise, for she fears to be pleased with any thing that is not Abelard, and rejects even celestial happiness as a thought unfaithful to him.

One more circumstance will justify in our eyes the order of ideas invariably followed in his correspondence by Abelard. He visited the Paraclete several times; he there found Heloise; he found there Lucie, his dear mother, as he calls her. It was in the presence of these that his heart laid aside the burden of evil days and overwhelming thoughts. What overflowings of soul, what delicate endearments must not those meetings have afforded! A sad joy, a sentiment full of melancholy pleasure, extinguished for Heloise the two brilliant torches of the past, and her decayed regrets exacted from Abelard only a small effort of courage. Absence brought back for her the malady; to the need of curing it must be referred the sublime firmness from which he never departed in his letters.

It is then that he speaks to her of immortality, of an imperishable union in the bosom of God; and he does it with an elevation of language, an authority

of conviction, a power of desire, which will show to
all ages his genius, his faith, his love.   In pressing
to his heart his mother and his wife, he had felt the
mysterious impulses of a life that cannot end, the
revelation of a world where the embracing itself must
be renewed.   Having returned to St. Gildas, he
wrote with a divine energy ; for he had read in their
eyes the assurance of a love that is stronger than
death, and is in possession of eternity.

Finally, when his faith is attacked, when the hur-
ricane sounds, when the winds rage, when the thun-
derbolts of a new council hang over his new heresy,
his first thought is for Heloise, his first care is to reassure her.   He feels that the moment has come for
drawing near to her.   It is not only the brother in
Christ who addresses his sister in the same Christ ;
it is the husband who speaks to his wife.   His voice
finds again the familiar tenderness of ancient days.
He comes to rest his head once more upon the heart
that has loved him so much.

We think that, according to the disposition of
readers, the letters of Abelard will always produce
two very different impressions.   We may compare
these letters to a prism which, at a distance, conceals
all the splendors of the light contained in its bosom,
but, seen near by, the crystal opens its precious casket,
illumines with its hues, and spreads over all things
flaming robes of gold, of azure and of crimson.   ,

The thought of Abelard always takes an ade-
quate form,—its gravity is never dishonored by a
vain ornament of words.   Like that of every poet,
his discourse flows in measure ; but it is firm, sober,
tranquil, free from every terrestrial agitation.

But love has no prescribed language.   Love trans-
figures every thing.   The most indifferent words may
become with it magnetic currents in which two souls
meet,—ways whereby the eye can follow them,—
bridges made of a single hair, over which they au-
daciously run without ever deviating.

If one is fortunate enough to have a hallucination
of the heart (*qui amant sibi somnia fingunt*), then
that dead text becomes animated, the blood and the
life circulate in the veins just now numb and color-
less; you feel their warm breath, your soul is flooded
with balm, and, by a marvel like those of history and
fiction, you see the rocky words softened, the rough
shell broken, and you can bathe your hands in fresh
waters, and let your ravished eyes wander over unexpected beauties.

These love-letters purified by Catholic incense,
will remind you of the ancient Spanish toils, under
which Zurbaran seems to gather all the shades and
all the melancholies of earth, in order to console them
from on high by a luxurious hope, and by the splendors of beatitude.   God is not there, although we see
only him ; man is alone there, though we see him not.

Over those pages, so nobly refused for the expression of human suffering, rolls invisible tears. All the branches of that myrtle, when you touch them, sigh or groan. Stop before the gladiator, after he has been overcome in the arena. Examine his face,—not a muscle is contracted; you listen at his mouth for a complaint, an imprecation, a word which will be the epopee of all his griefs,—the word does not come; you hold your breath; the patient is about to die, he is dead . . . . . you have heard nothing.

And nevertheless, you find that all has not been told.

A truth until then unperceived, has just been revealed to you. The calmness of the man appears to you more terrible than a tempest, and it is not without fright that you contemplate that impassive exterior, when you see within him his heart in agony, his hopes wounded to death until the last, and his mind in tears,—all filled with a dear image, and the rending agonies of an eternal adieu.

Heloise and Abelard entered upon life through high and brilliant portals, love and glory;—their route was accursed; and that no consecration might be wanting to them, to that of misfortune is added that of sanctity.

We draw near them with a lively and eager curiosity; we would see the palpitation of the heart that crucifies itself, hear what report a love so celebrated made in its own time, and understand the spirit that had the power to vivify the tomb. But when we come in contact with those high souls, that enter into relation with us only on those sides by which we are elevated and ennobled, we feel suddenly penetrated with respect. In presence of those embalmed remains of a religious memory and an eternal hope, it seems that the life of love and genius, which animated them in times gone by, comes to us in a harmonious wail and in tears divine. We find in those two great initiates of sorrow a striking image of humanity, with its virtues elevated to heroism, and its weaknesses sometimes as admirable as its virtues.

XXXI.

"DUST TO DUST."

POSTERITY, for the most part, is careful to preserve the remains, as well as the memory, of the noble dead.

Abelard and Heloise were at first buried in the same crypt. Three centuries rolled away ere any one thought of separating the two lovers, who had been so closely united in life, whom their last will had united in death.* Nevertheless, in 1497, on account of a ridiculous scruple, their bones were put in two different tombs which were placed on opposite sides of the choir in the great chapel of the abbey. They remained there about two centuries, when Marie de la Rochefoucauld had them placed, in 1630, in the chapel of the Trinity.

One hundred and thirty-six years afterwards, Marie de Roucy de la Rochefoucauld conceived the idea, at once pious and philosophic, of erecting a new monument to the memory of the two lovers, one of whom

* Letters of Abelard and Heloise, traduits sur les manuscrits de la Bibliotheque Royal, par E. Oddoul: precedées d'un essay Historique, par M. et Me. Guizot, vol. 1, p. cviii.

had been the founder and the other the first abbess of Paraclete. In 1766, she wrote to the Academie des Inscriptions, asking for an epitaph with which to adorn the tomb of Abelard and Heloise. Madame de Roucy de la Rochefoucauld, niece of the former, and the last abbess of Paraclete, caused the following epitaph to be engraved on their common tomb :

HIO,

SUB EODEM MARMORE, JACENT,

HUJUS MONASTERII

CONDITOR, PETRUS ABÆLARDUS,

ET ABBATISSA PRIMA, HELOISA,

OLIM STUDIIS, INGENIO, AMORE, INFAUSTIS NUPTIIS,
ET POENITENTIA,

NUNO AETERNO, QUOD SPERAMUS, FELICITATE,
CONJUNCTI.

PETRUS OBIIT XX PRIMA APRILIS MOXLII,

HELOISA, XVII MAII MCLXIII.

HERE,

UNDER THE SAME STONE, REPOSE,

OF THIS MONASTERY

THE FOUNDER, PETER ABELARD,

AND THE FIRST ABBESS, HELOISE,

HERETOFORE IN STUDY, GENIUS, LOVE, INAUSPICIOUS
MARRIAGE AND REPENTANCE,

NOW, AS WE HOPE, IN ETERNAL HAPPINESS,
UNITED.

PETER DIED APRIL XXI, MOXLII.

HELOISE, MAY XVII, MOLXIII.

All the convents in France were destroyed by a decree of 1792. The Paraclete was included in their number, but the authorities of Nogent made an exception in favor of the two lovers. The bones of Abelard and Heloise were taken from their resting-place with great ceremony, in the presence of the curé of the parish and the notables of the place. A magnificent procession conducted their lifeless remains to the church, where a discourse was pronounced, and funeral hymns were sung. Their coffin, in which their bones were separated by a partition of lead, were deposited in a vault of the Chapel of St. Ledger.

Under the ministry of a Lucien Bonaparte, it was ordered, in 1800, that the united remains of the two celebrated lovers should be removed to the *jardin du Musée Français*, where M. Alexander Lenoir, the founder of that establishment, had a very elegant sepulchral chapel constructed for them, out of the best remnants of Paraclete and of the abbey of St. Denis.

In 1815, the government ceded to the Mont-de-Piété a large portion of the ground first assigned to the Musée Français, and, consequently, it was necessary to remove the new monument of the lovers, ever united, never at rest! They were deposited for a season in the third court of that national establishment.

In 1817, their ashes were removed to the cemetery of Mont Louis, in one of the halls of the ancient house of Père Lachaise, which served them as an asylum about five months. On the sixth of November, the same year, they were placed, in presence of the commissary of police, in the cemetery of Père Lachaise. Lovers may there find their place of sojourn by inquiring for the *chapelle sepulcrale d'Héloise et d'Abailard.*

M. Lenoir says, speaking of Heloise: "The inspection of the bones of her body, which we have examined with care, has convinced us that she was, like Abelard, of large stature, and finely proportioned.

"I have remarked, as well as M. Delaunay, in regard to the stature of Abelard, that his bones are strong and very large. The head of Heloise is finely proportioned; the forehead, smoothly formed, well rounded, and in harmony with the other parts of the face, still expresses perfect beauty. This head, which was so well organized, has been moulded under my own eyes for the execution of the bust of Heloise, which has been modelled by M. de Seine."

We must now leave thee, noble Heloise; and, somehow, the very thought that we have completed our pilgrimage with thee, gives us an indescribable heaviness of heart. Willingly would we journey to the ends of the earth, if we could learn some magic art, by which to summon thee in living reality before us just as imagination now pictures thee. Thy pres-

12

ence is queenly, thy brow is like that given by sculptors of old to the Goddess of Wisdom; thy voice is softly tremulous and all-informed with melody; the " nectared sweets " of sentiment flow from thy tongue; the "honey dews of thought" distil from thy quivering lips, and in thy deep clear eyes so much is seen that speech cannot reveal. Remain with us for ever. Alas! we are clasping a phantom, and before us—just retribution!—there is nothing but a skull, with its toothless, bony jaws, with its bottomless eye-sockets instead of eyes—and that, too, is a phantom!

Bones may last for a season, but dust will not be cheated out of its kindred dust.

My brother, let thy going forth be with reverence, for thou art treading upon the decayed hearts of those who have loved as we love, who have struggled as we are struggling, who have sinned as we sin, who have vanished as we at length shall vanish. Above thee is arched God's great sky, over thee the night stars keep silent watch; in all and through all is the spirit that is soul of thy soul, life of thy life; and elsewhere than in the flesh are intelligences more nearly akin to us than we think.

XXXII.

RECAPITULATION IN THE LANGUAGE OF A POET.°

LOVE is one of the leading influences of our nature; and when this sentiment is elevated by female devotion, when it is irradiated by beauty, excused by weakness, expiated by misfortune, transformed by repentance, sanctified by religion, rendered popular through a long epoch by genius, perpetuated by constancy on earth, and aspirations of immortality hereafter—this passion almost resolves itself into virtue, and raises to the level of heroic saints, two lovers, whose adventures became the theme, and their tears the sorrows of an age. Such is the story, or rather the poem of Heloise and Abelard. During eight centuries no other has so profoundly touched the human heart. Whatever moves men long and deeply, forms a portion of their history; for human nature is equally compounded of mind and feeling. All that softens, improves. Admiration and pity affect the heart, and the heart is the safest and strongest organ of virtue. These two lives comprise a single one; they are so interwoven that each existence is a perpetual rebound

* Lamartine.

of the other; the same event, the same sensation, reflected back again in a double echo, produces the
same undivided interest. Let us now commence our
narration.

Peter Abelard was the son of a knight of Brittany,
named Beranger, whose family had long possessed, in
the neighborhood of Nantes, the castle and village
of Palais. Beranger exercised, like all the gentle-
men of his day, the noble trade of war. His son was
brought up to arms; but the piety of his race, attested by the religious habit which Beranger, his wife
and daughters assumed in their old age, associated
with the military education of the youthful Abelard,
the study of letters, philosophy, and theology. The
leading, and the only intellectual profession of that
period, the Church, attracted to her ranks all the
young men who felt within themselves the seeds of
poetry, or eloquence, the love of fame, and the ambition of mental supremacy. Abelard was more hap-
pily endowed than any other individual of his time.
He disdained the rude life of a mere warrior, and
resigned to his brothers his rights of primogeniture
over the domains and vassals of the house. He
quitted the paternal mansion, and went from school
to school, from master to master, gathering all those
buried treasures of Greek and Roman literature, which
France and Italy had begun to disinter from manuscripts, to restore to light, and to worship as the profane

mysteries of human genius. His warm heart and fervid imagination were not satisfied with the dead languages : he wrote and spoke in Greek and Latin, but he sang in French.

The verses, for which he composed the music himself, that the passion by which they were inspired should convey its full effect to the soul by two senses at a time, became the manual of all poets. They spread with the rapidity of an echo, which multiplies its own sound; they formed the conversation of men of letters, the delight of women, the secret language of lovers, the interpreters of undeclared sentiments, the popular songs of cities, castles, cottages; they carried the name of the young musician and familiar poet throughout the provinces of France. He enjoyed a personal fame during the spring of life, in the secret souls of all who loved, dreamed, sighed, or sang. A melodious voice which gave animation to language and music; a youth precocious in celebrity; a Grecian regularity of features, a tall and graceful figure, a noble bearing, a natural modesty, in which the bashfulness of early years blushed for the maturity of talent—all these qualities, combined in Abelard attraction with renown. He was ever present to the eyes, the ears, the hearts of the women who had seen him, or had even heard his name pronounced. It was thus that Heloise recalled his image to her heart long after the ruin of her illusions and her love.

But in his early verses, he sang of feelings which he
had not yet experienced personally. His love sonnets
were flights of imagination, imitated from the ancient
poets. They breathed the accents of the heart, but
not the heart of the writer. He lived apart from the
world, in study, in piety, and in the perspective of future
glory. His songs were his recreation ; philosophy and
eloquence exclusively enchained his faculties. His language softened by poetry ; his eloquence harmonized
by music, the rich, spontaneous fertility of his imagination ; his memory fed and strengthened by universal reading ; the brilliancy, propriety, and novelty
of the images into which he sculptured his ideas, to
render them palpable to his auditors ; such were the
endowments which made this young man (seated at
the feet of the most celebrated chairs of the University
of Paris) the master of masters, and the popular orator
of the schools. In that day the schools constituted the
forum of the human race. They were all that knowledge, science, religion, opinion, the press, the tribune,
became in after ages. The true word, scarcely recovered, governed the world, but under the exclusive domin-
ation of the Church. Eloquence, philosophy, and faith,
were only exercised on the same recurring texts.
There was one continued struggle in disputes, which
are now unintelligible, to produce the triumph of revelation by arguments drawn from profane reason,
and to call in Plato and the ancient sages to bear tes-

timony to Christ and the Apostles. It is easy to understand to what dialectic subtleties the minds of men were sharpened by such disquisitions. But these controversies, for other views of Providence, are sometimes intended as exercises to strengthen human intellect, and to supply the world with high examples of talent and reputation.

The young orator followed the stream of his age. He ascended the tribune of the day, the pulpits of the public schools, round which the people crowded with greater eagerness, as they were only emerging from profound ignorance, and expected the approach of some unknown light, just then beginning to appear. Abelard, at first an humble and docile disciple, raised himself by degrees, on the applause and encouragement of his listeners, to a level with the oracles of the schools, and soon began to dispute and oppose their dogmas. Finally he subverted them all, founded a new college of philosophy at Melun, carried away in his train the young students, fanaticized by his genius; by his increasing popularity spread consternation among his rivals, who were almost deserted in Paris; consumed himself with the fire he had kindled in public imagination; excited the envy of the learned in the University and the Church; retired for two years to the obscurity of his native district, to fortify his powers; and reappeared in Paris, stronger, more celebrated, and more controlling than before. He pitched his camp,

or rather his school, on the eminence, then almost
solitary, on which now stands the church of St. Gene-
viève.

This became the Mount Aventine of a people of disciples, quitting the ancient seminaries, to imbibe eagerly the fresh and fearless eloquence of Abelard. Each
of his followers paid a small fee to the philosopher—
the humble tribute of a nation thirsting for truth.
This salary, multiplied by the incalculable number of
contributors, elevated the fortune of Abelard as high
as his fame. He was in the flower of his years, of his
glory,· of his virtue; for up to this period he had in-
dulged in no passion except his passion for truth and
faith. The pride so natural to one who is looked up to
by men, and the seductive charm attendant on female
admiration, exalted and weakened him at the same
moment. A double snare awaited him as he reached
the maturity of his genius and reputation. He was
then thirty-eight. He reigned by eloquence over the
spirit of youth; by beauty, over the regard of women;
by his love-songs, which penetrated all hearts; and by
his musical melodies, which were repeated in every
mouth. Let us imagine in a single man, the first orator, the first philosopher, the first poet, the first musician of his age; Antinoüs, Cicero, Petrarch, Schubert,
united in one living celebrity, and we can then form
an idea of the popularity of Abelard at this period of
his life.

At that time there dwelt in Paris a rich and powerful canon of the cathedral, Fulbert, who resided in the learned quarter of the city. He had a niece living with him (some say she was his daughter), whom he loved with paternal affection. This niece, aged eighteen, and consequently twenty years younger than Abelard, was already much noticed in Paris for her beauty and early genius. Her uncle, the canon, had treated her with all those blind indulgences, which, while they adorned a chosen nature, with every gift of intelligence and education, he saw not, in the weakness of age, would prepare a more signal victory for seduction, love, and misfortune. Her name was Heloise. The medallions and the statue which perpetuate her, according to contemporary traditions, and the casts taken after death in her sepulchre, represent a young female, tall in stature, and exquisitely formed. An oval head, slightly depressed towards the temples by the conflict of thought; a high and smooth forehead, where intelligence revelled without impediment, like a ray of light, unchecked by an obstructing angle, on the smooth surface of a marble slab; eyes deeply set within their arch, and the balls of which reflected the azure tint of heaven; a small nose, slightly raised towards the nostrils, such as sculpture models from nature in the statues of women immortalized by the feelings of the heart; a mouth where breathed, between brilliant teeth, the smiles of genius and the

12*

tenderness of sympathy; a short chin, slightly dim-
pled in the middle, as if by the finger of reflection often placed upon the lips; a long, flexible neck, which
carried the head as the lotus bears the flower, while
undulating with the motion of the wave; falling shoulders, gracefully moulded, and blending into the same
line with the arms; slender fingers, flowing curls,
delicate, anatomical articulations, the feet of a goddess
upon her pedestal, such is the statue, by which we
may judge of the woman! Let the life, the complexion, the look, the attitude, the youth, the languor, the
passion, the paleness, the blush, the thought, the feeling, the accent, the smile, the tears be restored to the
skeleton of this other Inèz de Castro, and we shall
again look on Heloise. Her features, according to the
historians of the time, and Abelard himself, were less
striking to the eye from beauty than from expression,
that graceful physiognomy of the heart, which draws,
invites, and compels a reciprocation of the love it offers
—supreme beauty, far superior to the charms which
command admiration only. Here we may use the words
of Abelard: "Her renown," says he, "had spread
throughout France. All that could seduce the imagination of men presented itself to me. Heloise became
the adored object of my dreams, and I persuaded myself that I could win her affection. I was then so celebrated, my youth and beauty so enhanced my fame,
that I thought it impossible any woman could reject

my proffered love. I abandoned myself to the intoxi-
cation of hope, the more readily that Heloise herself
was accomplished in letters, in the sciences, and the
arts. A poetical correspondence had already commenced between us, and I ventured to write to her
with greater freedom than I could have spoken. I
yielded entirely to this passion, and sought every possible means of establishing familiar relations and opportunities of intercourse."

Nothing was more easy of accomplishment. The
uncle and niece, without the knowledge of Abelard,
conspired to assist him ; the niece by her charms, the
uncle by his pride. The friendship of such an illustrious man was a distinction for any family. Abelard,
through mutual friends, intimated to Fulbert that the
care of his domestic affairs interfered with his studies
and predominating love of learning, and that he wished
to seek the hospitality of an honorable and enlightened
family, where he might live like a son under the roof
of his father. Fulbert, overjoyed and flattered by
these proposals, at once offered his hearth to Abelard.
He should reap, he said, the double advantage of intimacy with the first man of the age, and finish the education of his niece without further expense. She, too,
by constant conversation with the oracle of his day,
would derive virtue and knowledge from their source.

We can readily believe, and the fact is attested by
the complaisance and subsequent rage of Fulbert, that

the uncle, an enthusiastic admirer of Abelard, and
hoping to win for his niece the only husband in his
opinion worthy of her, lent himself with paternal interest to an intercourse from which might spring the
mutual attachment and union of these young hearts.

Be this as it may, Abelard became an inmate in the
house of Fulbert. This domestic familiarity, authorized by the uncle of the fair disciple, offered to both
the opportunity, and, we may almost say, imposed the
necessity, of mutual love. Far from objecting to a
close intimacy between the master and his pupil, Fulbert entreated Abelard to impart to his niece all his
secrets of learning, and all his rare acquirements in
oratory, poetry, and theology; so as to complete in
her the intellectual prodigy which nature had commenced, and France admired with unwonted astonishment in a woman. He yielded up to him entirely his
paternal authority over Heloise, and, in accordance
with the rude discipline of the age, authorized him
even to correct her with blows, if she failed either in
obedience or attention. In a word, he reduced
Heloise to a state of mental thraldom, and constituted
Abelard an absolute master. Heloise was readily disposed to acknowledge not only a preceptor but a
divinity, in the handsomest and most celebrated man
of his age. Her rapid progress kept pace with the
wishes of her uncle. She labored no longer for the
world, but for Abelard alone; her sole ambition cen-

tred in the wish to please him. Nature, love, and
genius, combined to render this young girl the wonder
of her time.

Abelard became intoxicated with his avocation.
Two souls, tempted by such opportunities, could not
fail to fall into the snare which want of foresight or
complicity had spread for them under such specious
pretexts and such alluring indulgences. The external
world disappeared before them—they loved. Abelard,
who now thought of Heloise alone, proclaimed his
passion in poems, in which the verses and the music,
tempered in the same fire, spread the name of Heloise
as a heavenly secret divulged to the earth, and which
the whole world confided to one another by repeating
these divine songs, until at last they reached the ears
of Fulbert himself.

But Fulbert affected not to hear, or to disbelieve,
this profanation of his domestic hearth. He replied,
that Abelard was, by his genius and piety, too much
elevated beyond ordinary mortals to descend, even
under the seductions of love, from the paradise of
science and glory which his exalted intellect shared
with the angels. Perhaps, also, he expected from day
to day, that Abelard, conquered by an increasing
charm, would demand of him the hand of his pupil,
which he would have been too happy to accord. In
the mean time, Abelard, divided between his passion
for Heloise and his love of fame, hesitated to declare

himself. He had feared, lest, by avowing the influence
of earthly beauty, he should sink in the eyes of the
world from the reputation for purity and Platonic self-
command, which an ethereal philosophy had established for him in early youth. He was unwilling, also,
to renounce, by marriage, the prospective dignities,
honors, and fortune which the Church held out to him,
and which he had already propitiated by some noviti-
atory ceremonies. His disciples no longer recognized
their master. In his heart, love combated painfully
against his genius. His friends complained loudly of
his decline ; the languor of his passion had affected his
eloquence ; the fire of his soul evaporated in sighs, and
his lessons contained only cinders. He felt so unlike
what he had once been, that he gave up unprepared
discourses, in which his lips reflected nothing but the
image and name of Heloise. He was compelled to
learn by heart the lectures he had formerly extempo-
rized, and to repeat his own compositions, lest he
should fall in public estimation. His rivals and his
enemies triumphed. He was pointed at with the
finger of scorn, as a wreck of himself; quoted as a reproach and scandal to human weakness, and trampled
under foot as a deity hurled from his pedestal.
Heloise was more afflicted than Abelard at this degra-
dation of one she adored for himself alone. She entreated him to sacrifice her to his fame ; to permit her
to adore him as a divinity, who receives the heart and

incense of mortals, without other intercourse with his worshippers than the homage which they offer him ; to love her no longer, if this love diminished his reputation by a single ray ; or, if the disinterested affection of Heloise had become a necessity and a consolation to his existence, to reduce her to the condition of those women despised by the world, whose sentiments are equally unconsecrated by religion and law—slaves of the heart, never liberated by the title of wives. The contempt of the universe, endured for Abelard, was, she declared, the only glory to which she aspired. Shame, at such a price, would constitute her pride.

Abelard, after lamentable hesitation, could neither determine to accept this suicide of Heloise, nor openly to declare his passion before the world. He still continued to reside under the roof of Fulbert. Dastardly at the same time towards affection and virtue, he floated between two weaknesses, and evinced neither the courage of love nor that of glory. In this instance, as in all others, the heart of the woman was manly, the heart of the man, feminine. But his infatuation, meanwhile, nourished itself upon these agonies. Fulbert, justly irritated by a silence which resembled contempt, and which rendered his hospitality suspicious, closed his doors against the offender. This separation tore the heart of Heloise, and humiliated that of Abelard. Neither the master nor the scholar could renounce a life in which the looks, the conversation, the studies, the songs, the thoughts of both had blended two into a single soul. They contrived secret meetings, a mysterious intercourse with which Fulbert was deeply enraged. Abelard carried Heloise away, and conducted her with all respect to Nantes, to his paternal mansion, where he confided her as his wife to the affection of his own sister. Returning immediately to Paris, he threw himself at the feet of Fulbert, implored his forgiveness, and obtained by contrition the hand of his niece. Heloise pardoned and restored at once to her uncle and her lover, became secretly the spouse of Abelard. "After a night passed in prayer," says he, "in one of the churches of Paris, on the following morning we received the nuptial blessing in the presence of the uncle of Heloise, and of several mutual friends. We then retired, without observation or noise, that this union, known only to God and a few intimates, should bring neither shame nor prejudice to my renown."

The newly-married pair—their happiness unknown to everybody—affected thenceforth to be seldom seen together, and labored to extinguish all preceding rumors of their attachment. The world, for the moment, was deceived, and Abelard enjoyed together the delights of love and the return of his reputation. But the servants of Fulbert, necessarily acquainted with his secret visits, noised abroad the circumstance of the marriage. The envious detractors of Abelard

triumphed in his weakness, and accused him of having
sacrificed philosophy, eloquence, and fame to a second
Delilah. His pride took offence; he denied his ties,
as if they had been a disgrace. The generous Heloise
herself, preferring the glory of her lover to her own
honor, proclaimed and encouraged the assertion that
she was only united to Abelard by admiration and
love, and cast a stain upon her own virtue to exalt the
virtue of her husband. These reports, so offensive to
Fulbert, induced him to utter bitter and merited reproaches against his niece, whose devoted falsehood
had thus dishonored his blood. Abelard, dreading the
resentment of her uncle, snatched her once more from
the guardianship of Fulbert, and conveyed her to Argenteuil, a village near Paris, where he placed her in a
monastery of women. These monasteries, like the
altars of antiquity, afforded the right of inviolable
sanctity to all unmarried females or wives who passed
their threshold. Here he persuaded her to take the
white veil of a novice, without yet pronouncing the
irrevocable vows. He devoted himself to a monastic
life and the priesthood, and as soon as he was invested
with this holy character, with his own hands he placed
on Heloise the habit of a professed nun, cut off her
hair, and yielded her up to God, having neither the
courage to claim her as his wife, nor to leave her in
the world, which he had renounced forever. Heloise,
happy in giving up her life to him to whom she had

already abandoned her honor, submitted without a murmur, as the victim who voluntarily places herself on the sacrificial altar. Every thing was acceptable to her, even the punishment she underwent by the election, and through the love, or rather through the pride of her husband. The gates of the convent of Argenteuil were closed upon the Sappho of the eleventh century. Beauty, genius, affection, all were buried in those catacombs; and during fifteen years, the best years of the immured sufferer, neither reproaches, regrets, nor sighs, were heard from within that living monument.

Abelard, free and purified in the eyes of his followers, resumed with fresh ardor and brilliancy the course of his lectures, and the empire of his popularity. But the anger of Fulbert brooded over vengeance. Thrice foiled in his tenderness for his niece by the seduction, the perfidy, and baseness of Abelard, he saw snatched from him by the same hand the company of his beloved pupil, the reputation of his family, his honor, and his happiness. He had educated with so much solicitude that prodigy of her sex, only to see her despised by the selected husband to whom he had resigned her, tainted as a concubine, repudiated, contemned in her devoted affection, and finally shut up as a penitent in a monastery; cut off in the flower of her youth from the number of the living, to keep away false shame from the forehead of an ungrateful seducer, and condemned to feed on her own tears, while he was hailed by the acclamations of the century. We do not justify the vindictive feelings of an outraged father, we only endeavor to explain them. He had forgiven all, to behold Heloise married to the first genius of his age, and after being acknowledged as a wife, she was now denied. Despair excited hatred, and hatred began to ponder on crime. The gates of Abelard's house were opened one night, through the purchased treachery of his domestics; executioners, directed and paid by Fulbert, surprised him in his sleep; they overwhelmed him with cruel insults, and left him degraded by his punishment. Humiliation and remorse, worse than the inflicted revenge, made Abelard detest the life which his enemies had spared as an additional pang. The light of day became hateful to him. His despair at this unpunished outrage equalled the vainglory by which he had been carried on to the base ingratitude of sacrificing Heloise; his only remaining object was to disappear from the world he had filled with his renown, and which now resounded with nothing but his shame.

"I called to mind painfully," he writes, "the brilliant reputation by which I was surrounded on the eve of that fatal day, and the prompt ignominy by which my glory was extinguished. I acknowledged the just chastisement of Heaven—the *just* retaliation by which

the man I had betrayed, betrayed me in his turn. I
already heard the malicious exultations of my enemies, the delight of my rivals at this retributive dispensation. I felt that I could no longer appear in
public without being pointed at as an object of ignominious pity. The sense of my degraded state covered
me with such confusion that I am forced to confess,
shame rather than pity, drove me into the solitude of
the cloister. I wished, however, before tearing myself from the world, to remove Heloise from it irrevocably. By my direction she pronounced the eternal
vows. Thus, both of us, on the same day, embraced
together the monastic life, she at Argenteuil, I in the
abbey of St. Denis. Moved by her youth and beauty,
the companions of Heloise endeavored in vain to win
her from the sacrifice she was induced to consummate.
She replied (with tears, shed for her husband, not for
herself), by those verses which the Roman poet places
in the mouth of Cornelia, the widow of Pompey the
Great: 'Oh, my illustrious partner, thou whose bed
I was not worthy of partaking, it is my evil destiny
which weighs upon thine! Why, wretch that I am,
have I formed the bonds which have drawn on thy
ruin? Receive, in the holocaust of thy wife, the expiation of the misfortunes my love has brought upon
thee!' Having pronounced these words, broken by
sighs, Heloise rushed to the altar, as if precipitat-
ing herself into an abyss; she seized the funeral

veil, already consecrated by the bishop, and dedicated herself from that moment, before the assembled people, to the service of the Deity who received her oath."

Such is the recital of the sacrifice of Heloise, given by Abelard himself. The shadow of the convent inclosed her for many years; a concealed, but an unextinguished flame.

Abelard carried to the monastery of St. Denis his inward uneasiness, his talents strengthened by concentrated study, his ambition, which had only changed its object, and the intolerant zeal of reformation, by which new proselytes too often expect to redeem their wanderings. The relaxed monks of St. Denis, and the abbot who permitted and shared their irregularities, became irritated at his censures, and compelled him to remove his severe innovations to a neighboring and dependent establishment at Deuil. He there resumed his pulpit of philosophy, and filled once more the schools and the church with the report of new doctrines in matters of faith. The Church became indignant at his boldness, as the monks had been offended by his reproofs. Some subtle essays on the *Unity* and *Trinity*, in which he endeavored to explain that mystery without appealing to faith in aid of human reasoning, sufficed as a pretext to the enemies leagued against this active innovator. He was summoned before a council at Soissons to render an account of his doctrines, and solemnly condemned. To expiate the error, he was shut up in the cloistered monastery of St. Medard, where he gave himself up to despair. "The treachery of Fulbert," he exclaimed, "was less intolerable than this fresh outrage." The legate of the pope, more impartial and tolerant, speedily remitted the punishment. On returning to the abbey of St. Denis, he found the monks converted to implacable foes. They pronounced him an enemy of the state, guilty of high treason against the nation, for having said that St. Dionysius, bishop of Athens, converted by St. Paul, was not identical with the St. Dionysius, first bishop of Paris. Compelled to self-banishment, notwithstanding the complaisance of a re-cantation, to which he submitted to disarm their animosity, he fled, with a single disciple, to a desert spot in Champagne. "There," said he, " on the banks of a narrow river, shaded by oaks, and bordered by reeds, called the *Arduze*, I constructed with my own hands a small oratory, built of branches, with a thatched roof. I was alone, and could cry aloud with the prophet, 'I have fled, I have removed from the habitations of men and dwell in solitude.'"

But he was not long left to himself. The spirit of dispute and the love of novelty were at that time so strongly excited in the world, that those who possessed the word of life, drew after them whole nations of followers and listeners. The youth of the age thirsted so eagerly for truth, that controversy alone seemed a step towards the important mystery, and from the shock of opposing doctrines they expected the bursting forth of the lightning which never came. "As soon as my retreat was discovered," says Abelard, " my disciples crowded round me from every quarter, to erect humble cells in the desert. They abandoned soft beds of down for couches of leaves, luxurious viands for coarse vegetables ; it was thus that, according to St. Jerome, the philosophers of antiquity fled from cities, gardens, rich fields and shady groves, the melody of birds, the freshness of fountains, the murmuring of streams, from all that could charm the eyes and ears, seduce the senses, or enervate virtue. Even so, the sons of the prophets lived as hermits in huts on the banks of the Jordan, feeding on roots and herbs, remote from towns and human passions. My followers constructed cells on the bank of the Arduze, rather after the fashion of anchorites than pupils. In proportion as their numbers augmented, their lives became more studious and holy, so that the shame of my enemies increased with my reputation. Nevertheless, it was poverty which forced me to re-establish my school. I was unaccustomed to dig the earth, and I could not humiliate myself to beg my bread. My disciples cultivated the fields, and built the cells. Soon they became insufficient to contain them. Then they erected a vast edifice of timber and masonry, which I called after the name of the God of consolation,—*The Paraclete.*"

But the enemies of Abelard envied him even the wilderness. They saw, or affected to see, in the name of the *Consoling Spirit,* to whom he had dedicated his monastery, a sort of philosophic invocation to the one Person of the Trinity, to the exclusion of the other two. St. Bernard marked him out for the vengeance of the Church. He was obliged to abandon the desert himself, and to seek at the extremity of the shores of Brittany, amongst the rocks and strands of the ocean, an asylum still more inaccessible to jealousy and persecution. This was the abbey of St. Gildas, in the diocese of Vannes. The monks who dwelt there had degenerated from the sanctity of earlier ages, and had converted their convent into a den of barbarism and vice. The rude aspect of the neighborhood was exceeded by the character of the inhabitants. The place was a promontory, incessantly beaten by the surges of a groaning sea. Mountains of foam broke over the resounding rocks, and on a coast hollowed into vaults and caverns by the constant action of the waves, which buried themselves as in yawning gulfs, and then rushed back again from other apertures, like torrents of lava issuing from a volcano. Perpendicular cliffs shut out the sight of the land below from the abbey, which might be compared to a vessel in perpetual shipwreck, on a shore inaccessible to pilots. "The life of these monks," says Abelard, their superior, "was dissolute and insubordinate. The gates of the abbey were ornamented with the feet of stags, bears, and wild boars, the trophies and emblems of their constant avocations. They were awakened by the sound of the horn and the barking of hounds. Cruel and unrestrained in their licentious habits, and constantly at war with the surrounding nobles, they were alternately oppressors or oppressed." They laughed at the indignation which Abelard expressed at their rude manners, until their hatred against the intruding reformer led them on to crime. Insulted, threatened, attacked in the forests, poisoned even in the holy chalice of the sacrament, with difficulty he preserved his life by flight. The barons of the district snatched him from the steel of the assassins. He sought shelter in a spot even more deserted than the domains of the abbey, and, like the prophets of old, called upon the Lord from the abyss of his calamity.

Fifteen years passed over the head of Abelard in these alternations of learning, glory, sanctity, and suffering, during which he bestowed no token of remembrance on the still young and living victim he had buried at Argenteuil. Heloise complained neither of his insensibility nor silence. The neglect and contempt of her husband, she respected as additional virtues, believing that earth, heaven, and her own feelings, were worthy only to be sacrificed to this first and most

13

adored of men.   Abelard remained forever the sole
object of worship on the altar she had erected to him
in her heart.   All her sighs ascended to Heaven for
him, but they were breathed without sound, lest an
uttered thought or regret should scandalize the world,
or disturb his sublime contemplations.   The gates of
the convent of Argenteuil divulged no particle of
that immeasurable love which survived within its walls.
Persecution burst those gates.   Suger, abbot of St.
Denis, pretended that the convent belonged to his order, and drove out the nuns like a flock without fold
or shepherd.   Their cry of distress reached Abelard.
Whether it was that his own misfortunes had softened
his heart, or the memory of early happiness had returned full upon him, as it often does in the evening
of life; or that a comparison between the devotion of
this immolated woman, the ingratitude of the world,
and the emptiness of glory had lit up again the embers
of an ill-extinguished affection, Abelard hastened from
his retreat to the succor of the wandering and persecuted Heloise.   He conducted her to the Paraclete
with her companions, bestowed on her the convent, of
which she became abbess, and often visited her, to re-
lieve by his presence and fortune the indigence to
which he had opened an asylum.   At the age of fifty-
eight, clothed in sacerdotal habit, a spiritual father
rather than a carnal husband, the world respected the
union of the two tender hearts, whose community of

faith permitted only sorrow for the past, prayers for the present, and hope of eternal happiness for the future.

But their enemies were still active, and disseminated odious slander respecting this mystical intercourse between Abelard and his former wife. To put an end to them, he retired once more to his desert in Brittany. He preferred offering his life anew to the poignard and the poisoned cup, rather than expose the virtue of Heloise to the bitter tongues of her calumniators. It was then that he wrote the memoirs from which we have extracted the principal events described in this narrative. The volume, confided to friendship, reached the eyes of Heloise. The remembrances it excited, made the heart speak which had remained fifteen years in silence. An epistolary correspondence, affectionate on the one side, cold on the other, commenced between the hapless pair, separated equally by the hand of God and man. The Christian Sappho, in these letters, pours forth, with irrepressible passion, the ardor of a love purified by sacrifice, and which nothing earthly could extinguish, as its sole nourishment proceeded from heavenly fire. The address alone of these letters comprises a hymn of infinite tenderness, as it betrays the impassioned hesitation of a female hand, which seeks, finds, and rejects by turns, every name capable of expressing the strongest attachments of the soul, without finding one sufficiently comprehensive,

and which ends by joining them all together, lest nature should retain a variety of affection which she
has not acknowledged. "To her lord, or rather to
her father, his slave, his daughter, his wife, his sister,
Heloise to Abelard!"

"Some one," says she, in her first letter, after having read the recital of their loves by Abelard, "some
one has recently brought me by chance the history
you have intrusted to a friend. As soon as I perceived, by the first words of the superscription, that it
came from you, I began to read it with eagerness,
even greater than the adoration I still cherish for the
writer. What I have lost, I thought I had found
again, as if the beloved image could reproduce itself in
the tracings of the hand. Sad and bitter, oh, my only
treasure, are the lines of this narrative, which describe
our conversion and inexhaustible misfortunes. They
cannot be read, even by the most indifferent person,
without exciting tears."

Then, in allusion to his new exile, and the persecutions with which he was surrounded at St. Gildas, she
adds :—"In the name of the Saviour, who seems still
to protect us, we, who are his humble slaves, as we
are yours, we implore you to tell us in frequent letters,
of the dangers by which you are still surrounded, that
we, who are bound only to you in the world, may partake your grief or satisfaction. Usually, to suffer with
the afflicted, is to console him. These letters will be

doubly tender to us, as they will bear testimony that
we are not forgotten. Oh, how delightful is the re-
ceipt of letters from absent friends! If the portraits
of those separated by distance, recall their memory,
and soften regret by a deceptive solace, how much
more efficacious are letters, which embody and declare
the living stamp of the soul itself! Thanks be to God
that hatred has not prevented us from being thus still
present to each other."

She then calls upon him, by the cares which he
owes as a father to his daughters in religion, to be
prodigal of letters, orders, and advice ; but we easily
discover that unconsciously she uses a pretext to take
upon herself the leading part in this acceptable intercourse. "Think," she writes, "without speaking of
others, think of the immense debt you have contracted towards me. Perhaps then, what you owe to all
those holy women together, you will the more readily
acquit yourself of towards one who lives for you alone.
And why," she continues, with a jealous and tender
reproach for so many years of oblivion and silence,
"why, when my soul is bowed down with anguish,
have you not endeavored to comfort me, in absence by
your letters, in presence, by your words ? This was a
duty to which you were called, as we are united by the
sacrament of marriage ; and your conduct towards me is
the more blamable, as the universe is my witness, I
have loved you with an immense and imperishable affec-

tion. You know, sole object of my regard, how much I
have lost in losing you! In proportion as my grief is
great, so ought to be my consolation. From no other,
but from you alone do I expect it. You owe it to me,
or you only possess the power to sadden, rejoice, or
calm me! Have I not implicitly complied with your
wishes? Have I not sacrificed myself to obey you? I
have even done more; my love has carried me to
falsehood and suicide. By your order, in assuming
these habits, I have changed my heart to prove that
you were its absolute sovereign.

"Never, as Heaven is my witness, have I sought
from you aught but yourself. Although the name of
wife was the most binding and holiest of titles, any other
would have satisfied my heart. The more I humiliated
myself, for your sake, the more I should have merited
a tender return, and the less I should have fretted your
genius and injured your glory.

"Again, I call on Heaven to testify, that if the master of the world had thought me worthy of his hand
and had offered me with his name the dominion of
the universe, the title of your slave would have been
to me preferable to that of empress. What kings
could be compared to you? what country, what town,
what village was not impatient to behold you? where
were the women that did not sigh to look on you?
where was the queen who envied not my happiness?

"Were you not endowed with two gifts which irresistibly fascinated the female heart—eloquence and song? By these faculties, when reposing from the severer studies of philosophy, you composed those love-sonnets, which, through the combined charms of poetry and music, have caused our names to be repeated by every mouth. Yes, the name of Heloise has been heard in many lands, and has excited much jealousy when coupled with yours. And by what rare perfections of mind and body was your youth adorned! I have injured you, and yet you know I was innocent. Tell me only, why, since you have chosen to immure me in a convent, you have punished me by neglect and oblivion; by depriving me of your presence, and even of your letters? Tell me, if you dare to answer the question! Alas! I know, and the world suspects the reason! Your affection was less pure, less disinterested than mine. Since you have ceased to desire a profane happiness, you have ceased to love.

"Comply, I beseech you, with my request; it is easy, and will cost you little. Speak to me at least from a distance, by those words which restore the illusion of your presence. I thought I deserved much from you, when, still in youth, I embraced, at your desire, the austerities of the cloister. What recompense have I looked for from God, for whose love I have done less than I have for yours? When you have advanced towards Heaven, I have followed in your track. As if you had remembered the wife of Lot, who turned back,

and looked behind her, you thought it necessary, when
you quitted the world yourself, to bind me equally by
monastic vows.   Alas! you have misjudged my character.   I have mourned and blushed for this proceeding.
Was it necessary to drive me when I was ready to
follow you, even to perdition?   My heart was with
you, not with myself.   Let it remain yours, I conjure
you, which it will forever, if you listen to my prayer,
and return me tenderness for tenderness.   Formerly,
the purity of the motives which bound me to you
were open to suspicion; but does not the end prove
the nature of my love from the beginning?   I have
severed myself from every earthly enjoyment; of
worldly blessings I have reserved but one, the right of
considering myself forever yours.

"I conjure you, in the name of that Deity to whom
you have devoted yourself, give me as much of your
presence as is permitted : write to me letters of consolation, fortified by which, I may increase my ardor in
the service of Heaven.   When you looked for profane
gratification, you addressed me in frequent epistles,
which taught the name of Heloise to many lips, and
made those syllables familiar in many places.   To raise
my soul to God, can you not exert the power which
you formerly exercised to excite earthly feelings?
Think of what I ask! I finish this long letter by a single sentence—my all, my sole possession, adieu!"

Moved by these entreaties, Abelard at length broke

through the silence of many years. "Oh, my sister,"
said he, addressing his wife, "you who were so dear to
me in the world, who are a thousand times more cherished in Christ, I send you the prayer you have demanded with such importunity. Offer up to God, with
your companions, a holocaust of invocation, to expiate
our heavy and innumerable faults, to charm away the
dangers which beset me at every moment." He then
proceeds to a long and cold dissertation on the efficacy
of collective prayer from communities of nuns. At the
close of the letter, love seems to have betrayed him
into a last wish, which postpones, until death, the
reunion so vainly hoped for during life.

"Oh, my sister," he exclaims, "if God should deliver me into the hands of my enemies, if they put me
to death, or if, in the ordinary course of nature, I reach
the common end of all men, let my body, wherever it
is buried or abandoned, be transported to your cemetery, that you, my daughters, my sisters in Jesus
Christ, having my tomb ever before your eyes, may
feel called upon to intercede for me more incessantly
by constant prayers. For a soul afflicted by so many
calamities, and penitent for so many errors, I know
not where to find a resting-place on earth more safe
and salutary than that which is dedicated to *The Consoling Spirit*, and which so well deserves the name.
They were women who, careful of the entombing of
the Saviour, embalmed him with perfumes, and watch-

13°

ed around his sepulchre. Thus they were the first who received consolation."

With the exception of this involuntary return of love after death, the letters of Abelard are dry, cold, and unfeeling. They breathe exclusive selfishness, while those of Heloise contain no thought but of him.

"*To my only thought after Jesus—to my only hope next to the Saviour*," thus she addresses him; "it is you alone who will celebrate our obsequies, you who will dismiss to the Almighty those you have assembled in his presence. Surely God will not permit us to survive you; but should you die before us, we shall think rather of following than of burying you, since, destined so soon to the grave ourselves, we shall want the strength to prepare your tomb. If I lose you, what hope remains to me! how shall I longer bear this pilgrimage of life, in which I am still sustained by nothing but the thought that you partake it with me? Am I not unfortunate beyond all precedent? Raised by you above the level of my sex, have I only reached this high renown to be precipitated from unmeasured felicity to unparalleled disaster? We lived in chastity: you in Paris, I at Argenteuil: we separated to devote ourselves entirely—you to your studies, I to prayer with the holy sisterhood who surrounded me. During this irreproachable life, the hand of crime was permitted to reach you. Ah! why did not the blow fall on both together? Both were guilty, but you

alone have borne the expiation; the least culpable
has received the punishment. What you have suffered for a moment, I ought to have endured for life!
If I must avow the weakness of my soul, I search in
vain for repentance there. My happiness was too
supreme to be rooted out from memory, or recollected
with horror. In sleep, even in the midst of devotional
ceremonies, the periods, the places, the incidents of
our blissful lives present themselves to my imagination.
They call me holy, who know not how I regret the
past. I am praised by men, but ah! how censurable
in the eyes of God, who reads all hearts! In every
action of my life, you well know, I have feared your
anger beyond that of God himself. Think not too
well of me, and never cease to intercede for me in your
prayers."

In the midst of an elaborate dissertation on " The
Canticle of Canticles," Abelard introduced some touching sentences in his answer. "Why," said he to Heloise, "do you reproach me with having made you
a participator in my sorrows, when you yourself have
forced me to this by your solicitations? Is it possible
that you could ever be happy while I am miserable?
Would you wish to be the companion of my enjoyment,
and not partake my anguish? Can you desire that I
should precede you to heaven, you who would have
followed me to the lowest depths of perdition?" He
then recalls in order his past iniquities, and commands

Heloise to return thanks to the Creator for the punishments which have assailed and changed him. "You,
O Lord, have joined and divided us," he thus con-
cludes; "those who, for a time you have separated in
this world, we beseech you to reunite forever in the
world to come!" At last, we find the husband once
more in the saint.

Persecution drove Abelard back to the Paraclete.
The odious insinuations of his enemies forced him from
that sanctuary a second time. "How is it," he exclaimed in his despair, "that suspicion still clings to
me, when misfortunes, years, and the holiness of the
monastic profession are my securities against crime?
I suffer more at present from calumny than I did
formerly from outrage."

But his persecutors thought to attack him more severely in his glory than in his love. His writings,
which increased daily, alarmed Rome herself, and were
considered heretical, since they spread forth the first
dawn of freedom in discussion. St. Bernard, the
censor, reformer, and avenger of the Church in France,
set himself vehemently in opposition to these new
tenets. Cited before the council of Sens, to answer
for his opinions, Abelard preserved silence. St. Bernard denounced his contumacy as an additional offence.

"This man," said he, addressing the sovereign pontiff, "boasts that he can explain by reason the most
profound mysteries. He mounts up to heaven, and

descends to the lowest abyss; he is great in his own
estimation. He scrutinizes the Divine Majesty, and
disseminates errors. One of his treatises has been
given to the fire. Accursed be the hand that gathers
up the fragments! Necessity demands a swift remedy
for this contagion, for the man has many followers.
He preaches a new gospel to the people,—a new faith
to the nations of the earth,—all is contradiction! The
exterior form of piety is displayed by a modest carriage
and humble garments. His disciples transform themselves into angels of light, while they are in fact so
many *Satans!* This *Goliath* (thus he denominates
Abelard) hath proposed to sustain against me perverse
dogmas. I refuse to argue, because I am a child in the
truth, and he is a great and terrible opponent. But
you, successor of the Apostles, you alone will judge,
whether he ought to find a refuge on the chair of St.
Peter. Consider what you owe to yourself! Why
have you been elevated to the throne, if not to root
out and plant anew. If God has permitted schism to
rear its head in your days, is it not that schism may be
overthrown? Behold, the foxes will spoil and tear up
the vineyard of the Lord, if you suffer them to increase
and multiply. If you strike them not, they will bring
trouble and despair to your successors. If you hesi-
tate to destroy them, we will destroy them ourselves."
Thus spoke this all-potent tribune of the Church of
France, to whom statues are erected after an interval

of eight centuries. A summons so imperious, supported by the popularity of St. Bernard, could not fail to be complied with by Rome, although the pope, of a gentle and indulgent nature, was unwilling to strike a teacher, whose sincerity in faith he acknowledged, while he admired his genius. Abelard was condemned to perpetual seclusion in a cloistered monastery. This sentence, officially promulgated in France, after considerable delay, but foreseen by the victim of it, removed him for the last time from the quiet security of the Paraclete and the tears of Heloise. He bade an eternal adieu to the retreat which he had first peopled with enthusiastic disciples, afterwards with pious maidens, and which had so often sheltered him from the storms of his troubled existence. Alone and on foot he travelled towards the Alps, to implore from the justice of the pope an asylum against his persecutor. In his journey he passed by Cluny, at that time a sovereign abbey, which administered hospitality without distinction to popes, kings, pilgrims, and mendicants, on their journey from Paris to Rome.

This celebrated monastery, of the order of St. Benedict, was founded by William, duke of Aquitaine, who possessed an extensive territory in the province of the Mâconnais. William, according to the practice of the princes and nobles of his time, expected to purchase eternal bliss by a gift of land to the cenobites, who, in return, offered up perpetual prayers for the salvation of

his soul. The monks, whom he had commissioned to
seek out the fittest place for the site of the intended
monastery, having traversed the hills and valleys of
his domains, fixed their choice upon a deep and narrow
defile, which runs behind the chain of mountains of the
Saône, between Dijon and Mâcon. "A place," as
they described it, "shut out from all communication
with the world, and so full of silence, repose, and
peace, that it presents, in some manner, an image of
celestial tranquillity!" These recluses possessed a natural instinct for solitude and contemplation. At that
time the hills were covered with thick forests, the
growth of centuries, which bounded the horizon, and
concealed the sun; the waters of the mountain torrents overflowing the flat lands, formed lakes, ponds,
and marshes, bordered by reeds. The only track that
led to this basin of water and foliage, was a narrow
path hollowed out by the feet of mules. Above the
summit of the woods arose the smoke of a few thinly-
scattered cottages, inhabited by hunters, fishermen, and
wood-cutters. The gorge of Cluny was the Thebais
of the Gauls.

"On this spot," said the monks to the Duke of
Aquitaine, "we will erect our monastery."

"No," replied the Duke, "it is a valley too much
overshadowed by thick forests, and full of fallow deer.
The hunters and their dogs, with their shrill cries and
barking, will disturb your silence."

" Then drive away the dogs, and introduce the monks," replied the holy men.

William consented; the dogs disappeared, and the monks supplied their places. In a few centuries, owing to the extent and fertility of the land, the pious disinterestedness which made many dying penitents bequeath their fortunes to the monastery, and the skilful government of the abbots, who proved themselves good worldly statesmen, the desert of Cluny beheld rising in lofty elevation, where once its forests stood, another forest of steeples, cloisters, domes, vaulted arches, Gothic battlements, and Byzantine windows, the ornaments and defences of a Basilica equal in extent to the largest ecclesiastical edifices of Imperial Rome.

The river which formerly inundated the valley, now inclosed within beds of stone, or drained off into ponds stocked with fish, conveyed fertility to extensive meadows, whitening with flocks and herds. A large town adjoined the abbey, under the protection of the monks. Popes had issued from its cells to rule the Christian world; monarchs came to visit, endow, and bestow privileges on this chosen sanctuary. Councils were assembled there, and the abbots ranked as sovereign princes. Pilgrims from all quarters of the globe besieged the gates, and were received with hospitality. At the time of Abelard's arrival, the monastery was governed by Peter the Venerable, a man supremely eminent in science, poetry, renown, and virtue. A living

contrast to St. Bernard, the Abbot of Cluny personified
the true charity of religion, while the other embodied
only the proselytism and terror.   Peter the Venerable
had been elected while still young to the command of
the order, through the reputation of his talents, and
the influence of his character; a poet, a philosopher,
an author, a negotiator; a statesman in piety, and a
religious man in politics; he was another Abelard, but
divested of his pride and weakness.   The impress of
his soul was stamped upon his features.   He was tall
and slender in figure, slow of step, beautiful in counte-
nance, of a gentle aspect, a composed expression, and
an affable demeanor.   Habitually silent, when he spoke
he became eloquent and persuasive.   Placed, as we may
say, by the elevation of his thoughts, on an interme-
diate point between heaven and earth, he divided his
attention equally between things temporal and things
eternal.   Representing the holiness of true Christianity,
he attracted thousands towards religion by the charm
of gentleness, instead of driving them away by the terror of severity.   The memory of his virtues was so in-
delibly impressed, that it has been handed down for
eight centuries, from father to son, in the town and
valley of Cluny.   A few years since, a tomb having
been discovered by chance, and supposed to be his, the
women and children eagerly contended for the dust it
contained, urged by a traditional affection acknowledged
throughout the district.   Peter the Venerable had held

disputes with St. Bernard, whose practice it was to quarrel with all he was unable to control. The Abbot of Cluny loved Abelard for his poetry, his eloquence, and, above all, for his misfortunes. Heloise he looked upon as the wonder of the age, and the ornament of the sanctuary. He had visited the Paraclete, rendered famous by the piety and tears of this widow of a living husband, and carried back from the interview edification, enthusiasm, and piety, which led him to commence and continue with her an epistolary correspondence. Such was the man of whom the fugitive Abelard solicited the shelter of a night's lodging.

He arrived, broken down by sorrow, fatigue, and sickness, at the gates of the abbey. Prompted by humility, he wished to throw himself at the feet of Peter the Venerable, who received him in his arms, and opened to him his house and his heart. Abelard, overpowered by a reception to which the persecutions of St. Bernard had disaccustomed him, related his recent vicissitudes, his sorrows, his condemnation to the cloister, and his resolve to proceed on foot to Rome, to throw himself on the justice and commiseration of the sovereign pontiff, formerly his personal friend. The Abbot of Cluny expressed warm compassion for his misfortunes, and encouraged his confidence in the pope. But, mistrusting the strength of his guest, weakened as it was by grief and fear, apprehensive lest this glory of France should perish miserably on some snow track

while begging his bread across the Alps, or that he
might fall a prisoner into the hands of his enemies beyond the mountains, he retained him at the monastery
under a variety of pious pretexts. During this interval, Peter the Venerable addressed the pope privately,
in a letter full of the tenderest and most disinterested
zeal for his friend. "The illustrious Abelard," said he
in this epistle, "well known to your Holiness, has
passed some days with me at Cluny, coming from
France. I questioned him as to where he was going.
'I am pursued,' replied he, 'by the persecutions of certain men, who have applied to me the name of heretic,
which I reject and detest. I have appealed from their
sentence to the justice of the supreme head of the
Church, and in that sanctuary I seek protection against
my enemies.' I have approved this project of Abelard,
and have strongly encouraged him to repair to your
presence, assuring him that neither justice nor kindness
would be withheld from such a suppliant, seeing that
both are freely accorded to the obscure pilgrim, or the
perfect stranger. I added also, that he might rely on
indulgence for unintentional errors. While he rested
at the abbey, the Abbot of Clairvaux arrived here. We
concerted together in all Christian charity, how to
reconcile Abelard, my guest, with the Abbot Bernard,
who has reduced him to this necessity of appealing to
your Holiness. I have used every effort in my power
to bring about this accommodation. I have advised

Abelard to expunge from his writings, under the supervision of Bernard himself, and other sagacious men,
every passage that offends against the scruples of the
true faith. Abelard has given his consent to this.
From that moment the reconciliation has been effected
by my agency, but much more through the inspiration
of Providence. Abelard, our guest, has bade farewell
forever to the agitation of controversy, and the schools;
he has selected Cluny for his last and permanent residence. I implore you then, I, the most humble and
devoted of your servants, the entire community of the
abbey implores you, and Abelard himself joins in the
entreaty,—by him, by us, by the messengers who bear
these letters, by the letters they carry, we all beseech
you to allow him to exhaust at Cluny the few days
which remain to him of his life, and his old age; and
few indeed those days are likely to number. We all
conjure you not to allow persecution *from any quarter*
to disturb or drive him forth again from this house,
under the roof of which, like the sparrow which seeks
a nest, he rejoices to have found an asylum, even as
the dove rejoiced when it found a dry spot on which
to rest its foot. Refuse not your holy protection to the
man whom you once distinguished by the title of your
friend!" Such a touching appeal of friendship, and the
living memory of the enthusiastic regard which he had
formerly felt for the orator and poet of his youth, could
not fail to reach the heart of the pope. He granted

to the prayer of Peter the Venerable the pardon and protection which he implored for Abelard. In his nominal imprisonment, Abelard had for superior and jailer the most tender and compassionate of friends.

Heloise, satisfied as to the worldly destiny of her husband, watched at a distance, by letters and prayers, over his declining health and immortal prospects. The last days of this distinguished man, who had inspired and lost the admiration of the world, but who had still preserved the undivided tenderness of a woman, and the attachment of a friend, passed over in poetical and religious conversations with Peter the Venerable, in the contemplation and study of futurity, in the contempt of those vanities which had not consoled him for the devotion of a single heart, and in the hope of the happy reunion which Heloise assured him would be assigned to them in heaven.

At the extremity of a desert alley, and at the foot of inclosing walls, flanked by the towers of the monastery, on the margin of extensive meadows closed in by woods, close to the murmuring stream, and the reeds of a dried-up marsh, through which the breezes whistled drearily, there is still existing an enormous lime-tree, under the shade of which Abelard was accustomed to sit and meditate, with his face turned towards the direction of the Paraclete. The monks, proud of having afforded the hospitality of their cloisters to the most shining light of the eleventh century, sedulously preserved this tradition. The fury of the French Revolution, which destroyed so much, respected this lime-tree and one or two of the spires of the monastery. The last of the ecclesiastics related the legend to the inhabitants of the town, who tell it again to accidental visitors. I myself possess, under a lime of three hundred years old, in my garden at Saint-Point, the bench of gray-stone, sonorous as a bell, on which, according to the tradition, Abelard sat under the more ancient tree of Cluny. I have also carried from thence a large table of the same stone, on which he reposed his head while composing his hymns, or meditating over his misfortunes and his love.

His soul, consumed by the fire of passion and the flame of genius, robbed of happiness by evil destiny, and of fame by persecution, exhausted itself before he reached an advanced period of life. He expired in the arms of his friend, two years and a few months after he had crossed the hospitable threshold of Cluny.

The disinterested attachment of Peter the Venerable ceased not until he had superintended the interment of his friend. Under the instinct of truly divine charity, he became an accomplice in the love which suffering, repentance, and tears had rendered sacred in his eyes. He felt that Abelard above, and Heloise on earth, demanded of him the last consolation of a reunion in the grave. He could not persuade himself that it was culpable to descend from the height of his sanctity, and participate in the weakness or illusion, which, while it was unable to blend two lives into one, might at least be permitted to mingle the mortal dust which once was animated. But, dreading even the shadow of scandal, he wrapped up in secresy the pious theft which he himself was about to commit on the cemetery of St. Marcel, an oratory belonging to the abbey, in which Abelard was interred.

He confided to no deputy the care of accompanying the remains of the deceased, and of remitting them to the guardianship of Heloise. No hands were worthy of touching this sacred deposit, except those of a saint and a wife. He rose in the dead of the night, exhumed the coffin, conveyed it to the Paraclete, and inscribed in verse the epitaph of his friend. "The Plato of our age" (thus he designates him in these lines), "equal or superior to his predecessors, sovereign master of thought, acknowledged throughout the universe for the variety and extent of his genius; he surpassed all men in the strength of his imagination and the power of his eloquence. His name was Abelard!" The pious abbot then assumed the paternal charge of an only son, who had been born to the unhappy pair during their temporary union, and before they had pronounced the monastic vows.

Heloise, having received with tears the coffin of Abelard, shut herself up in the cemetery of the Paraclete, in the vault, where she assumed her conjugal place by the couch of death. Peter the Venerable himself performed the funeral rites, and departed after he had placed the mortal relics of his friend under the guardianship of an unextinguishable love. This mutual reverence for the memory of the same object drew still closer the ties of admiration and gratitude which attached the abbot of Cluny to the widow of the Para-clete. Heloise, who longed to be assured of the eternal happiness of Abelard, as passionately as she had mourned his earthly sorrows, entreated from the venerable father a written attestation that her anxious desires were accomplished. "I conjure you," she wrote to him after his return, "to send me open documents, stamped with your seal, containing the full absolution of my departed lord, that these evidences of felicity may be suspended over his tomb. Remember, too," she added, "to consider as your own son the son of Abelard and Heloise."

Peter the Venerable yielded to this last anxious scruple of affection, and forwarded to the Paraclete the letters of absolution demanded from him. He also, with his own hand, in an epistle to Heloise replete with evangelical love, recapitulated every circumstance attending the last days of Abelard, which might tend to console the anguish of an eternal widowhood. "It is not on this day," says he, "oh, my sister, that I begin to love you, for I have loved you long already! I had scarcely passed my early youth and reached the age of manhood, when the fame reached me, not then of your exalted piety, but of your unrivalled genius. It was related everywhere that a young female, in the first bloom of youth and beauty, had distinguished herself, unlike her sex in general, by poetry, eloquence, and philosophy. Neither the love of pleasure, nor the attractions of the time, could obtain-dominion in her heart over pursuits which were grand in intellect, and beautiful in science. The world, stagnating in base and slothful ignorance, beheld with astonishment how, not only among women, but in the assemblies of men, Heloise exhibited and maintained her vast superiority. Soon (to speak in the words of the Apostle) He who had suffered you to issue from the bosom of your mother, by divine grace, attracted you entirely to himself. You exchanged the study of perishable knowledge for the science of eternity; for Plato you adopted Christ; and in place of the academy you selected the cloister. Would that it had been permitted that Cluny should have possessed you! that you should have shared our sweet imprisonment of Marcigny, with the female servants of the Lord, who pant only for celestial liberty! But, although Providence withheld this favor from us, we have been distinguished by receiving him who in life belonged to you : him whom we must ever honor and remember with respect,—the philosopher of the gospel, the Abelard who, by Divine permission, was sent to close his days in our monastery.

14

" It is no easy task, my sister, to describe in a few short lines the holiness, the humility, the self-denial he exhibited to us, and of which the collected brotherhood have borne witness. If I do not deceive myself, never did I behold a life and deportment so thoroughly submissive. I placed him in an elevated rank in our community, but he appeared the lowest of all by the simplicity of his dress. It was equally so with his diet, and all that regarded the enjoyment of the senses. I speak not of luxury, which was a stranger to him : he refused every thing but what was indispensable to the sustenance of life. His conduct and his words were irreproachable, either as regarded himself, or as an example to others.

" He read continually, prayed often, and never spoke, except when literary controversy or holy discussion compelled him to break silence. What can I tell you more ? His mind, his tongue, his meditations were entirely concentrated on, and promoted, literary, philosophical, and divine instruction. Simple, straightforward, reflecting on eternal judgment, and shunning all evil, he consecrated to God the closing days of an illustrious life.

" To afford him a little recreation, and to recruit his failing health, I dispatched him to Saint Marcel, near Châlons. I purposely selected this country, the most attractive in Burgundy, and a convent close to the town, from which it is only separated by the course of the Saône. There, as much as his strength permitted, he resumed the cherished studies of his youth, and as has been also said of Gregory the Great, he suffered not a single moment to pass that was not occupied either in prayer, in reading, in writing, or in dictation.

" While occupied with these holy avocations, death, the missionary of the Divine, came to seek him. He found him not asleep, like many others, but awake, up, and ready, and conveyed him joyfully to the marriage feast. He carried with him his lamp replenished with oil, his conscience filled with the testimony of a holy life. A mortal sickness seized and reduced him to extremity; he felt that he had reached the term of his mortal existence, and was about to render up the common tribute. Then, with what fervent piety, what ardent inspiration, did he make the last confession of his sins! with what fervor did he receive the promise of eternal being! with what confidence did he recommend his body and his soul to the tender mercy of the Saviour! Such was the death of Abelard! And thus has the man who had rendered himself illustrious throughout the world by the miracles of his knowledge, and his lessons, passed, according to my conviction, into the presence of his Creator.

" And you, my sister, loved and venerated in God, you who were united to him in worldly bonds, before you enter on a second union cemented by divine affection; you who have so long devoted yourself to the

Lord with him, and by his direction, remember him ever in your prayers, and in your communion with the Saviour. Christ shelters you both in the asylum of his heart: he warms you again in his bosom; and when his day arrives, announced by the voice of the archangel, he will restore Abelard to you, and never more will you be separated."

Religion should have erected a statue to the man who could indite this letter. Never did divine tenderness unite itself with more indulgence to human affection. Never did sanctity evince greater condescension, or virtue soften into more amiable compassion. We observe, with what delicacy of sentiment and expression he recalls, even in death, the image of an eternal marriage, so inseparably wound up with the aspirations of Heloise. The oil of the Samaritan did not penetrate with more healing influence into the wounds of the body, than these words of true piety alleviate the sufferings of the heart. The friendship of such a man as Peter the Venerable, and the love of such a woman as Heloise, are of themselves sufficient evidences that Abelard deserved better of his age than posterity is willing to believe.

Heloise survived her husband twenty years, a priestess of God, devoted to the worship of a sepulchre in the solitude of the Paraclete. When she felt the near approach of the death she had so long invoked, she directed the sisterhood to place her body by the side of that of her husband, in the same coffin. The love which had united and separated them during life, by so many prodigies of passion and constancy, appeared to signalize their burial by a fresh miracle. At the moment when the coffin of Abelard was opened, to lay within it the body of Heloise, it was said that the arm of the skeleton, compressed for twenty years under the weight of the lid, stretched itself out, opened, and appeared to be reanimated, to receive the spouse restored by heavenly love to an eternal embrace. This credulity of the age, transformed into an actual occurrence, was related by historians and sung by poets, and consecrated in the imagination of the people the holiness of the reunited pair.

They reposed for five hundred years in one of the aisles of the Paraclete, sometimes separated by the scruples of the abbess, and subsequently united again in compliance with the conjugal desire, strongly expressed in life as in death, and which was repeated even from the tomb.

The French Revolution, which scattered to the winds the dust of the kings and princes of the church, respected the remains of these unfortunate lovers. In 1792, the Paraclete having been sold as ecclesiastical property, the town of Nogent removed the tombs, and sheltered them in the nave of their own church. In 1800, Lucien Bonaparte, a zealous advocate of letters, and collector of ancient relics, instructed a re-

spectable artist, M. Lenoir, to transport the coffin of
Abelard and Heloise to the museum of French monu-
ments in Paris. When the lead was opened, the wit-
nesses present declared "that the two bodies had been
of elevated stature and beautifully proportioned." "The
head of Heloise," according to M. Lenoir, "is of admirable contour, and the rounded forehead expresses still
the most perfect beauty. The recumbent statues carved
on the tomb have been moulded from these recomposed
remains by the imagination of the sculptor. A few
years later, the mortuary chapel in which the tomb
was inclosed became the principal ornament of the
garden of the museum." The visitors were frequent
and numerous. In 1815, the government of the Bour-
bons, which carefully preserved all sepulchral vestiges,
to bring the people back to the ancient worship, was
desirous of removing the coffin of Abelard and Heloise
to the abbey of St. Denis, a sanctuary to which it no
more belonged than the proscribed does to the pro-
scriber. General opinion protested against this burying
within a closed church a monument which all claimed
as public property. It was then finally placed in the
great necropolis of Paris, the cemetery of Père-la-
Chaise. There may be seen the statues of Abelard
and Heloise, lying side by side, decked with flowers
and funereal coronets, perpetually renewed by invisible
hands. Succeeding generations appear to claim an
eternal relationship with the illustrious departed. The

votive offerings proceed from kindred souls, separated by death, persecution, or worldly impediments, from those to whom they are attached on earth, or mourn in heaven. They thus mysteriously convey their ad miration for truth and constancy, and their sympathy with the posthumous union of two hearts, who transposed conjugal tenderness from the senses to the soul, who spiritualized the most ardent and sensual of human passions, and changed love itself into a holocaust, a martyrdom, and a holy sacrifice.

THE END.

www.ingramcontent.com/pod-product-compliance
Lightning Source LLC
Chambersburg PA
CBHW060536030726
47498CB00004B/1217